Mystery
at
Southwood
School

BOOKS BY CLARE CHASE

Mystery
at
Southwood
School

CLARE CHASE

bookouture

Published by Bookouture in 2022

An imprint of Storyfire Ltd.
Carmelite House
50 Victoria Embankment
London EC4Y 0DZ

www.bookouture.com

ISBN: 978-1-80314-409-2
eBook ISBN:978-1-80314-408-5

To Ruth, with heartfelt thanks

PROLOGUE

The killer knew Natalie Somerson would be early to the clandestine meeting. It was in her character to break into the hidden room rather than waiting for someone with a key. It was what she'd done when she was a student at Southwood School thirty-seven years earlier, and she hadn't changed. They felt a jolt of fury as they glanced over their shoulder. Natalie was all showy arrogance and finally she'd pay the price.

Night had fallen hours since, though the lights in the boarders' blocks shone brightly. But the killer was confident, walking between the imposing Victorian buildings. Although the main pathways glowed in lamplight, there were plenty of shadows, and a fog had settled as the cold autumn night took hold. They'd planned their route carefully – knew exactly how long it would take them, and how to avoid any straggling boarders as they scurried back to their rooms. The odd few the killer saw clutched their coats around them against the dank evening. The autumn term was long and arduous, summer all but forgotten. But the killer didn't feel the cold – they were warmed by thoughts of their mission.

Under their academic gown, they carried the murder

weapon – a hammer they'd sought out earlier. It was a brutal way to kill. A method few would even contemplate, except in the heat of the moment. But the figure wasn't daunted. They were eager.

It wouldn't be long now...

1

ONE DAY EARLIER

It was late lunchtime, and Eve Mallow was following her friend, Viv, through the grounds of Southwood School, across the courtyard known as Great Quad. It was quiet, but in the distance Eve could hear the sound of children playing.

'They're not allowed in the quad unless they're on their way to a lesson.' Viv, as a former Southwood student, knew the drill. 'I got detention once for showing my nose here during the lunch break.'

The pair of them were on their way to meet with what Viv called 'the coven' – the committee that ran the place. Eve's stomach was quivering like a pan of water just coming to the boil. It was partly interested anticipation, but partly tension too. Viv's memories of the place weren't encouraging; the austerity she'd described went with the imposing Victorian architecture: formal red-brick walls and stone window settings.

Eve shivered and pulled her coat more tightly around her. 'How did they come to be known as the coven?'

'I can't remember who started it, but even they refer to themselves that way now.' Viv hung back so she and Eve could talk privately. 'They take a pride in it, and none of them trust

each other. You ought to have a field day observing them all.
Multiple weirdos in one room.'

As an obituary writer, people-watching ran through Eve's
veins.

'Don't you worry about me as you enjoy yourself,' Viv said.
'I'll just sit quietly and endure my flashbacks.'

She'd been a boarder at Southwood over thirty years earlier.

'Why didn't you ask to leave, if it was that bad?'

'I could have. Mum and Dad would have taken me out, but
the cookery facilities were exceptional, so I stuck with it.'

Viv's baking skills were the reason for their presence.
Tomorrow was Founders' Day at Southwood, and Viv, as a
former student and owner of Monty's teashop, was providing
the refreshments. Eve was there as her colleague. Freelance
journalism was an uncertain business, and part-time work at
Monty's gave her financial security. Viv had brought her on
board to whip the business into shape, an offer Eve couldn't
resist. Viv would score full marks for her baking but negative
points for admin. Eve had twitched as she'd watched Viv make
a hash of it. Anyone would. Surely.

In between shifts, Eve unpicked the lives of the dead, and
the relatives they left behind. It was fascinating.

Eve and Viv weren't the only ones on their way to meet the
coven. Ahead of them was the reason Viv had been hanging
back: Sabina Montague, mother of her late husband Oliver.
Monty's had been his business originally, and Sabina still
watched developments there like a hawk. She was all thin lips
and disapproving, hooded eyes.

Sabina was also a former Southwood student, and one of the
lay committee members who got involved in school events. Viv
and Oliver had formed a bond when he came along to a summer
fete at the school, much to Sabina's disgust.

'And that was before I started with the multicoloured hair
thing,' Viv had said, running her fingers through this season's

mane, which was an autumnal red-orange. 'How she and Edward produced such a fun-loving and relaxed son, I'll never know. I used to tease him about it. Tell him there must have been a mix-up at the hospital.' There was a rare catch in her voice. Eve had given her a hug.

Sabina strutted ahead of them in her high-heeled patent leather shoes, her coat swishing around her calves, somehow conveying that she was already annoyed. She turned and glanced at the pair of them as though she'd been lumbered with two rotten apples – all that was left in the supermarket crate.

'Hurry up! They're busy people, you know.'

But they weren't the last. Over to their left, Eve spotted Southwood's headmaster, who would also be in the meeting. He stood next to a woman she guessed must be his wife. They had two girls with them, muffled up against the autumn chill, with duffel coats and emerald-green scarves. They were far too young to be Southwood students. Probably their own children, in fact, perhaps home after a morning at infant school. The relationship was confirmed a moment later as one of them grasped the headmaster's hands.

'Again, Daddy!'

He laughed, his cheeks rosy from the cold, a red silk cravat showing at his throat – a bright patch above his black wool coat. 'One more time then!' He swung her out so her feet left the ground and she whooped as the second child queued up for a go.

The woman ruffled the hair of the first girl after she'd finished and kissed her.

'*They* don't seem to be rushing!' Viv muttered, loudly. She'd never mastered the art of whispering.

They didn't seem like weirdos either, Eve thought. Perfectly human on the face of it.

Sabina tutted, at both Viv and the headmaster, Eve reckoned. She was mid-disapproving snort when another person appeared behind all of them, sauntering across the grass.

Eve had no trouble recognising the newcomer. It was Natalie Somerson, the famous talk-show host, there as a former Southwood student and its guest of honour this year. Her bountiful blonde curls fell over the padded shoulders of her leather jacket. She'd teamed it with faded black jeans, decorated with studs and the odd tear.

Sabina looked away pointedly as she approached, muttering something about exhibitionists. Natalie gave a catlike smile.

She'd caught the head teacher's attention too. He was frowning.

'I'm sorry, my dears,' he sighed, looking down at his daughters, 'Mummy and I need to sort out Southwood's big day now. You run along with Mimi.'

A dark-haired young woman had appeared and took the girls' hands, promising mugs of milk and a jigsaw puzzle.

Sabina stood back to let the head and his wife enter the administrative section of the school first, holding out an arm to block Eve and Viv, as if they might have pushed forward otherwise. Eve took a deep breath to counteract the effect the woman had on her, but it wasn't quite enough.

Sabina let Natalie go first too, but with a look of such disdain that a lesser person would have shrivelled.

'Thank you so much!' Natalie swished through the door with a relaxed grin.

Sabina's face was a picture and Eve couldn't help enjoying it, though she was uncertain about Natalie. She couldn't think of her talk show without judging her. No topic was too sensitive; Eve imagined ratings overrode other concerns.

At last, Eve and Viv followed Sabina's clacking heels up some stone steps and through an archway. A moment later, they entered the room where the others had gathered.

The place was dark, with its mullioned windows and wood

panelling, and the portraits of past head teachers made Eve feel watched.

The assembled group looked like a secret society. Ahead of them, the head and his wife were still in the process of putting on academic gowns, with a certain amount of ceremony. The rest of the coven wore them too – only the visitors were without.

One lamp hung low over a long table, illuminating the assembled group.

The headmaster motioned Natalie Somerson to a seat at the head of the table, furthest from the door.

'Your place as this year's Founders' Day Champion,' he said, rather stiffly.

'Thank you.' Natalie didn't react to his tone as she arranged herself. 'I'm delighted to be here.'

Someone scoffed, but Eve didn't see who.

The whole situation was weird. She'd asked Viv about Natalie's role beforehand and learned it was a twelve-month appointment, involving a speech on the day and visits after-wards. Apparently the champions helped Southwood with publicity and fundraising. Of course, Natalie had a national platform, but she struck Eve as a risky choice. In the last week, the press had been full of an affair she was meant to be having with an actor. Someone had snapped them with a long lens. The photos weren't conclusive, but they'd had their arms around each other, their heads close, a bottle of champagne in view. Natalie's hair mussed up. Eve didn't imagine it had gone down well with her husband. Or with the coven members who'd voted for her as champion at the end of the summer term. It was the sort of buzz the school could do without, though Natalie had blown up at the photographer and insisted it wasn't how it looked. Eve found that hard to believe.

But it wasn't just Natalie's antics that made her risky. Sitting amongst the coven, her blue eyes radiated mischief. Eve could understand that. Sabina alone made her feel rebellious and the gown-wearing and formality seemed over the top in this day and age. But if Natalie decided to ruffle feathers, her reach was far wider then Eve's. Her TV show focused on exposing damaging scandals. Southwood had better hope it had no skeletons in its cupboard.

It made Eve wonder why on earth they'd invited her. The downsides seemed to outweigh the potential benefits.

2

It took a while to get everyone settled. Viv's mother-in-law pulled out the chair furthest from Natalie and slowly removed her coat before sitting down. It meant Eve and Viv had to wait to get past, and it looked pointed. It would have been so much easier if she'd simply taken the chair next to the TV star.

But Natalie seemed unaffected once again, chatting animatedly with the woman on her other side. Eve knew Natalie was five years Viv's senior, which put her at fifty-five, but you'd never guess it. Could she have had a facelift?

Eve found herself sitting up a little straighter. Her tweed trouser suit was a lot smarter than Natalie's outfit (meeting a coven seemed to demand it) but she suddenly felt drab. Natalie's perfume wafted across the table: Christian Dior's Poison. Eve remembered hankering after a bottle as a student, but it had been too expensive.

'Thank you for joining us.' The headmaster addressed the room.

Eve had looked him up earlier out of curiosity. It was relatively rare to have a male head of an all-girls' school, and Martin Leverett was Southwood's first. He was probably a decade or so younger than she was – around forty maybe – with broad shoulders, dark hair and deep brown eyes. As she took out her notebook, she wondered how many of the sixth-formers had crushes on him, and how difficult that must be for him and his wife.

He smiled as his gaze swept the room, though Eve noticed his look narrow as it landed on Natalie. 'Let's get down to business.'

As they talked about timings, visitor numbers and logistics, Eve made copious notes. It wasn't all relevant to her role, but she liked to be prepared, and Viv looked overly relaxed.

Eve's research had told her who was attending this current meeting. She'd found their mugshots on the school website beforehand, but guessed some of them were years out of date. The woman to Natalie's left was easily recognisable, though. Anastasia Twite, the bursar. She had cropped silver hair, bright sparkling eyes and subtle but smart make-up. Eve guessed she was well beyond retirement age, but she fizzed with energy, leaning forward to express a point, and snorting with laughter at a woman to her left, who was talking fussily about place settings. Eve identified the fussy woman as the head of the sixth form. She had grey hair too, but hers was in a bob. Her face was lined in that way that indicates a life of worry – or possibly natural grumpiness. Eve guessed she might be a little younger than Anastasia, but she had none of her vitality. Whenever she wasn't engaged in conversation her gaze moved to Natalie and her jaw tightened, her body rigid. Eve wouldn't like to be looked at like that. Her expression was venomous.

Next to the grumpy head of sixth sat Southwood's head girl, her red hair spilling over her shoulders, eyes made up, and wearing a rust-coloured dress. Eighteen, but trying to look ten years older.

'Surely it won't work if we make the parents file in via the central aisle,' she said now, leaning forward, eager to share her wisdom. 'There'll be a terrible bottleneck. Approaching the front seats via the side aisles is the answer.' Her patronising smile set Eve's teeth on edge.

It was Anastasia who replied. 'My dear, if they do that, they will have to walk through the orchestra. The last time we allowed it, someone knocked over a music stand and trod on the lead violinist's bow. The parents will use the central aisle and that's an end to it.' The way she spoke left the matter in no doubt, though she did it with a twinkle in her eye.

The head girl flushed all the same. It was anger as much as embarrassment, Eve decided.

'Anastasia's absolutely right, of course,' the headmaster's wife said, her dark wavy bob swishing as she turned towards the head girl. 'You must be prepared for the rough and tumble of the coven. You speak your mind and if your suggestions aren't accepted, I know you'll take it on the chin.'

'Like a true Southwoodian,' Natalie said, with an ironic smile, as the head girl continued to scowl.

The head of sixth form stared down the table at her. 'Not something you'd know much about, Natalie.'

The TV star turned to her languidly. 'Whereas you epitomise everything I associate with the school. I'm so glad you're still here, carrying on into your dotage.'

Natalie's words had clearly been meant to hurt, but the older woman's reaction was violent. She snatched up her water glass and rose from her seat, her hand shaking. For a moment, Eve thought she was going to dash the contents in Natalie's face. Natalie raised an eyebrow as though daring her to go ahead. She looked like she'd relish it. Eve wondered what the heck had happened between them in the past.

And why had Natalie agreed to act as Founders' Day Champion if she thought so little of Southwood? It made the whole situation more extraordinary.

No one moved. Eve saw Anastasia exchange a glance with the headmaster. But then the head of sixth form subsided, like a sheet that had been billowing in the wind when the gust suddenly dropped.

Viv reached for Eve's notepad, wrote *More fun than I'd thought*, and passed it back. To her horror, Eve realised that Natalie had seen it, but her only response was a stifled laugh.

Eve and Viv's cakes were well down the agenda, but at last the pair of them were drawn into the conversation.

'I understand you're baking our traditional fruit and peel cakes and icing them with the Southwood crest?' The headmaster smiled at Viv.

'That's right. And Eve's making a recipe that will be unique for this year.'

And now the head's friendly gaze was on her. 'Perhaps you could tell us more?'

'They're spiced pumpkin cakes, with ginger – warming and seasonal.'

'Pumpkin?' Viv's mother-in-law turned to Viv as if Eve had said arsenic. 'You didn't tell me that.'

But the headmaster and Anastasia spoke over her. 'Marvellous.'

'It sounds perfect.'

Eve rejoiced as Sabina's mouth snapped shut.

'What's a Seattleite doing in deepest Suffolk?'

Natalie Somerson's question caught Eve off guard. The chat-show host was looking at her just as she looked at her TV guests, her eyes full of curiosity and anticipation. It was the look that drew people out – just before she turned on them and they regretted relaxing.

'You've a good ear for an accent.'

'I love Seattle. My first husband was born there. So what's your story?'

Eve's stomach clenched. She was used to interviewing other people. Having the tables turned wasn't great, especially in front of a roomful of strangers. 'My dad's British. He encouraged me to study in London.'

'And you loved it so much you stayed?'

'That's right.'

'Except now you're in Suffolk.'

Everyone was waiting for her to answer; she couldn't just clam up.

'I came to one of the nearby villages, Saxford St Peter, for work a couple of years ago and I decided to relocate.'

'I won her over with my job offer at the teashop,' Viv put in.

Sabina seemed eager to fill in the blanks. 'She was in Suffolk writing about a murdered cellist,' she said. 'She's an obituary writer with a taste for sensationalism.'

Love you too, Sabina. The comment was completely unfair. Eve always treated her subjects sensitively and with respect.

'She's helped the police identify several murderers,' Viv said, patting Eve on the back.

This was getting worse.

'Her husband left her. That was why she moved from London,' Sabina leaped back in.

She could only have got that from... Viv shot Eve a sidelong glance and mouthed 'sorry'.

'Although he walked out, he wouldn't stop dropping in to check up on me. It was driving me up the wall.' Eve's words came in a rush. Instantly she felt herself flush, as though she was naked in front of them.

Natalie laughed. 'I would have cut and run too. Good on you. As for husbands, I have a collection of exes as you probably know. I don't think anyone should be expected to get it right first time.' There was a look of camaraderie in the woman's eyes but the tuts in the room were audible again.

At last, the meeting wrapped up and everyone filed out of the room, the bursar switching off the light behind them, her bright eyes catching Eve's for a moment.

'The meetings are always like that,' she said. 'I sometimes feel outsiders should be warned. And about the directness of the questions and comments.'

It was kindly meant, but Eve felt caught out once again. Anastasia was sharp. She could see how uncomfortable Eve had felt.

'I'm going to find a loo,' Eve said to Viv, a moment later.

'You're not going to leave me alone with the gorgon, are you?' Viv whispered loudly, glancing over her shoulder at Sabina, who was chatting to the still-frowning head of sixth form. 'She wants to check our operation in the kitchens.'

They'd been given one of the home economics classrooms until Founders' Day was over.

'I'll be there before you know it, though washing my hands might take a while. Cleanliness is so important.'

'Beast.' Viv turned to dash after her mother-in-law.

Eve followed a sign marked 'ladies', down a dark corridor which smelled of paint and dust, given off by the huge old-fashioned radiators. She entered the bathroom and was just about to pass through an inner door when she heard someone take a sharp breath. Nervous-sounding, eager.

'I think it's inspiring that you rebelled when you were here, Natalie. I'm glad the coven voted for you as Founders' Day Champion. We're always told we should be independent spirits at Southwood, and you'll lead the way.'

The head girl. Her voice was unmistakable: a little breathless and young, yet slightly husky.

There was a short pause before Natalie replied in her confident drawl. 'I'm sorry, sweetie, but you sound like such a creep.' She laughed a cold, harsh laugh. 'If you really believed in rebellion, you'd hardly be head girl. I've had enough of your pestering. You and I have nothing in common, so please don't try to imply otherwise. Ever.'

Eve heard the head girl gasp, then her footfalls as she dashed towards the door.

Eve just had time to dart back into the corridor and press herself against a wall. She wasn't hidden but the head girl was too shocked to notice her and turned in the opposite direction, back the way she'd come.

At that moment a bell rang. Time for afternoon lessons, Eve guessed. The head girl pulled out a tissue as she rushed away, blowing her nose angrily.

3

'I'm sorry I told Sabina about Ian walking out on you,' Viv said, as Eve entered their temporary kitchen. 'It was right near the beginning when she gave me the third degree about your background. I should have told her to buzz off – it's none of her business anyway – but it seemed quicker to give in. She's already gone, by the way,' she added, as Eve glanced to check. 'Do you forgive me?'

'I'll consider it.'

'Thank you.' Viv perked up immediately. 'Fun meeting, wasn't it? Sizzling with suppressed violence.'

'We have to talk about your likes and dislikes. My trip to the bathroom was eventful too.' As she pulled on her apron, she relayed the details. 'I only managed to make use of the facilities after Natalie left.'

'Poor Scarlett,' Viv said. 'Though she is a bit hard to take. What a know-all. The head girl in my day was much more down to earth. Irritatingly clever and talented, obviously, but I could forgive her for it.'

'Scarlett must have hidden depths, presumably.'

'I wouldn't be so sure. Her father's a major donor to the school.'

Eve met Viv's eye. 'You think they'd make her head girl because of that?'

'I should say so. Not everyone's as upstanding as you are. The coven might not all approve but someone will have pushed for it, I'll bet. And if it means Southwood can afford a new tennis court or an extra teacher, they probably think it's worth it.'

It was a stark way of putting it. 'After sitting through that meeting, Scarlett being head girl isn't the only mystery. I'm all the more surprised the coven chose Natalie for Founders' Day Champion.'

'I know what you mean. It's like a load of mice inviting a snake to visit. They've been up in arms since her affair came out, of course. Maybe they'd have withdrawn their offer if the news had broken earlier.'

'Yet a majority wanted her, back in the summer. I assume Scarlett must have voted in favour, though I'd guess she's regretting it now. Did Sabina get a vote?' She'd have been against, clearly.

But Viv shook her head. 'She's only here as part of the events committee. She'd love a bossier role, obviously, but being in the coven goes with your job. The head, the bursar, the head of pastoral care and the head of sixth form are the four staff who're always represented' – she counted them off on her fingers – 'and the head girl's included to represent the students.'

'The head of sixth form must have voted against, unless she wanted her here to dash water in her face. I'm guessing they have a past.'

Viv let out a snort. 'Eliza Gregory and Natalie? I'll say they do. Eliza was just an English teacher back in mine and Natalie's day. Founders' Day's a bit of a flashpoint for her.'

Eve weighed out some flour. 'How come?'

'Natalie had been picked to recite a poem in front of the parents one year. She stood up, looking like butter wouldn't melt, and began to read. The verse started out quite touching, but as it went on it became clear it was about Anthony Leverett, the current headmaster's father. So far, so embarrassing. I imagine the teachers wanted to stop the reading, but it was crowded and the whole thing played out in seconds. Most of them looked too stunned to react. And then it got worse.'

'Explain.'

'The third verse was a lot more... sensual in nature.' She glanced at Eve. 'Imagine something as extreme as you can, then add a bit.'

'Heck.'

'Then, when Natalie reached the end, she said: "I didn't write this, of course; I found it in the English block. But I thought it was beautiful. So much better than what I produce. I never get good marks in English." She laughed and turned over the paper, then put a hand over her mouth. It was a pretty good act. After that, she looked straight at Eliza Gregory and said: "I'm so sorry. I had no idea. Oh, my goodness. I'll return this to you immediately."'

'Eliza wrote it? She'd fallen for Martin's father?'

Viv nodded. 'I doubt she really signed it. I imagine that bit was for show, but there was no doubt; Natalie must have recognised her handwriting. Eliza tried to bluster it out, of course, but no one believed her. She was already puce before Natalie made it clear she was the author.'

An image of Eliza came to mind, very much younger, the centre of attention in a huge hall crammed with parents and staff. Had they laughed? Been embarrassed? Both, probably. Whatever happened it would have been excruciating for Eliza. Eve felt her toes curl at the thought. How had she lived it down? Eve would have been tempted to apply for another job. That kind of gossip could have made life hard to bear.

'Was Martin's dad there?'

'Yep. He was bursar then – part of the coven of the day, along with Bridget, his headmistress wife. Anthony's dead now, but Bridget still lives on site.'

Worse and worse.

'No wonder Eliza hates Natalie.'

Viv shrugged. 'It was probably revenge. Eliza was by far and away the cruellest teacher I had while I was here. Humiliation was her punishment of choice. She made me stand on a chair with my back to the class for an hour once, and encouraged my frenemies to discuss my shortcomings while I listened. Everyone spoke in loud whispers. I could hear the comments, but I couldn't work out who said what. Of course, I wasn't allowed to answer back.'

Viv spoke lightly but it was clear the memory still affected her. Eve had been weighing out butter but put it down and gave her friend a hug. 'That's appalling. Did you tell your parents?' Eve would have been incensed if it had happened to one of her twins. They were adults now, but the thought still made her go hot all over. You had to keep order, but never in a million years like that.

Viv shook her head. 'It would have felt like letting her win. I wanted her to think I didn't care.' She took a deep breath. 'I hope she never realises how much I did. I can't believe she's still here. I always assumed she detested the job.'

Eve felt a rush of discomfort at having to be polite to the woman while she was at Southwood. She was glad they'd be back in Saxford the day after Founders' Day. She was missing home and her dachshund, Gus, though he'd be in seventh heaven, round at her neighbours' house.

Viv bit her lip. 'I know Natalie's merciless on TV, but she was a bit of a role model for me, back in the day. I know better now, but at the time she seemed so sophisticated and I loved her rebelliousness. She hated Southwood and I felt much the same.

She came back regularly after she'd left too. Turned up in a fast car, smoking in the grounds, always wearing that bright red lipstick.'

'Why on earth would she come back?'

'Anastasia's her aunt – she came to visit her. They're both descendants of Emily Fox, one of the two founders of this place. Anastasia owns a half share of Southwood, and it passes down the female line. Natalie will inherit when she dies.'

'Heck.' The coven must love that idea. 'Who owns the other half?'

'You remember the young girls you saw playing on the lawn with the headmaster? The older one of them. She's a direct descendant of the other founder.'

'But she must only be four or something.'

'I know. Crazy, isn't it? It'll be held in trust for her until she's of age, but that's the result of the mad rules the founders put in place. She and Natalie will run the place together in the fullness of time.'

It was a weird thought. 'But I doubt Natalie wants to get embroiled. And why has she accepted the role of champion when she clearly despises the school? She said Eliza epitomises everything she associates with Southwood. That didn't come across as a compliment.'

Viv laughed, then frowned. 'It is a bit odd, now you mention it. She must have a reason.'

'I noticed Anastasia seems to get on all right with Natalie.'

Viv nodded. 'She's not at all stuffy or traditional. That and being related must help.'

The bursar's heritage might explain why she hadn't retired yet. The school was in her blood, and it sounded like she loved her work. Eve thought of her bright eyes again, and her stylishly cropped white hair. There was a pizzazz about her – she was full of zest for life.

'I can see why Natalie came back to see her after she'd left school,' Viv went on. 'Anastasia's probably quite acceptable, as aunts go. The weird thing is, Natalie used to visit Eliza too. I saw her going into her office more than once. I mean, who would do that? Can you imagine actively seeking her out if you'd escaped her clutches? And after crossing her like that?'

Eve agreed. That really was odd.

4

It was mid-afternoon when Eve went for a break after putting another batch of pumpkin spice cakes into the oven. Strolling through Southwood's grounds, she tried to imagine attending such a grand school. Beyond the lawns towards the front of the site there were mature trees, their leaves turning with the change in season. Walking a little further, she could just see the lake she'd heard about too.

Turning again, she saw a face she recognised and her pulse quickened. Robin. She knew he was on site, of course. His profession as a gardener had brought him there. Southwood's regular groundskeeper was off sick and the school had needed a short-term stand-in. Robin did the gardens for most of Saxford St Peter and came recommended.

As she watched him rake leaves in the cold, his grey-streaked hair falling over his eyes, he glanced up and caught her look.

She checked over her shoulder to make certain they were alone, but all was quiet. Afternoon break had finished; the students and teachers were busy in their classrooms.

Eve and Robin were secret lovers, though not for any of the

usual reasons. Viv was one of the few people who knew they were an item. Eve kept her voice low as she approached him. 'Do you have a sixth sense or something? I thought I was being quiet.' The grass was soft and wet under her boots.

He grinned. 'Old habits die hard. It's safest to be aware of your surroundings.' It was thirteen years since he'd left his job as a detective inspector in London, but Eve could still see the policeman behind the gardener. Uncovering a network of corrupt officers and their criminal contacts had forced him underground. He'd changed his name as well as his job. 'How are your preparations going?'

She was halfway through telling him about the coven when he put a hand on her arm and glanced over her shoulder, making her look too.

Someone was coming. She could see a shadow in the trees. It put her on high alert. She knew she'd get pestered with questions about Robin's background if they went public about their relationship. Slipping up could put him in danger. It was safer to meet in secret.

'I'll make myself scarce.'

Eve nipped out of the clearing but then paused. If she carried on walking, the person approaching would probably see her. In the end, she hid close by, behind a tree. She kept still, not peering around the trunk to get a look. But the voice told her all she needed to know.

'Hello there.' It was Natalie's sensual, confident drawl.

If there was one person at Southwood who'd want to avoid her searching questions it was Robin.

His reply was little more than a grunt.

'It's been bugging me,' Natalie said. 'I feel like I've met you before. I thought I'd seek you out – see if the details come back to me. Or perhaps you remember?' Her tone was playful.

'I'm afraid I don't.' Robin's voice was clear now. 'And I'm sure I would.'

'Thank you.'

Eve didn't think Robin had meant it as a compliment. She hoped not, anyway.

'Don't worry,' Natalie went on, 'I'm sure it'll come to me. Maybe we knew each other in a past life.'

Eve hoped she was just flirting. Not that she liked it; it sent her pulse into overdrive. But it was better than the alternative: that she'd known Robin years back, when he was DI Robert Kelly. The thought sent a chill through Eve's core.

'Anyway...' Natalie drew the word out, 'I came because I want to proposition you.'

Was this about to get worse? Eve hated the sound of her ingratiating voice.

Robin didn't reply and at last she went on. 'How would you fancy coming on my show? I could wine and dine you in London at the same time. It would be fun.'

Eve was desperate to look round at them. She had visions of Natalie touching Robin, staring up into his eyes. She liked power over people – her TV show made that clear. Eve imagined it extended to captivating the men she met.

'What on earth would you want with me?'

'Are you kidding?' Natalie's laugh rang out. 'A male gardener, slaving away at an all-girls' school, probably underpaid, in order to make the grounds look pretty for a gang of privileged young things? My viewers would be fascinated.'

'And you imagine I'd get to keep my job afterwards?'

She laughed again. 'I'm sure you'd be discreet.'

But Natalie would do everything she could to avoid that.

'Thanks anyway, but I'm only temporary cover here. The head gardener's off with a bad back.'

'All the better. You'll have an outsider's eye, and you won't have to worry about future employment.'

At last, Eve risked peering at them.

Natalie was right up close, well into Robin's personal space.

'There's a fee, you know,' she said, taking a leather-bound note-book and gold pen from her bag. 'Can I at least put your details in my address book? I'm only here until tomorrow. I can leave you to think it over for a day or two, then give you a call.'

'No thanks.'

But she just laughed again. 'I'll see you before I go; I'm determined to change your mind. And in the meantime, I'm going to work out where I know you from.'

Two minutes later, Robin found Eve, seemingly knowing exactly where she'd hidden.

'Do you remember her?'

He shook his head. 'She seems pretty certain though.' He looked pale.

'What are you going to do?'

'Work out where we met before she places me. It's a long time ago now, but if my identity gets out...' He shook his head. 'The people I crossed have long memories and they aren't the sort to forgive. They make examples of people. If news gets out that I'm Robert Kelly it won't just be me that's in danger. You would be too. I can't let that happen.'

After they parted, Eve continued her walk, her pace quick-ening along with her heartbeat. Natalie's words spun in her head. Was she a danger to Robin? Had she known him as Robert Kelly? If she had, Eve could imagine what she'd do with the information. Finding an ex-police officer who'd uncovered corruption would be irresistible to her. She wouldn't care about his safety.

Her stomach was in knots by the time she approached the school building again, ready to rescue her cakes. She rounded the corner in time to see Robin head indoors ahead of her, drop-ping his rake off in a shed on the way.

And there, off to one side, stood Natalie, staring after him, chewing her lip. She was still trying to work out how she knew him, Eve guessed. How long before she remembered?

After a moment the talk-show host strode off in the direction Robin had taken.

Eve hoped to goodness she hadn't worked it out already. Watching left her feeling powerless.

She nipped along the path that ran next to the school and cautiously opened the door they'd disappeared through, glancing up and down a long corridor. She didn't want Natalie to see her. She'd been planning to go straight back to the home economics room, but the urge to see what happened next was overwhelming. She glanced at her watch. Five minutes before the cakes burned. There was no sign of Robin or Natalie, but Eve heard a creak and gave in to temptation by following it. Down a dark side corridor, she caught sight of Natalie's golden curls as she rounded a corner into an unknown room.

Had she followed Robin? Eve couldn't imagine what he'd be doing in there. Before she could stop herself, she made for the room the presenter had entered. It had no windows facing the corridor. Eve stood uneasily at the door, shifting from foot to foot, looking around, her breathing rather fast. She knew she should go.

She could hear someone talking inside but they kept their voice low; she couldn't tell who it was.

After a pause, Natalie answered. 'Well, guess what? I don't care! It's right that you pay, and believe you me, you haven't paid remotely enough. If you know what's good for you, you'll carry on just as before.'

Not Robin – he would have answered back, loud and clear – but it was a dangerous conversation nonetheless. It sounded a lot like blackmail.

Eve's heart was thudding as she inched back along the corridor. Being a known witness would be very unwise indeed.

5

As Eve returned to the home economics classroom, she saw Robin through a window. He must have sneaked out of a different door to dodge Natalie. She was glad he'd avoided her, but it meant he wouldn't have seen who she was talking to. The question played on Eve's mind as she put her cakes to cool and a bell sounded, marking the end of lessons for the day.

She and Viv had baked themselves silly by the time Sabina came and interrupted them at six.

She peered at their produce and went to sniff the pumpkin cakes Eve had made. A dissatisfied frown furrowed her brow as she stood upright again and turned her cool gaze on the pair of them.

'I've been invited to stay for supper. Seven sharp. I'll see you both in the refectory.'

'Oh no! So sorry, Sabina.' Viv stepped in front of Eve, blocking her. 'I'm afraid we can't possibly break for food at a time like this. I've brought us sandwiches. We'll work through.'

'For heaven's sake. Can you really not come and show your faces?'

'Really not. We want everything to be perfect for tomorrow.'

Sabina huffed. 'Well, honestly! Edward and I will see you at Founders' Day then.' She turned on her heel and swept out of the room.

Eve turned to Viv. 'Have you really brought us sandwiches?'

'Not exactly. But we do have an awful lot of cake.' It was true. As well as Eve's signature pumpkin spice cakes and Viv's fruit and peel, they'd made chocolate brownies, apricot flapjacks, florentines and sticky ginger biscuits.

Viv gave her best winning smile. 'And I brought a bottle of wine.'

Eve's stomach felt hollow. 'We've finished the baking, haven't we?'

Viv steered her to a chair. 'Yes, but it's supper with Sabina we're talking about. A fate far worse than cake overdose.' She presented Eve with a plateful of their bakes and poured her a helping of red in a measuring cup.

Eve's shoulders started to unknot as she accepted the situation. She hadn't relished another dose of Sabina either, and she'd get to see more of the coven the following day.

'This is actually an important part of our work,' Viv said, settling down to a flapjack. 'We can't serve this stuff tomorrow without testing it first.'

A while later, Eve was glancing out of the window onto Great Quad as she finished a final brownie. 'Supper's breaking up.'

Old-fashioned lamps illuminated hordes of students, piling out of the door from the refectory. They slowed their pace as a teacher called them to order. Most of the adults appeared after the main throng, their gowns fluttering in the breeze.

Viv appeared at Eve's side, then flinched. 'Oh no. I'd know that strutting walk anywhere.'

She was right. Sabina was marching across the grass towards their block.

'Quick!' Viv dashed to the door of the classroom and locked it, switching off the light.

In a second, she was back next to Eve, peering for Sabina, but she'd already disappeared inside their wing of the school.

'She'll be walking up our corridor this very minute,' Viv hissed. 'Keep absolutely still and quiet.'

Eve tried not to giggle. 'I can't believe we're hiding from your mother-in-law.'

'You'd hide if she was yours.'

At that moment the door rattled as someone tried to get in, and they both froze.

'Hello?' Sabina's snappy cut-glass voice called through the keyhole. 'Vivien? Eve?'

Nerves bubbled inside Eve's chest, almost pushing the laugh in her throat out.

Just when she thought she might burst, they heard Sabina's high-heeled footfalls echoing away down the corridor.

'Phew!' Viv leaned against the wall.

'Don't rejoice too soon. We'd better keep the light off. She's bound to wonder where we've gone. She might come into the quad to check again.'

They waited, peering into the night. As they watched, the final straggling students disappeared, urged on by the staff. Eve's stomach still felt quivery with suppressed laughter.

After a full five minutes, the bit of the quad nearest them was deserted.

Viv moved away from the window. 'Do you think we can turn the light back on now?'

'Hang on a minute.'

'You are the most cautious person I know.'

'It's not that. Come and look at this.'

Eve had spotted two adults leaving the refectory building later than everyone else, one wearing an academic gown, one not. They were heading across the grass in the direction of the cookery classroom Eve and Viv occupied.

'Is that one of the staff with Natalie?'

'Looks like it.' There was no mistaking the outline of the TV star's hair, and her boxy leather jacket. It would be cold out there, but Eve guessed she was too fashion conscious to add a coat. 'I think it's Martin's wife.'

'Lucia? Really. That's interesting.'

The pair looked deep in conversation, Natalie's arm through Lucia Leverett's.

'Why, especially?'

Viv glanced at Eve. 'Sabina told me Lucia voted against Natalie as Founders' Day Champion. She and Eliza were the dissenters. All the rest supported the move. But they look pretty pally now.'

'They do.' As they watched, the pair drew nearer to where they were hiding. Eve guessed they must be after a quiet place to talk. She felt shifty, standing there watching them, but she couldn't tear her eyes away. Natalie looked indignant now. Angry, in fact. But not with Lucia. She put an arm around her shoulders and gave her a squeeze, shaking her head in controlled fury. 'Looks as though Lucia's pouring out her woes and Natalie's sympathising. Whatever she's told her seems to have got Natalie worked up. Why confide in someone like her?' It seemed like a dangerous option.

'Very weird. Let's hope it's about something boring, or else—'

'Wait a moment.' Eve put a hand on Viv's arm and pointed past the pair. 'Is someone there?' She'd spotted a change in the shadows. A slight deepening in the darkness. Someone in a gown?

She and Viv peered at the spot now, Lucia and Natalie temporarily forgotten.

And then the clouds shifted, the moon lit the quad and Eve spotted a glimmer of red hair.

'It's the head girl.'

'Scarlett Holland. So it is.' Viv took a deep breath.

'What on earth is she doing, trailing after Natalie and Lucia?' Natalie's words came back to her: *I've had enough of your pestering.*

But the moonlight had spooked Scarlett. The red hair disappeared – she must have put her hood up – and she darted into the shadows. Lucia and Natalie had turned away now too, towards the tunnel that led between the library and the hall, through to Old Quad.

'It's where the guest quarters are,' Viv said. 'The ones for proper visitors. Not like us.'

Later that evening, Eve reflected on the bedroom she'd been allocated, in Great Quad, above the administrative offices. It was a classic spartan student room, with a narrow bed, a desk with a reading lamp and an empty set of shelves. A draught worked its way round the damper in the fireplace. Eve pulled it down further in a vain attempt to seal it off.

It was hardly luxury accommodation. A moment later, she'd googled the school's fees. Handsome was putting it mildly, but it certainly wasn't comfort they paid for.

As she lay in bed, she missed her cosy seventeenth-century cottage in Saxford, her snug duvet, and most of all Gus.

She didn't sleep well that night. She wasn't quite warm enough and thoughts tumbled in her mind like a jumble of laundry in a washing machine. Natalie's cruel words to the head girl, Scarlett Holland. Her threats to an unknown person. Her interest in Robin and secret chat with Lucia Leverett, who'd voted against her presence. Why was she really at Southwood? What had made her accept the role of champion?

At last, Eve dropped off, but within a couple of hours she was awake again. She sat up and grabbed a dressing gown from the chair by her bed, ready for the trip down the draughty corridor to the loo.

When she returned to her room, she was drawn to the window by the moonlight, illuminating a patch of floorboard under the dark curtain.

She pulled the curtains back a little and looked at the building opposite, its roof enclosed by battlements. On the ground floor was the library and the school hall; above it, acres of empty classrooms. And over to her right, another Victorian block – full of student bedrooms. She thought of the young people behind all those curtains. Did they suffer at Eliza Gregory's hands, just as Viv had? Why didn't the woman retire? Could Natalie be blackmailing her, so she couldn't afford to? It would explain her regular visits to the head of sixth form. But if it was true, what hold did Natalie have over her?

The thought of the TV star's ruthlessness made Eve feel sick. She'd cause so much damage if she knew Robin's past.

The quad had blurred in front of her, but suddenly, she focused again, made alert by movement.

Someone was slipping between the school buildings opposite – not using the main archway but a narrow tunnel to its right. It was impossible to tell who it was. They wore an academic gown, but all the staff had them, and the sixth formers too. It seemed formal to put one on for a night-time walk, but Eve had rapidly realised Southwood was like that. If staff or students were entitled to wear one, they tended to. Eve imagined it made some, like Scarlett, feel important. Whereas others, like Lucia, might put one on so that students could instantly identify a senior member of the school. Someone they could trust. The only time she'd seen her without one was just before the coven meeting, when she'd been briefly off-duty, playing with her children.

But could this night-time wanderer be trusted? What were they up to? Eve knew the passageway led to Old Quad, then on to the wider grounds. Were they returning to their rooms or just heading out? Eve checked her watch. It was gone three: an odd time to be up.

Suddenly, she was reminded of being at home in Saxford, in her bedroom at Elizabeth's Cottage. A number of times now, she'd woken after dreaming of thudding footsteps outside her window. There was never anyone there and each time she had to shake herself and remember that it was just a nightmare. Hearing the footsteps was said to signify danger. It was how her road, Haunted Lane, had got its name.

Tonight she was away from home and she'd heard no footsteps, but out below, someone was making their way stealthily through the grounds. Eve felt every bit as anxious as she did after the dream.

6

On Founders' Day morning, Eve sat next to Viv in the refectory, eating breakfast. They were being treated to the same menu as the staff – almond pastries and good coffee – but sitting at high table didn't cut out the echoing noise from the rest of the room. She found the clamour from the students hard to take on so little sleep, though the caffeine was helping.

Martin sat close to Lucia, their daughters between them, with an older woman Eve hadn't met opposite.

'Martin's mother,' Viv said, in a stage whisper.

Eve pieced the information together. So this was Bridget Leverett, the former headmistress. She'd watched Natalie reading out Eliza's love poem about her husband. What must the atmosphere be like at Southwood? Yet there was something reserved about Martin's mother. She was elegant, with layered grey hair done in an up-to-the-minute style, teardrop earrings and expensive-looking make-up. An outer veneer. She was looking towards her granddaughters and smiling slightly, but her expression wasn't focused or sentimental. Eve was fairly sure she was thinking of something else.

At that moment, a gowned woman appeared at Lucia's side and whispered in her ear.

Eve raised an eyebrow at Viv.

'One of the teachers, I think,' she said. 'Too young to have been here in my day.'

'Of course, of course.' Lucia shifted uneasily in her seat. Turning to her nearest daughter, she kissed her soft hair, then stood up to do the same to the other one. 'Will you two be good for Daddy? Mimi will come and join you soon. There's someone who needs my help.'

Martin glanced up at her. 'Really?' He held her hand for a moment. 'Can't it wait ten minutes?'

'It doesn't sound like it.' Lucia looked pale.

'Who is it?'

Her face was pained. 'You know I can't tell you that.'

Martin's shoulders sagged. 'All right.'

Anastasia had appeared. 'Why don't I take your place until Mimi comes?'

The older girl bounced in her seat and patted Lucia's vacant chair, but Bridget was up now. 'I am here, you know, Anastasia. If the children need someone to sit with them then I will do it.'

The older girl bit her lip and the younger one's smile faded, but Bridget took the vacated seat. Anastasia nodded and went to sit with Natalie at the other end of the table.

Bridget wasn't natural granny material, but she sure as heck didn't want to be supplanted by the bursar.

As for Lucia, Eve knew she was in the coven thanks to her role as head of pastoral care. From Martin's expression she guessed these interruptions were common. Running South-wood was a full-time job. They must be glad of Mimi.

By two o'clock that afternoon, Eve and Viv had all their cakes
marshalled, ready for kitchen staff to carry into Southwood's
grand library once the speeches were over.

'Why don't they use the hall?' Eve asked, as they left the
cookery classroom. It was just as handy.

'The library's older, and the founders viewed it as their
greatest achievement,' Viv said. 'It's a lot more ornate than the
hall, and the books impress the parents. I've always liked it –
and there's a huge open space in the middle for talks, so it lends
itself to the job all right.'

As they entered the vast room, Eve saw what Viv meant.
The place was grand, with a high vaulted ceiling. Trestle tables
covered in white cloths lined the central open space. They were
already set with stacks of fine bone china.

'I wish they'd let us bring the food in ourselves,' Viv said.
'We could have avoided the speeches altogether.'

Sabina, who was on Viv's other side, gave her an acidic look.
Just beyond her, Eve could see her husband Edward, with his
permanently puce face, nose high in the air, mouth
downturned.

As for Eve, she was curious to hear Natalie's speech. She'd
made history at one Founders' Day; she'd probably want to
make her mark this time, too.

It took a while to find out. The orchestra played as the
remainder of the audience filed in, then an unknown woman
introduced the head, Martin Leverett, who spoke first. After
him came Lucia, then the bursar, and the leader of the parent
council. Eve's mind drifted. She started to see the beautiful
library behind the Founders' Day paraphernalia. Beyond a
screen displaying photographs taken during the previous year,
the rows of books soared up towards the ceiling, a mahogany
library ladder propped against them. She was filled with a
desire to explore – find out what was there.

As Natalie finally took to the podium, Eve looked directly

above her and noticed a huge silver cup sitting high in an alcove created by a small arched window. The cup was close to the edge and Eve found herself obsessing over it toppling down and crushing Natalie's head.

She shook herself. Ridiculous. It wasn't going to fly off on its own. But the notion made her think of things hanging in the balance.

Natalie was talking about her school days. She used no notes. There was some laughter as she said her message would be 'do as I say, not as I did'.

'You all know what I do for a living,' she added. 'So if any sixth formers over the age of eighteen – or the staff of course – fancy unburdening yourselves about your experiences at Southwood on television, come and see me.'

'The very idea.' Sabina's whisper travelled.

Natalie returned to tradition as she finished off, paying tribute to the school and its staff. It was out of character and ought to have acted as a warning.

'Eliza Gregory and I had our differences when I was a student here, but I'm thrilled that she's still teaching. We have a gem too in our wonderful bursar, my aunt, Anastasia Twite, and I know we're all filled with admiration for Martin, just as we were for his mother, and also his father, Anthony.' Then she nodded at Eliza Gregory. 'Some of us even more than others. But it's not unnatural. Who can resist those wonderful Leverett looks?'

She laughed, and all heads turned towards the head of sixth form. Eve could only see her rear view, her shoulders tensed, her body absolutely still.

Anthony was no longer around to hear Natalie remind everyone of Eliza's crush, but his wife was. Eve turned to look at her. She didn't appear vulnerable, standing there, her trim figure smart in a black suit. But Eve could tell from her face that she was angry.

7

Uniformed kitchen staff put out tray after tray of Viv and Eve's bakes, slipping around to each of the trestle tables, noiselessly setting down their burdens and returning with more as the speeches went on. Trolleys arrived with urns of tea and huge coffee pots.

The moment the speeches ended, the hush turned to mayhem. Parents spotted each other across the crowded space and shuffled round the rows of chairs, tripping over abandoned bags, trailing coats and awkwardly placed umbrellas. It took Eve and Viv a while to reach a trestle table and sample their own wares a second time. Eve had just taken her first sip of tea when Viv plucked at her sleeve.

'Sabina and Edward have followed us. Let's make a run for it.'

They moved through the crowd.

'I had a good snooze during the speeches,' Viv said. 'Though I came to in time to hear Natalie's dig at Eliza.'

'That was definitely the standout bit.' Eve couldn't imagine Eliza's response when Natalie was proposed as Founders' Day Champion. And the others must know the story, yet they'd gone ahead. They might not sympathise with Eliza – she sounded cruel – but Natalie didn't strike Eve as much better. Eve wondered again who'd thought she was a good idea, and how they'd managed to get a majority to vote in favour.

As she pondered the puzzle, she tried to spot Natalie in the crowd. At last she saw her, surrounded by a cluster of dads. The mums held back, chatting to each other, looking on with unfriendly eyes.

But in amongst the throng walked Scarlett Holland, the head girl. She made her way up to Natalie, all strutting confidence, and rather than shooing her away, Natalie turned her back on her fan club and smiled at Scarlett.

'Look at that.' Eve gave a subtle nod in their direction.

Viv frowned. 'Are you sure it was them you heard in the loos yesterday?'

'Certain.' But you'd never guess it now. Natalie had her arm around Scarlett's shoulders, her eyes on hers, chatting animatedly. Then she laughed and clapped Scarlett on the back. The head girl looked lively too – excited, eager.

'They're suddenly best friends?'

'Maybe Scarlett's offered herself up for a slot on Natalie's talk show.'

'I'm surprised Natalie looks so enthusiastic. She'll want dirt, not a head girl's perspective.'

It was true. But maybe there was more to Scarlett than met the eye. Viv had hinted her selection had been biased, because her father was a major Southwood donor. Perhaps her dad thought you could buy anything at a price. Scarlett might be just as unprincipled. Willing to gossip about the school for five minutes of fame. Of course, if Natalie unveiled a Southwood scandal, she'd reduce the value of Anastasia's half share in the school – the share she was due to inherit. But Eve doubted she'd care. She had a jaundiced view of the place and she'd made a mint through her TV career, according to the press.

A little later on, Eve found herself alone as Viv chatted to a contemporary with a daughter at Southwood. She was drawn to the quieter areas of the library. A bank of museum-style display cases beyond the last bookcase caught her attention. She wandered over and found they contained a series of ancient first editions.

She spent some time quietly studying them, and was turning away after she'd finished when she caught movement out of the corner of her eye. It made her start. She'd thought she was alone in that section of the library, but someone had just entered the avenue of books beyond where she stood. She'd caught sight of the hem of an academic gown.

What was a member of staff doing hiding away when the library was crammed with parents? But maybe it was one of the sixth formers, after some peace and quiet.

Eve walked along, browsing the solid-backed bookcases nearest her, until she reached the end closest to the windows. She could wander round to the next row now, but the thought of the unknown gowned figure made her hesitate. Maybe they didn't want to be disturbed. For some unaccountable reason she felt nervous, and then a sudden angry voice coming from the next row made her jump.

'She told me all about it. It's heartless of you! How could you treat her so badly?'

That was Natalie. She must be talking to the person in the gown. Eve was glad she'd kept to her row.

Holding her breath, she crouched down, and pretended to examine a book on the bottom shelf. She didn't want to be at eye level. A moment later, she peered around the end of the bookcase and glanced cautiously up at the people talking. It was Natalie and Martin Leverett. The chat-show host had her back to her. She was standing opposite the headmaster.

Slowly, Eve withdrew behind the bookcase again, still crouched down.

She didn't catch all of Martin's reply, but the words 'no idea what you're talking about' were clear.

'You're saying it's not true?'

'Of course it isn't.'

'Forgive me if I don't believe you.' Natalie's tone was barely controlled. '*She* was in no doubt.'

And then Eve heard it, a slap. Hand on skin. She was quite sure. Natalie had hit Martin – or he'd hit her.

She heard a gasp. It sounded like the headmaster. She stood up and travelled down her side of the bookcase again. A moment later she watched him emerge, walking quickly, a hand to his cheek. He didn't rejoin the throng but went through a door marked 'staff'.

Natalie appeared too. She was shaking slightly, but went back to the crowds, laughing as she joined one of the adoring dads.

Eve followed at a distance, her mind full of what she'd overheard.

What had the pair been talking about? Was it something to do with Scarlett? Natalie had been talking to her most recently. But Eve doubted it; she hadn't seen any tension between the head girl and Martin. Maybe it related to the heart-to-heart Natalie had had with Martin's wife the night before then. Had Martin let Lucia down in some way? Or was this to do with one of the students? Whatever it was, it must be significant. Natalie had been properly angry.

8

There was no avoiding supper with the coven that night. They'd made it clear that Viv and Eve would be expected to join them. It was intended as a thank you, which Viv had said was 'deeply ironic'. She'd come up with a number of creative excuses to get out of it, but Eve had pushed back. It had seemed too rude. At least Sabina had gone home. ('Small mercies,' Viv said.)

Eve was preoccupied by Natalie's conversation with the headmaster. If she *had* been referring to what Lucia told her it begged new questions. Did she and Lucia have a secret connection? But if they were close, why had Lucia voted against her as champion?

'I said please pass the salt.' Eliza fixed Eve with her cold blue eyes, her skin pale, lips pursed.

'I'm sorry.' She obliged, then tried to apply herself to her melba toast and duck pâté.

Eliza had taken a seat as far away from Natalie as possible. No surprises there. Scarlett had distanced herself from Southwood's special guest too, but Eve noticed their eyes meet periodically, as if they were sharing a private joke. Eve had felt for

Scarlett when Natalie was so rude to her, but in general, she found it hard to warm to the head girl. Her smile was superior, and her attempts to lay down the law at the coven meeting suggested she was used to getting her own way.

Eve was curious to see how Martin and Natalie interacted after their earlier confrontation. The answer was, not much at all. Martin was attentive towards his wife, Lucia, and she smiled in reply, but she seemed tense and rather stiff.

Martin's mother, Bridget, was next to her daughter-in-law. 'How are the children?' she asked.

'Perfect,' Lucia said. 'They're having a story and hot choco-late with Mimi before bed. Founders' Day always wears them out.'

'How old are they?' Eve asked across the table.

'Pip's three and Ada's four and a half,' Lucia said.

'Ada owns a half share in the school, if you can believe it,' Bridget put in. 'Her "privilege" as a female descendant of Alice Blyth, who co-founded Southwood with Emily Fox. Of course, it's held in trust until she's of age. But all the same, it's a mad arrangement, you must admit.'

Martin looked up, frowning. 'Dad didn't think so.'

'I of all people know that, Martin.' Her tone was tart. Perhaps it was her husband who'd persuaded her to come and teach at Southwood so that he could be involved in the family enterprise. As a man, he wouldn't inherit, but it sounded as though he'd believed in the school. It was interesting that Bridget still lived there if she was less convinced. Maybe it was because of the grandchildren. She seemed territorial – she hadn't liked it when Anastasia offered to keep them entertained.

The whole thing was a bizarre set-up. Eve felt sorry for Ada, destined to run the school alongside a cynical, uninterested Natalie, fifty-odd years her senior. What an arrangement to be saddled with.

. . .

Southwood looked different after dark. Eve and Viv had been back to their rooms after supper, but had bumped into the bursar when they emerged for the final event of the day: evening drinks. Now, Anastasia was leading them along one edge of Great Quad. The lamplight created deep shadows in dark corners. The wind stirred the odd brittle leaf, trapped near the forbidding buildings. Anastasia's heeled shoes clipped along, her long gown blowing out behind her, making her look like a bat. As Eve caught up, the bursar's eyes glinted in the low light. She looked even more awake at night.

They were nearing the door to the staff common room, leading off a corner of the quad. 'There will be brandy and coffee on offer,' Anastasia said. 'Well deserved after another successful Founders' Day, and all your hard work. And of course, I have to drink to my ancestor, Emily Fox. Her achievements are well worth toasting. In fact, I—'

But then she broke off. The light was on in the library. Eve assumed someone was still clearing up in there, though the event had finished hours ago. But now, Natalie's silhouette appeared behind a blind – the long curly hair and her boxy leather jacket.

Anastasia paused. 'I wonder what she's up to. Perhaps I should go and find out.'

But at that moment, Eve saw a second figure stop abruptly outside the library, near the door, deep in shadow. She couldn't see who it was, except that they wore an academic gown, just like Anastasia. And all the other staff and sixth formers. In a moment, they were under the porticoed entrance, their hood up. Eve saw them turn a fraction, checking behind them, but not enough to reveal their face. They paused for what felt like forever before entering the building. Nervous perhaps? They hadn't spotted Eve, Viv and Anastasia. The three of them were at the entrance to the staff area now, deep in shadow.

As they watched, the second figure appeared inside the

library in silhouette. Their hesitancy was all gone, they passed three windows at speed, an arm up.

For a moment, Eve wondered if they meant to harm Natalie. Her mouth went dry, but whoever it was didn't attack her. There was definitely a row going on, though. Natalie threw her hands up and shuddered. It seemed she could barely control herself.

'I apologise,' Anastasia said. 'Sometimes my job is to step in, but I also need to know when to step back. At the moment, I have to confess, I'm torn.'

As she spoke, the person who'd joined Natalie appeared in the same window as her, their hood down now, and their two silhouettes became one. The newcomer was holding her and she was letting them.

Anastasia shook her head. She still looked white in the lamplight and Eve guessed she'd been scared, just like her. 'I think that answers my question.' But still she frowned. 'Let's carry on to the common room and have that brandy.'

9

Eve and Viv followed Anastasia into the staff common room. They were the first people to arrive.

'Let's not stand on ceremony!' The bursar turned her twinkly smile on them, then strode over to a table with decanters and a variety of glasses. 'Brandy for you both?'

'Thank you.'

Beyond where she stood, pouring their drinks, a fire blazed in a huge chimney breast, crackling, a log subsiding as it turned to charcoal.

'Here.' Anastasia held out a glass for each of them and poured her own. Soon after she'd finished, Martin and Lucia appeared at the door and Anastasia took their drink orders too, by which time Eliza had also joined the group.

'Well,' Anastasia said, 'another Founders' Day over.' She passed the head of sixth form a glass and raised her own. 'It went off all right, in the end. Here's to us all and to Southwood.'

Martin raised his glass, but Eliza stood stiffly to one side. 'All right for whom?'

Lucia moved closer to her and put a hand on her arm, which Eliza shook off.

'Natalie's a tricky customer, I grant you,' Anastasia said, 'but you already know why I wanted to bring her in.' She turned to Eve and Viv. 'Before the vote, her share in the school was on my mind.' She paused. 'I argued that it was no use keeping a future owner at arm's length, given the influential nature of the position.'

Eliza spluttered. 'Oh believe me, she already has plenty of influence. And nothing's going to change that.'

'What do you mean?' Lucia was very still, and Eve noticed Martin had drunk his brandy in one go.

Eliza seemed to shrink slightly and there was a pause before she replied. 'Well, she's here as Founders' Day Champion, isn't she? Despite being wholly unsuitable.'

'Careful.' Anastasia glanced at the door. 'She might come in any moment.' She glanced at Viv and Eve, and raised an eyebrow. 'Though she looked rather busy when I last saw her, it has to be said.' She downed her brandy too.

'What— What was she up to?' Martin's voice was low. He'd had to clear his throat and restart his question. Lucia glanced at him sharply.

'Nothing for you to worry about,' Anastasia said.

Lucia hitched up her sleeve and glanced at her watch. It was a moment before she spoke. 'She and Scarlett are taking their time.'

'I expect they're talking about Scarlett's future career in the media,' Eliza said, closing her eyes as though to reject the image that was forming in her head. 'I over-heard Scarlett chattering about it, following in Natalie's wake.'

If that was Scarlett's plan, it explained her efforts to get close to Natalie. Though not her sudden success.

'But Natalie spoke to me about Scarlett only yesterday.' Lucia was frowning. 'It was shortly after the coven met. She was horrible about the girl. I had to pull her up about it.' She glanced at the bursar. 'Sorry, Anastasia. I know she's your niece, but there are limits.'

Once again, Eve wondered why Lucia had confided in Natalie if her opinion of her was so poor.

The bursar held up her hand as Martin's mother, Bridget, entered the common room.

'You know I don't offend easily, Lucia.' She turned to Southwood's former headmistress. 'Can I get you a drink, Bridget?'

But Bridget marched straight up to the decanters herself. 'I'm sure I can manage.' She gripped the neck of the cut glass tightly and poured herself a large brandy.

'We were just saying how Natalie and Scarlett are apparently best of friends today,' Eliza said. 'It seems Natalie has agreed to help Scarlett launch a TV career. I daresay they deserve each other.'

Eve couldn't believe she was being so unguarded about her feelings. Had the coven really just made Scarlett head girl because of her father? She realised she'd been hoping it was at least a blurred issue. Scarlett might have a rich dad, yet still be one of the top students. 'I assumed Scarlett must be a figure-head for the school, as head girl?'

Eliza stood there, stony-faced. 'We'll see, won't we?'

This was worse than Eve had imagined. It seemed that Eliza thought of Scarlett as a liability.

Bridget tutted. Perhaps she felt the head of sixth form had said too much.

'Scarlett's a little bit hard to take at the moment,' Anastasia said, 'but that's not uncommon for someone of her age. She gets excellent grades – genuinely a marvellous all-rounder.' The bursar struck Eve as practical enough to realise the sort of rumours that might be circulating. She'd found a way to justify Scarlett's appointment, though Eve sensed it hadn't been her idea. Her tone was slightly strained. 'Even Natalie brings in some fresh air,' the bursar went on. 'Challenges us. It's right that we should be kept on our toes.'

Eliza shook her head, slammed her glass down on a side table and stalked out of the room, her head held high.

Eve and Viv didn't manage to extricate themselves from the common room until gone eleven. Despite the long period sitting listening to the speeches, Eve felt bone-achingly tired. She couldn't wait to get into her narrow creaky bed and close her eyes. Yet still she couldn't sleep when the time came. The question of who had met Natalie that evening floated through her mind. There were a few male teachers, she knew, as well as some maintenance staff, a caretaker, and the various dads who attended Founders' Day. One of them might have come back. But did that fit?

The scene in silhouette had looked like an emotional standoff, followed by a passionate reconciliation.

At last, she got out of bed, pulled on a thick navy sweater and went to look out of the window, just as she had the night before. There was something mesmerising about the school after dark, as if time had stood still. Across the way she could see the grand library – in darkness now.

She had her bedroom light off and sat between the closed curtains and the glass, feeling the cold from the single-glazed window. She'd stopped being conscious of the scene in front of her when movement yanked her attention back. It was like the previous evening was playing on repeat.

A figure in an academic gown was walking in the shadows again. Was it the same person? This time they'd appeared from the passageway that ran under the rooms opposite, rather than disappearing into it, but Eve thought their gait looked the same.

And then they turned a corner, and for just a moment, they

were lit by moonlight. Their hood was down, and Eve could see their hair.

It was Anastasia Twite, walking purposefully towards the building to Eve's right. Returning to her rooms, Eve suspected. But where had she been?

10

Eve got through three cups of coffee in double-quick time the following morning. She was sitting with Viv and the coven again, at high table in the refectory. She'd read somewhere that you could replace sleep with food, so she'd tucked into the full English breakfast served on Sundays rather desperately. She still felt shattered as she put down her knife and fork. It was a relief to think she'd be able to go home soon.

Over the rim of her coffee cup, she peered at Anastasia. The woman looked as bright-eyed and vibrant as ever, her white hair neat and stylish, subtle make-up carefully applied. How did she stay so energised after wandering the school at night? Maybe she was the sort who got by with four hours' sleep. Eve was dying to ask, but she didn't want to admit she'd been peering at her.

Scarlett arrived at that moment. Eve saw her pause mid-stride in the refectory doorway, her eyes on high table. Maybe she'd been hoping it would be empty by this time, and she'd be able to sit with her friends.

As it was, Scarlett slowed her pace but brought her tray over once she'd loaded it.

'You're a little late, Scarlett,' Lucia Leverett said.

Martin had already gone to get ready for the weekly service at the chapel. He always gave a reading, apparently.

'And what happened to you last night?' Eliza put in, turning her sharp face towards the head girl.

'I had to study.'

Eliza's eyebrows shot up and Scarlett flushed.

It was clear she doubted her, yet Anastasia had said she got excellent grades. It didn't make sense.

'We missed you at common room drinks,' the bursar said, mildly.

'I meant to say I couldn't make it at dinner. I'm sorry.'

'Natalie didn't turn up either.' Eliza sniffed and dabbed the corners of her mouth very precisely with her napkin. 'And now she's not here again.'

'I don't know about that. I didn't see her.' Scarlett's reply was abrupt. She looked down and busied herself with her bacon and tomatoes, her red hair falling forward, covering her face.

Eliza sat, her back ramrod straight, and stared at Scarlett. 'But you visited her, didn't you?'

Scarlett looked up and blinked.

'I was further down her corridor. I saw you outside her rooms, mid-evening. I must say, it's delightful if surprising that you two are best of friends now.'

Scarlett looked down again. It was a moment before she spoke. 'She's been very kind – agreed to help me make contacts in television. That's why I was visiting her. But I don't know where she went later in the evening, that's what I meant.'

But Eve could see she'd been caught out. She'd clearly had no idea anyone had seen her visit Natalie and it was obvious that Eliza's attention was unwelcome. Yet she'd come up with an excuse readily enough. Why not say that in the first place? Eve could only conclude she had good reason to keep her entire visit secret.

'It's a bit odd that she hasn't joined us for breakfast,' Anastasia said. 'I know she's a law unto herself, but it's her last day here and she likes to make her presence felt.'

They looked towards the refectory door, then at each other.

'Has anyone seen her this morning?' the bursar added.

Heads shook all round.

'Perhaps she's having a lie-in.' Anastasia gave Eve and Viv a meaningful look.

Eve took her point. After the scene in the library, it seemed possible that she'd enjoyed a night of passion, and was sleeping it off.

'I think I might give her a ring.' Anastasia took a mobile from her pocket and dialled, but the call went to voicemail. A couple of minutes later, a uniformed member of staff approached her side and spoke quietly in her ear.

'That's odd,' she said, as the young woman slipped off again. 'Natalie requested help with her luggage yesterday, but when the domestic team knocked on her door ten minutes ago there was no reply. They ended up using their own keys in case she'd left her bags for them to collect, but she hasn't even packed. They say her bed doesn't look slept in.' Again, the bursar glanced at Eve and Viv. 'I can think of possible reasons for that, but she said she was catching the ten o'clock train.' She frowned. 'I wonder if we should look for her.'

As the four coven members got up, Anastasia hung back with Eve and Viv.

'I've asked the domestic team to knock on the doors of the male staff who live on site,' she said in an undertone. 'I suppose they might find her there, but I don't know... It's not like her to let affairs of the heart change plans that affect her business. She's due in the studio later.'

The day was breezy, but much sunnier than of late. Clouds scudded across the sky as they walked through the quads, checking the library, the kitchens and the classrooms.

Everywhere was deserted.

'Everyone will be heading to the chapel for the service.' Lucia tucked her tangled bob behind her ears as they headed outside again, but the wind pulled it free within a minute.

'I think we can safely say she won't be there,' Anastasia replied. 'The gardens, perhaps?'

Eve had visions of Natalie deep in conversation with Robin, asking more probing questions.

But it was Sunday, of course. He'd be back in Saxford. There was no one in the gardens but them.

Anastasia's mobile rang. 'Any sign of her?' she said without a pause. 'Ah... I see. Well, thanks for doing the rounds.' She turned to the rest of them. 'The domestic team have had a hunt, but no luck. Where else might she be?' She closed her eyes for a moment. 'We all know her well enough. Where could she be hiding?' She looked at Eliza.

'What about the hidden room? She spent enough time there as a student.' The head of sixth form's tone was bitter.

It seemed to Eve that both Lucia and Scarlett reacted to the name, stopping in their tracks, absolutely still.

Anastasia raised her eyes to heaven and turned to Eve and Viv. 'The students break in there sometimes. It's not really hidden, but it's out of the way and out of bounds. The perfect goal for a rebellious child. It's at attic level and leads to one of the battlements on the roof, so you can see why it's forbidden.' She turned back to Eliza. 'You think she might go there for old times' sake?'

The woman shrugged. 'Or out of devilment. I've never found her sentimental.'

'I can't imagine her staying there overnight. It's not very comfortable. Still, perhaps we should check.' Anastasia took a purposeful step towards an arched doorway in the corner tower of a nearby building. The others moved more slowly.

They entered, and Eve filed up a spiral staircase just behind the bursar.

'I've never liked this place,' Eliza said. 'Too many memories of coming here to scold Natalie for wantonly disobeying the rules.'

It was dark and gloomy too, but Eve could imagine the appeal to students. She'd been boringly law-abiding as a child, but a narrow spiral staircase leading to the rooftops would have been beguiling.

At the very top was a solid oak door.

'It's kept locked of course,' Anastasia said, 'but I'm afraid the occasional student excels at lock picking.'

'Natalie certainly did,' Eliza said.

Anastasia tested the door, and Eve could see Eliza had been right. Or at least, someone had managed to get it open. Eve could see light through the chink the bursar had made. She knocked before going any further.

When there was no reply, she pushed the door wide and stepped inside, the rest of them on her tail.

They came to an abrupt halt when the bursar did. Her eyes were fixed on the floor across the room.

Natalie lay there, dead.

11

Eve closed her eyes, but not before she'd registered an image that would never leave her. Natalie's head was in a terrible mess. She could see blood and other detail her brain didn't even want to compute.

As she stood there, dizzy, her breathing ragged, Anastasia called the police. Eve could hear her voice as though from a long way off, mechanical, tight – barely controlled. Somehow, they managed to back out of the space, though no one seemed to coordinate it. The bursar locked the door behind them, but only on the second attempt. Her hands were shaking. Their quivering echoed the nausea jittering in Eve's stomach.

As they trod slowly down the spiral staircase, like sleep-walkers, Eve could hear Lucia's breathing just in front of her, fast and uneven.

Eve's stomach was still turning. The image of the room flashed in her mind: a door which must lead to the roof, a low bench by a squat attic window and a bundle of flags, stuffed into an umbrella stand in one corner. They must fly them on special occasions.

And Natalie. Eve's mind created a blurred impression of

her, shutting out the details.

The police were quick. Eve saw the first cars arrive through the staff common room window. She was in there with Scarlett, Viv and Eliza. Lucia had gone to her husband to warn him to keep the students in the chapel. Anastasia had darted off to talk to the police. Eve could see her now, striding towards a patrol car.

Eve had texted Robin to tell him the news. She wondered if anyone had seen him and Natalie together. Thoughts of him embroiled in the investigation sent her insides to jelly. On the local police, it was only Greg Boles who knew Robin's true identity. Greg happened to be married to Robin's cousin. The others were in the dark and she knew it was important it stayed that way. Colleagues of Robin's who'd seemed like friends had turned out to be foes. Who knew what dodgy connections members of the local force might have?

Eve had contacted her neighbours too, to warn them she might be late picking up Gus. Thoughts of giving both Robin and the dachshund a hug hovered in her mind, out of reach.

'They'll want to speak to you urgently, I imagine, Scarlett.' Eliza brought Eve's thoughts back to the room. 'You were one of the last people to see Natalie alive. Maybe *the* last.' Her cold eyes held a spark of malice. 'It was a little after nine when I saw you outside her room. Were you on your way in, or had you just left?'

'I don't remember.' Scarlett had her hands over her eyes.

'Were you on your way to talk to Natalie as well?' Eve tried not to make the question sound like a challenge. The urgency to find Natalie's murderer was all-consuming with Robin tangentially involved, and Eliza's presence needed explaining. Eve and Viv had been given rooms in the main blocks, but Natalie had a proper suite, away from the staff apartments and student quarters. It wasn't a place you just happened to pass through.

The noise Eliza made reminded Eve of a turkey. 'I was. Not that it's any of your business. When I saw Scarlett, I realised Natalie was already engaged and went off again.'

Eve's question seemed to have rallied the head girl.

'Oh, really?' She stared at the head of sixth form. 'Perhaps you came back later. Perhaps *you* were the last person to see her.'

Angry red patches tinged Eliza's pale skin. 'I didn't! I wasn't!'

But she was picking at the sleeve of her dress. Eve wasn't sure she was telling the truth.

'Either way,' Scarlett went on, 'I'm sure the police will be just as keen to talk to you as to me. Everyone knows how much you hated poor Natalie. And yet you sought her out the night she died. That seems very odd.'

'And she held you in the utmost contempt until her mysterious change of heart on Founders' Day,' Eliza shot back. 'I'm sure the police will find that detail of interest too.'

All that was true, but of course, Eve, Viv and Anastasia had seen Natalie in the library, later than when Scarlett had visited her. Eve wondered whether to say so, but the police might prefer her to keep it quiet. And now Eve knew Natalie was dead, another possibility occurred to her.

Perhaps the silhouette in the library hadn't been her at all, but the killer or their accomplice dressed to look like her. It would only have taken a wig to mimic those bouncy curls. Eve traced the thought back to what had triggered it. It was the staginess of the scene which made her wonder. Natalie was a dramatic person of course, but it still left Eve feeling uncertain. And if the scene had been faked, then there were two people who knew the truth about Natalie's death.

It would be interesting to know exactly when she'd died.

· · ·

Eve's interview was with DC Olivia Dawkins, a quiet, conscientious detective who Eve had met before. So much better than getting her old foe, Detective Inspector Nigel Palmer. She'd seen him through a classroom window, talking to Martin Leverett, and felt a small twinge of sympathy. Palmer was a lazy, narrow-minded toad in human form. From a selfish point of view, she'd been glad he was occupied. Despite his seniority, he often interviewed her personally so he could warn her off. She'd written the obituaries of several murder victims now, unearthing crucial information which had helped the police. Rather than being grateful, Palmer hated her for it.

On the upside, he was careless and sometimes let details slip about the case. Dawkins was much more cautious, though she provided a rough time of death. Eve was asked to account for her movements between six thirty and eleven the previous night.

She told DC Dawkins everything she could remember, from attending dinner to witnessing the silhouettes in the library window at nine thirty and joining the coven for drinks until she left at eleven fifteen.

By the time the interview was over, the news of Natalie's death had reached the media. Overblown tributes were pouring in on Twitter, though there were some nasty comments too.

Eve's mobile went as she was on her way to the bathroom, breathing deeply to steady herself.

'*Eve, it's Portia Coldwell.*' Portia was her contact on *Icon* magazine. '*We've just heard about Natalie Somerson. I gather she died in your neck of the woods and some of her closest connections are there. We wondered if you'd be willing to write her obituary for us?*'

'I'm at Southwood School now.' Eve explained the background.

'*How perfect,*' Portia said. '*I'll pop you over a contract.*'

How perfect. Eve felt sicker still.

12

Eve and Viv drove back to Saxford St Peter together. Within forty minutes, they were sitting safe and cocooned in Elizabeth's Cottage.

Gus was behaving as though Eve had been gone for months, scampering around the living room excitedly, then rushing up to make sure she was still there, putting an anxious paw on her leg. She'd given him lots of reassuring cuddles and had found them just as sustaining herself.

He followed her through to the kitchen as she went to make mugs of tea and piles of toast.

'Thanks,' Viv said, drawing up a chair at the kitchen table. 'I've only just realised how hungry I am.'

'I know. I thought toast might settle our stomachs. There's mushroom pâté as well, if you're up to it.'

Viv's eyes lit up. 'It's probably best to maintain our strength.'

Eve had asked Tammy and Lars, old hands at Viv's teashop, to cover the Sunday afternoon shift. It meant she and Viv had time to pause and take stock. Thank goodness Lars had extended his stay in Saxford for love of Tammy. He was planning to go home to take a degree in psychology eventually. He'd be hard to replace; a sizeable proportion of Monty's clientele was in love with him.

'Who do you think did it?' Viv spread a thick layer of pâté on the sourdough toast.

'Give me a chance!'

'My money's on Eliza.' She paused to swig her tea. 'She's definitely ruthless enough – I've seen that from my own experience. And she's friends with my mother-in-law. They were probably in it together. Case closed.'

'People can be appalling yet innocent of murder.'

Viv tutted. 'If you say so. So, what's the plan?'

Eve reached for her laptop, which was on the kitchen dresser, and flipped it open. A moment later, she'd created two spreadsheets, one for the obituary and one for the murder investigation. She set up tabs for each of the key players.

'We need to order the information we have.' Neatly recording every detail would help her feel in control. She'd want to have it ready to share with Robin, too. Butterflies fluttered their way around her stomach as she thought of him. He'd texted to say he'd been interviewed by Greg Boles, but given no further detail. Her imagination filled in the blanks. Someone had seen him with Natalie. Their behaviour looked suspicious. He was high on the list of suspects... His words after his talk with Natalie came back to her. *If news gets out that I'm Robert Kelly it won't just be me that's in danger. You would be too. I can't let that happen.*

She knew he'd never kill to protect the status quo, but anyone who discovered the background might not be so sure.

She badly wanted an update. They'd arranged to meet later.

In the meantime, she needed to focus. 'Let's pool ideas. But first, tell me again how the ownership of Southwood works. Who will get Natalie's share now she's dead, and what powers would she have had, if she'd come into her inheritance?' Financial gain or a desire to protect the school seemed like two possible motives for her murder.

Viv puffed out her cheeks. 'Okay. So, there were two founders, Emily Fox and Alice Blyth. They decreed that their half shares in the school should pass down the female line, because they were flying the flag for their sex. They wanted the institution run by women, for women.'

'Got it.'

'In the present day, the descendants who own the half shares are Anastasia Twite and little Ada Leverett, whose portion's held in trust until she comes of age.'

'Do you know who the trustees are?'

'I think Lucia's one of them, as her mother, but there's some independent lawyer too, according to Sabina. She was telling me all about it. She doesn't like it because the lawyer's male.'

'And what will happen to Anastasia's share, now Natalie's gone?'

Viv gave her a meaningful look. 'Here's where it gets interesting. Natalie was the last of her line. Her half share will go to Ada, and the whole thing will pass down to her female heirs.'

'Wow.'

'Think Martin or Lucia would kill to benefit their daughter?'

Eve frowned. 'They don't seem ruthless enough, and it would only accelerate what would happen anyway, in the fullness of time. I suppose worry over Natalie's effect on the school could have urged them on though. How much control would she have had?'

'Well, the coven do all the day-to-day running of the place, but they have to get sign-off for any major financial decisions. The heirs can veto all significant changes, so the coven has to keep them sweet.'

'Natalie could have been a real thorn in their side then, if she was intent on making trouble. Devalued the school, perhaps, so that Ada's inheritance dwindled to almost nothing.' Eve was sure Natalie would have been out to vex the coven at every turn. Objectively, she could see Martin and Lucia's motive, but instinct still told her they were unlikely. Committing murder would have been a far greater risk to their family than a possible downturn in the school's fortunes.

Eve could imagine the pair resorting to violence in response to a desperate, urgent threat, but it was hard to envisage otherwise. She noted down everything Viv had told her. After that, they threw out memories and dragged up details until the tabs on the spreadsheets were crammed with information. Eve breathed a little more easily. At least they were getting it down while it was fresh.

'What about back in the old days?' she asked Viv. 'Did Natalie have any special friends at Southwood? Or other enemies beyond Eliza?'

Viv wrinkled her nose. 'I'd say she had acolytes, rather than friends. People gathered round because they felt it was safer to be on her side than not. I never saw her let anyone get truly close.'

It was interesting. What had made her isolate herself? And why had she been so intimidating to others?

She checked the notes she'd made. 'So, we've covered Southwood, and Martin and Lucia benefit from Natalie's death indirectly, via Ada. But we need to consider Natalie's personal fortune too. She was loaded, by all accounts – one of those celebrities whose annual income makes the papers. We need to know who might inherit that. I suppose her husband's the most likely. Let's get googling. We need information on him and their domestic life.'

Viv took out her phone so they could work in parallel.

'Heck.' Eve had found an article entitled 'At Home with Natalie Somerson'. 'She lives in a seven-bedroom, four-bathroom mansion this side of Ipswich. When she's not down in

London filming, that is. She's got an apartment there too, apparently.'

Viv peered at the photos Eve had found. The country house was huge, with tall chimneys and mature trees in the grounds. 'I am so in the wrong business,' she said. 'I'm sure baking ought to pay better than humiliating people in front of a live audience.'

Eve was scanning more results about Natalie. 'Speaking of her day job, she's had a number of death threats in the past, according to this article.'

She couldn't imagine how she'd managed to block them out. They must have sat there permanently in some corner of her mind. Whatever she'd been like, the abuse was horrific.

'So those people will be suspects.'

Eve nodded. 'But we can't hope to tackle them. Besides, Palmer will give them a thorough going-over.'

'Palmer? Thorough? Are we talking about the same person?'

But Eve was sure of her ground. 'He won't do it personally, but he'll look at non-Southwood suspects as a priority. He'll want it to be an outsider – not someone from a well-to-do school, educating the children of the local great and good. Ruffling feathers there might affect his career. And because Southwood's privately owned, the senior staff are inextricably linked with the school's identity.'

If Robin was a suspect, it meant Palmer would focus on him too. Arresting a local gardener would be a lot more appealing than one of the coven. Her insides shrank at the thought of it.

'I've found husband number four,' Viv said, turning her phone so Eve could see. 'They married nine months ago, apparently.'

Eve scanned the details. The man was Gavin Vale. Good-looking with dark hair and brown eyes, but there was something untrustworthy in the twinkle he'd aimed at the camera. Or maybe Eve was being cynical. Vale was a musician apparently.

'I'll google his band.' It was called Winged Flight. Eve had never heard of them, but that didn't mean anything.

A few minutes later, she looked up at Viv again. 'They're old-timers, but the band was a big name back in the day and Vale still plays live gigs. He's continued to be part of the rock-and-roll scene by the sound of it. Scandalous, drug-fuelled parties and the like. If his royalties have dried up, he might be glad of Natalie's money. And he's probably jealous too. There are several recent articles about the affair she supposedly had with that actor, Calvin Wright.' The accompanying photos showed Natalie's furious face, part-blocked by her hand, up to the camera lens. *Natalie says no – she's not having an affair.* 'It looks like Wright's abroad right now, so he's not a suspect. As for Vale, I've got every reason to interview him, as her husband. But of course, he might not be her beneficiary.' They hadn't been married long.

'Will you get to see inside Natalie's house?' Viv asked wistfully.

'That could be useful if I can swing it.'

'If you need anyone to take notes, please let me know.'

'You'd only fidget.'

13

_____

After Viv left, Eve sent an email to Gavin Vale's agent, asking to interview him about Natalie. She hoped the sniff of publicity in a high-profile magazine like *Icon* might tempt him, even if paying tribute to his wife didn't. Relations might have been poor between them, given the recent news coverage.

She pondered him as a suspect. The country house wasn't so far from Southwood. He could have sneaked onto the school site to meet Natalie. Pinched a gown maybe, to slip around unnoticed. If the silhouette in the library was genuine, he could have been the other figure. He and Natalie had probably been rowing over her rumoured infidelity. Maybe he'd pretended he was desperate to see her. And then she – flattered by his attention – had held his hand and guided him up to the hidden room, where he'd taken a horrific revenge.

But did that really fit? Gavin Vale couldn't have relied on finding a murder weapon at the crime scene. Eve wondered what the killer had used. She'd been in shock, but she hadn't noticed anything. Whatever it was, she guessed the murderer had removed it.

If Vale had brought a weapon with him, wouldn't Natalie

have felt it under his gown when they embraced? She shook her head. It might depend on where it was, and how they'd held each other. And of course, it could have been a spur-of-the-moment killing. The brutal method made it seem likely. Perhaps Vale had genuinely wanted a reconciliation, but their meeting had turned sour after they'd arrived in the hidden room. He might have found a weapon there. But if he'd never intended to kill, why disguise himself by wearing a gown on his way to the library? She shook her head. Even if he was guilty, he might not be the second silhouette. There were too many variables. She needed to know more.

At last, she turned her mind to Natalie's three ex-husbands. She managed to find them by googling. A multimillionaire property developer, now based in New York, a novelist who'd died of a heart attack five years after they'd divorced, and a former celebrity chef who ran a luxury hotel in Edinburgh. She rang the hotel and asked to speak to husband number three. She had plenty of excuse to call, what with the obituary, and she wanted to know if he was at home, in Scotland.

The hotel receptionist was sympathetic, friendly, and shocked at the news of Natalie Somerson's death, which the staff had all seen on social media. She confirmed the star's ex-husband had his own apartment at the hotel, but didn't normally work on Sundays and had gone out to play golf. Could he call her back the following morning?

He could still have killed Natalie, then driven through the night to get back to Scotland, but Eve thought it was unlikely. She agreed to a call the following day at nine.

After that, she turned her attention to the property developer, researching him, then emailing to convey her condolences and explain about the obituary. She wanted his input, but she didn't think he could have killed her either. She'd found press reports of him attending a topping-out ceremony on Friday in Brooklyn. He could have taken a flight back to the UK the following day, but why would he? If he wanted to kill his ex-wife, sneaking into Southwood would add an avoidable challenge.

It was different for Natalie's current husband, Gavin Vale. He wouldn't want to kill Natalie on home turf. And he'd have talked to her recently. He might know the ongoing tensions with Eliza Gregory at Southwood. Killing Natalie there could have seemed like a good way to misdirect the police.

Eve would be busy while she waited for the husbands to reply. She had interviews to prepare for at Southwood the following day. Anastasia had agreed to talk the moment she'd asked – the bursar would be able to provide a good overview. Eve wanted to understand Natalie's relations with the coven, especially Eliza. But as a family member, Anastasia might shed some light on Gavin Vale too. They'd probably met.

Scarlett had agreed to an interview as well, though she'd looked like a rabbit in headlights when Eve suggested it. Eve wanted to know what had caused the dramatic change in relations between her and Natalie over twenty-four short hours.

Next, Eve focused on background research. According to Natalie's Wikipedia page, she'd been sent away to boarding school at the age of seven. The thought tugged at Eve's heart. She'd been so young. Eve remembered Viv's description of Natalie's social circle at Southwood. The way she'd kept everyone at arm's length. Was it that first experience of boarding school that forced her to put up barriers? Had she decided it was her against the world? She imagined Natalie, uprooted. Thrust into a new environment, far from home. And she had been far flung. Her parents had lived in Oxfordshire, but her first school was in the Scottish Borders.

Wikipedia told Eve that Natalie's mum had died when she was fourteen, after she'd started at Southwood. But she'd been ill for some years. Perhaps Natalie's dad had decided she'd be best off away at school. But a seven-year-old would have been far too young to understand his thinking.

There was no broader detail of Natalie's schooldays on Wikipedia. It wasn't surprising. She hadn't had much time for Southwood, after all. The poem she'd read out on Founders' Day marked her out as a rebel with a creative, vindictive streak. Once again, Eve thought how surprising it was that she'd accepted the role of Founders' Day Champion. She must have had her own agenda. Had her motive for coming led to her death? It seemed possible, but what had she been up to?

She went on to focus on Natalie's early career. She'd worked as an assistant on a film-review show, then moved on to work for Dirk Acton, her current producer, on a late-night chat show. Eventually, she'd made the move on screen, and to prime time. Acton would be well worth talking to; they went back a long way.

She googled for contact details and sent him an email, asking for an interview.

After that, she went back to scanning Wikipedia. The page revelled in the controversies and scandals of the *Natalie Somerson Show*. Paternity test results and affairs revealed in front of a live audience, drug addiction and abuse unveiled, weaknesses and vulnerability exploited, families torn apart.

Eve watched some clips of the show. Everything controlled for maximum confrontation and tension, with Natalie laying into her guests with razor-sharp comments.

Being shipped off to boarding school at seven might have made her tough, but surely nothing could justify the way she'd treated the people who went on her show.

After checking the obvious avenues to get an overview of Natalie's background, Eve did some more circuitous browsing. Aside from photos with her current and ex-husbands, and the actor Calvin Wright, there wasn't much to indicate a wider social life. Her producer Dirk Acton was the one other person who'd occasionally been snapped alongside her. Eve found no sign that she and Lucia had a connection beyond Southwood. Nothing which would explain their heart-to-heart.

The only other interesting snippet Eve discovered dated back to Natalie's school days. Southwood had put on a show at a theatre in Ipswich. Someone had digitised the programmes and Eve saw Natalie had been down to play Sandy in the musical *Grease*. It was interesting to know she'd been keen on acting and singing as well as interviewing.

She googled for reviews of the show and struck lucky. But scanning the text, she found a different person, Jane Parker, was credited as Sandy. She must have taken Natalie's place at the last minute. Jane had done well, according to the reviewer. Natalie wasn't mentioned.

The information she'd gathered circled in Eve's head as she walked Gus through the darkness of Blind Eye Wood, thick with fallen leaves, to reach Robin's house. Moonlight made patterns on the ground and bare branches reached up like bent fingers. Somewhere, an owl hooted.

As usual, they approached Robin's fisherman's cottage via the back garden, to avoid prying eyes.

Gus mobbed him the moment he opened up and he bent to tickle his tummy, then rose to hold Eve in his arms. She let the feeling of warm, solid comfort flow over her, but it didn't last. She could see the worry in his eyes.

'How did it go with Greg?'

He closed the door behind her. 'So-so. Glass of wine?'

'Thanks.'

His eyes met hers as he unscrewed a bottle of Merlot. 'The police have witnesses who saw Natalie pursuing me. Now Palmer's got it into his head that she was pressuring me in some way. And to be fair, she was. She caught me again after you saw us together. I'm afraid I'm definitely on Palmer's radar.'

14

_____

Eve's mouth had gone dry; she had to swallow before she replied. 'I'm so sorry.'

She wondered who'd seen Robin and Natalie together – and if they'd caught sight of her with Robin too.

'I've worked out where Natalie knew me from.' Robin handed her a glass and poured one for himself. 'Turns out I worked on a burglary at her place, three husbands back. She had a different surname, and she wasn't famous then. I didn't make the connection until I did some digging. I don't know if she remembered before she was killed.' He closed his eyes for a moment.

Eve knew what was at stake. If his identity got out it would ruin the life he'd carved out in Saxford. He'd probably insist on disappearing again, to a new area, with no contacts. He wouldn't risk her safety.

Inside Eve, panic threatened, making her chest tight. Memories of their time together flitted through her head. The first moment she'd seen him in Saxford, standing in a stranger's garden, when she hadn't known to trust him – nor he her. Then snatched conversations in secret places, the estuary path and

Blind Eye Wood. The growing feeling of connection. The point
when she'd realised she could tell him anything. Quiet
moments on deserted stretches of beach, early in the day. Love.
Their relationship had always had limits, thanks to the need for
secrecy, but it was infinitely precious.

'We just need to work quickly and find out who's guilty.'
She tried to keep her voice steady, to project confidence she
didn't feel.

He gave a flicker of a smile. 'It does focus the mind. We
won't have Greg's input unfortunately – not in the way we
normally do.'

Greg found DI Palmer just as lazy and blinkered as Eve did.
To let off steam, he often talked cases over with Robin. Given he
was married to his cousin, Eve guessed it felt like keeping it in
the family. The details Greg fed Robin had helped keep Eve
safe as she'd researched murder victims in the past.

'Our chats are always against the rules, of course,' Robin
said, 'but it would be a bridge too far to pass on confidential
information to one of the suspects. But I'm getting ahead of
myself.' He hugged Eve again, even more tightly. 'We can tackle
this, but you need to get warmed up and eat a proper supper. It
must have been horrific, finding Natalie's body.'

He let her go and pulled out a chair at the kitchen table,
next to the log fire he'd got going. It was kicking out a
comforting heat, but the chill inside Eve wasn't just physical.

'I think I blanked it for a while afterwards.' Eve winced as
her mind went back to the hidden room, but she needed to
focus. It was the one possible way through this frightening mess.
'I can visualise her body again now.' She shuddered. 'The attack
was brutal. I'd guess the killer was channelling a load of pent-up
anger. Either that or they were so ruthless and determined they
could override their horror at bashing someone's head in.' She
felt sick again.

'Sip the wine,' Robin said. 'Unless you'd prefer brandy?'

She shook her head but did as he suggested with the Merlot.

'I made us coq au vin and baked potatoes. I'll put a plate in front of you. Just see what you can manage and let's talk.'

For a second, the smell turned her stomach, but as she took a deep breath the feeling lessened.

'Do you want to tell me what you saw while you were at Southwood?' Robin held her hand for a moment. 'Anything and everything?'

She nodded. 'I noted my memories with Viv this afternoon, then wrote a timeline after she left.' Viv hated that sort of detail. It had been best to wait for peace and quiet.

Eve called up her files on her phone. 'Okay. So starting with the basic facts, we have some key timings. I assume Natalie died between six thirty and eleven, since that's the window I was asked to account for by Olivia Dawkins. She probably allowed a bit of leeway either side, so maybe it's more like seven to ten thirty.'

Robin nodded. 'Sounds about right.'

'Here's the timeline.' She handed him the phone.

6.30 p.m.: the coven, Viv, Natalie & I had drinks in the staff common room, next to the refectory.

7.00 p.m.: We all went into dinner at high table.

8.30 p.m.: Viv and I went to our rooms, with an arrangement to meet again at 9.25 in Great Quad, ready for drinks in the common room. The others could have been anywhere but...

9.05 p.m. approx: Eliza Gregory spotted Scarlett Holland in the corridor outside Natalie's room.

Robin raised an eyebrow as he read. 'Does Scarlett admit to visiting Natalie?'

Eve nodded. 'She claims she was meeting her to discuss a future in TV. Eliza says *she* was there because she wanted to talk to Natalie too, but left when she saw Scarlett. According to her, she never went back, but she looked panicky when Scarlett asked her about it. I'm not sure I believe her.'

Robin nodded, and carried on reading.

9.30 p.m.: Viv and I bumped into Anastasia in Great Quad where we saw a silhouette (apparently Natalie) in the library. Then a hooded figure stopped just outside, paused in the porch, then entered. It looked like the pair argued quite violently, but it resolved quickly and the two silhouettes embraced.

9.33 p.m. approx: Viv, Anastasia and I arrived in the staff common room for drinks.

Robin paused and looked up. 'Anyone else in the common room when you arrived?'

'No, we were first. I'm afraid all the timings from now on are best guesses. Except for the hour Viv and I left the common room. I was desperate to go to bed, so I'd been looking at my watch.'

9.40 p.m. approx: Lucia and Martin Leverett joined us in the common room.

9.42 p.m. approx: Eliza Gregory arrived.

9.45 p.m. approx: Bridget Leverett also arrived.

10 p.m. approx: Eliza Gregory left the common room in a huff about Natalie and the influence she had at Southwood.

Robin frowned. 'What's this about the influence Natalie had?'

'I'm not sure. When someone challenged Eliza on it, she blustered and claimed she meant as Founders' Day Champion.'

'Worth noting.' Robin nodded, and finished reading.

11.15 p.m.: Viv and I left Anastasia, Bridget, Martin and Lucia in the common room and went to bed.

2.30 a.m. approx: I saw Anastasia walk from Old Quad into Great Quad.

Eve's eyes met Robin's as he handed her phone back. 'I presume Anastasia's also the figure I saw the night before, wandering the grounds. It's outside the six thirty to eleven p.m. window, obviously, but it seemed worth mentioning.'

'Absolutely.'

Eve took a tentative forkful of the coq au vin. Talking facts had helped. Made her believe they might somehow get a grip on all this. Suddenly, the rich gravy was making her stomach rumble.

'It's amazing.' She nodded down at the food. 'I can feel my brain waking up already.' But she was worried her voice sounded falsely bright.

Robin gave her a crooked smile. 'How did Anastasia behave during her late-night strolls?'

Eve thought back. 'She kept to the shadows, but she wasn't hiding. And she didn't have her hood up. I could see her hair.'

He nodded. 'What about suspects?'

Eve thought of the vast school. 'In theory, there might be hundreds. Any of the teachers or students could have done it.

But in reality, the brutality of the murder makes it seem deeply personal. I'm sure it'll be a known, close connection.'

He nodded.

'And the location makes a difference too,' Eve continued. 'It suggests a secret assignation. Perhaps she arranged to meet someone in the hidden room, or took them there. Either way, it had to be someone she trusted.

'So with that said, the suspects fall into two sets, depending on whether the silhouette was really Natalie or not. If it was, then Scarlett and Eliza had the opportunity. Eliza left the drinks by ten, or thereabouts, and Scarlett never showed up. And we also have Natalie's husband, Gavin Vale, assuming he has no alibi, though it would have been less straightforward for him, living off site. I'd say Eliza and the husband are the most likely in terms of motive. Eliza hated Natalie and the husband had reason to be jealous.'

'The rest of the group would be out of it?'

'I think so. The school's a big place. I'll check when I go back, but I guess it would have taken Natalie five minutes or so to walk from the library to the hidden room. She couldn't have been killed before nine thirty-eight, even if she'd gone there immediately after we saw her.

'Bridget Leverett might just have managed it, if she'd been lying in wait and had run to the common room afterwards, but in reality, it doesn't seem possible. She wouldn't have had time to wipe her hands, let alone get over the shock, and she didn't look ruffled when she came for her drink. She wasn't even out of breath.'

Robin nodded.

'But if someone dressed up as Natalie, and stood in the library window to create a false alibi, then all the bets are off.'

He closed his eyes for a moment. 'Right. Talk me through it.'

15

Eve gathered her thoughts. 'Okay. If the silhouette in the library was a fake, any of the suspects could have done it, as far as I'm aware. There's a period after supper, before drinks, when they all go off and do their own thing. They'd have needed an accomplice as the second silhouette though.'

'Eliza seeing Scarlett outside Natalie's door just after nine complicates things,' Robin said.

Eve thought it through. 'I'm not sure it makes much difference. Scarlett could have lied about Natalie being in her room, either because she'd already killed her, or for another more innocent reason. For instance, if Natalie was being elusive and Scarlett had been hanging around outside her door like a stalker, she might not like to admit it. She could have claimed they'd had a lovely pally meet-up, just to save face. It would have seemed like an unimportant fib until Natalie's body was found. If Eliza had killed Natalie earlier in the evening, she'd have been delighted when Scarlett lied about the meet-up. It would be one more bit of evidence to blur the time of death, on top of the staged silhouette scene.'

Robin frowned. 'True... Though if either of them killed Natalie earlier, why would they go to her room?'

'Good question. Because they finally felt safe and wanted to hear the silence? Or because they wanted access to something which belonged to her?'

He nodded. 'Could be. And the possibility that Scarlett lied means the others could have killed Natalie before five past nine too.'

'That's right. Whatever the case, Scarlett was very shifty when she realised Eliza had spotted her outside Natalie's room.'

'Fair enough. Thinking about timing again, Martin, Lucia and Eliza joined you very quickly for drinks. If any of them was one of the silhouettes, could they have made it in time?'

'I think so. If they'd stopped play-acting as we went inside, or just after. The library's only across the quad from the staff common room.'

'Anastasia's a special case, of course,' Eve went on. 'If she's guilty she'd have needed two helpers, because she was with us when we saw the pair in the library. She's not as likely, but not out of it, either. Natalie wasn't well liked.'

'Fair point. But if you were a betting woman?'

'Eliza Gregory still feels like a key suspect. I think Natalie was blackmailing someone – quite possibly her.' Eve reiterated what she knew about the pair's history.

'That would fit then. If it was blackmail, I guess Natalie must have acted out of hate.'

'True. She didn't need the cash. If Eliza was her target, it could explain why Natalie always sought her out when she came to visit Southwood. She'd want to keep turning the knife in the wound – make sure Eliza hadn't forgotten the threat she was under. And it might tie in with Eliza's comment yesterday, about Natalie already having plenty of influence. She was echoing Anastasia's words, but she said it with such force, I think influence might equal control. I've told Olivia Dawkins I suspected Natalie of blackmail, but not that I think Eliza might be her victim. It's only a hunch. But Eliza was on her way to see Natalie last night.'

Robin nodded. 'And you think Eliza could have made herself look like Natalie, to create the silhouette?'

Eve visualised her. 'They're very different physically. Natalie was curvaceous, whereas Eliza's all bony angles. But in a wig and a padded jacket? Yes, I think she could have done it, then dumped the disguise. But I don't know who her accomplice might be.'

'Are you sure it was a man?'

'No – not at all. It was just the impression the view created. Martin Leverett is the only male in the coven, of course. There are other male members of staff but they seem less likely. I never saw them interact with Natalie.'

Robin lifted his wine and reflected flames danced on the glass. 'Did Martin have any reason to want her dead, do you think?'

'In theory.' Eve told him how Ada would inherit the entire school on Anastasia's death now. 'That motive applies to Lucia too, of course. They might believe Natalie would have damaged Southwood if she'd inherited her share. Either of them could have killed to save it in its current form for Ada. They could have acted the silhouette scene together. They knew there'd be a gang of us making our way to common room drinks at that point. If it was a charade, they could reasonably assume we'd see it as we crossed the quad. The sticking point is their objective. I can't honestly imagine them bludgeoning Natalie for that reason. It's not as though they knew for sure that she'd trash the school. Their motive doesn't seem compelling enough and the risks were huge.

'But there's an oddity to relate about them too. Martin's wife Lucia didn't want Natalie as Founders' Day Champion, but despite that, I saw them having a secret heart-to-heart on Friday

evening. I wonder if it was about Martin. Natalie met him in a
secluded part of the library and tore a strip off him yesterday.
I'm pretty sure she slapped him.'

Robin raised an eyebrow.

Eve glanced at the notes on her phone. 'She said: "She told
me all about it. It's heartless of you! How could you treat her so
badly?" If I'm right, then the heart-to-heart and that conversation are related. The "her" could be one of the students Lucia
counsels, I suppose, but my bet is it's Lucia herself. I can't see
her sharing information about one of her charges. She seems too
conscientious. Either way, Martin can't have killed to keep a
secret from Lucia – it seems she knew already, and Natalie was
wading in on her behalf. She was certainly angry.'

'Interesting.'

Eve took more of the casserole as Gus shifted at her feet. As
she peered at him, she saw his eyes close. She yearned for his
peaceful situation, basking by the fire, untroubled by worries.
Why did this have to happen? The thought made her feel
guilty. She had the privilege of still being alive.

She made an effort to focus. 'Then there's Scarlett. Great
for opportunity, but I'm not sure about motive. Natalie was
hateful to her on Friday, but by Saturday they were best
buddies.' She shook her head. 'Then again, an oddity like that
might mean everything. I want to understand Natalie's change
of heart. She invited anyone from Southwood to talk about the
school on her show. It's possible Scarlett signed up. She's after
a career in TV – she might be willing to tell Southwood's
secrets in return. She'd have no reason to kill Natalie, just the
opposite, but relations between them were volatile.' The head
girl's image filled Eve's head. 'She makes me uneasy. She
seems to have got her position in part due to her father's
generous donations to the school. Maybe she thinks money
can buy you anything. I could imagine things getting ugly if
she was crossed.' The small disagreement at the coven

meeting still stuck in Eve's mind. Her anger had been dispro-
portionate.

She sighed. 'Plus she was creeping around after Natalie
when she was chatting with Lucia. If she was hoping to talk to
her again, it looks like she felt the need to ambush her. Or, if she
was tailing her to listen in, then she was after something. It's
possible she killed Natalie because of what Lucia told her, but I
can't quite see it. She'd need to kill Lucia too, if she wanted
something hushed up. But something made her shifty, before
we found Natalie's body. I need to know what.'

Robin rubbed his chin. 'Food for thought. And what about
Natalie's personal fortune as a motive? I'd imagine she was
loaded.'

'She was, by all accounts. I'm wondering if her current
husband is also her heir.' Eve explained what she and Viv had
discovered.

'He definitely sounds interesting. If you talk to him at their
mansion, I'll hang around the grounds as backup. It sounds
isolated.'

'Thanks.' It would mean a rare day out with him. One of the
last, maybe... An hour or so of treasured time, talking to him in
the car. She blinked quickly and shook herself. 'I mustn't forget
Bridget – the former head and Martin's mother. She was angry
when Natalie brought up Eliza Gregory's love poem again at
Founders' Day. It's hardly a motive, but she's intimately
involved with the school. She needs to stay on the list. They
all do.'

Robin swallowed a mouthful of food. 'So what's next?'

'Multiple interviews, starting with one of Natalie's exes first
thing tomorrow, followed by a chat with Anastasia, then Scarlett. Anastasia seemed tolerant of Natalie, and she was her aunt,
but I'd like to know what she was doing, wandering the school
grounds by moonlight.' Eve was considering following her one
night. She knew it was risky, but she was desperate to get to the

truth quickly. Only that would keep Robin safe. She didn't want to tell him. He'd tell her not to, or insist on coming along. Under the circumstances that wouldn't be wise. How would it look if they were discovered? The police focus on him would be a hundred times worse.

16

Natalie's ex-husband number three, Duncan Ross, the celebrity chef-turned-hotelier, called her at nine the following morning as promised.

'I'm so sorry for your loss.'

He gave a dry laugh, but it cracked partway through. *'We didn't part on good terms, but the finality of what's happened... Well, it takes some getting used to.'*

'If you feel up to giving me your impressions of her, it would be hugely helpful.'

She heard his sigh down the line. *'Natalie was damaged. I should have realised it before we married; all the signs were there. I suppose I thought our partnership would be different from the ones which went before. But it went too deep.'*

She wouldn't take his word for it – it was just his opinion, but he'd known her well. 'What do you think caused it?'

'I had a go at pop psychology, of course. Maybe it was her dad sending her away to school at such a young age. Whatever it was, she was primed to lash out first. Pre-emptive strikes.'

'How do you mean?'

'When she felt someone might double-cross her, betray her,

abandon her. She anticipated those things happening as a matter of course, even when they weren't on the cards. I had no intention of leaving her. But our back-stabbing social circle made things difficult.'

'What happened?'

'My TV show had been going from strength to strength. I had book deals, and people would stop me in the street. I was nowhere near overshadowing Natalie, but we were becoming equals. And I was better liked.'

'And that altered the dynamic?'

'It seemed to. I overheard one of our so-called friends at a drinks party, wondering why I stayed with her and speculating that I'd move on. I suspect she heard too. And I had talked to her about her career. Asked if she might be happier looking for another role. She knew I didn't approve of what she did to her guests. But I still loved her. The show was part of her. I'd take it, if that's what being with her meant.

'Shortly after the drinks party, she said she wanted a divorce. Accused me of infidelity, which was crazy, and she knew it. I told her I loved her. That I still wanted to make a go of it. But she shut down all discussion. She said she was learning with each marriage. It makes me wonder what it's been like for her current husband, Gavin Vale. After we divorced—' She'd been able to hear the passion in his voice but now he stopped suddenly.

'What is it?'

'I don't know if I can say. I can't prove any of it. It's unprintable.'

'If you'd like to tell me privately, I promise I won't refer to it in my article. It will just inform my overall impression of Natalie.'

There was a long pause. *'I looked up your work when I got the message you left yesterday,'* he said at last. *'I trust you. In confidence then, after we divorced, Natalie seduced the producer* of my show. She persuaded him to drop me and put the word around that I was terrible to work with. A bully.'

His voice was shaking. 'She told me what she'd done and watched my pain. I hated her at the time. I could have killed her myself. I'm not entirely surprised someone else did in the end. I saw a therapist later and it helped me to let it go. I'm happier than I've ever been, up here, running the hotel. It was a strain, being married to Natalie.'

'How long is it since your break-up?'

'Ten years. Long enough to take a step back.'

But she could still hear the judder in his voice. As she ended the call, her heart ached for him. The therapist must have done a good job, but the hurt and anger were still there. And underneath it all she felt a twinge for Natalie. Too damaged to hang on to a man who'd wanted to stick by her. A kind man, on the face of it, who might have had the patience and dedication to make her happy if she'd let him.

An hour later, after a call from Natalie's husband, Gavin Vale, agreeing to see her that afternoon, Eve was at Southwood, waiting outside Anastasia's office. She thought of her sweeping through the grounds by moonlight. It was tempting to ask about it, but it was best the bursar didn't know she'd been seen. If Eve was going to follow her, she didn't want her watchful or altering her behaviour.

She abandoned the thought as Anastasia's assistant arrived to show her in.

'I'm so sorry for your loss,' she said as the bursar motioned her to a seat and the assistant retreated.

'Thank you.' Anastasia put her head in her hands for a moment. 'I still can't take it in. Things have changed out of all recognition since yesterday.'

Eve wondered what effect Natalie's death had had on the

wider school. 'It must be a terrible shock – and for the students too. Parents have been getting in touch, I guess.'

Anastasia's look turned wry. 'You guess correctly. It's understandable, of course, but the phones have been ringing off the hook. I've been taking it in turns with Martin and Lucia to field calls. Some are already asking to take their children out.'

Eve had imagined that might happen. 'I'm so sorry.'

But Anastasia sounded calm. 'Natalie had a lot of enemies outside the school. I think we've managed to calm everyone down, and I'm sure the children are perfectly safe. I imagine this was personal.'

That didn't rule out a Southwood killer, though.

Eve fished for her notebook and pen and glanced around the room. Anastasia looked comfortable at her old mahogany desk, with its leather inlay. She must keep a firm grip on Southwood's finances but there was an informality about her workspace. Along with all the files and papers, she'd collected random sentimental oddments in an emerald-green bowl. There was a painted pebble depicting a sailing boat, a round metal token with a hole in it decorated with a baby rabbit and a dumpy-looking bird, and a small doll made from a pipe cleaner.

Anastasia's eyes followed her gaze and she smiled. 'The token was a present from an old boyfriend. A bit twee, I know. We adored each other but our timing was terrible. It still makes me happy to have it there. And Ada made me the doll. I think she gave one to Bridget too. I'm privileged!'

Eve bet Bridget hadn't got hers on display.

At that moment, the bursar's assistant reappeared with coffee. 'Thank you very much, Sue. And chocolate digestives! My favourite. Just what we need at a time like this.'

As the door closed again, Eve caught sight of a painting of a stormy sea, the turbulent waves a mass of indigo, grey and white. In the bottom corner was an inscription. 'To Anthony'. It was signed Mary Leverett.

'It's quite something, isn't it?' Anastasia said. 'Mary was Martin's grandmother, but she painted that for his father, of course. He was bursar before me. I love that picture, so I kept it up.' She smiled. 'But that's in keeping with Southwood. Nothing changes very quickly.' She shrugged. 'You can imagine.'

'You'd like it to change faster?'

The twinkle was back. 'I'm a reformer. I pushed for Martin to be our first male head, for instance. The school founders stipulated that shares in Southwood should pass down the female line and that was all well and good. Women only gained the right to control their own property in 1882. But we're in the twenty-first century now. We need to take the next step. The girls need to know it's reasonable to expect men to champion their cause. And boasting apart, I think Martin proves my point. He's been excellent for Southwood.'

'There was a lot of opposition?'

'Most people saw my argument. Eliza was very much opposed, I'm afraid, along with several parents. But I won in the end. I pushed for Bridget, Martin's mother, to be head before him too. Prior to that, we'd only chosen descendants of one of the founders. Senseless. I've always loved Southwood. I was born and brought up here; it's in my blood, but I'm clear-sighted enough to know when to break with tradition.' She shook her head. 'Bridget would have left if we hadn't offered her the role. She was already head of sixth form at the time. She naturally wanted the next step up. I talked sense into the coven, and we hung on to her.'

'And she's still here now.'

'Her apartment's available for her lifetime and she likes to keep an eye on things.'

It was interesting she'd put it like that – not that she wanted to stay near her son and grandchildren. It was the impression Eve had too – that she didn't want to leave and miss out. Have other people taking over in her absence, not least Anastasia. Eve suspected it had irked Bridget when Ada made the bursar a doll.

'Have most of the founders' heirs worked at the school, just like you?' Eve wanted to know if Natalie was unusual in choosing another career.

'All of them so far. My mother was head in her time. She put every ounce of energy she had into this place.' She reached out and patted the wall as though the school was a living thing.

Natalie must have been a complete shock to the system then – the first prospective heir not to make Southwood her be-all and end-all.

Eve turned her mind back to her questions. She needed to understand Anastasia's true feelings towards her niece. 'At drinks last night, you mentioned you were keen to have Natalie as Founders' Day Champion, even though she was a controversial choice?'

Her lively blue eyes met Eve's. 'I didn't know *how* controversial until the newspapers broke the story of her affair. As I mentioned, I felt it was no use sticking our heads in the sand. Natalie was set to inherit, whatever anyone thought. It made sense to bring her in. Have her challenge our ideas. But my view was based on low cunning, I'm afraid. Natalie liked to be heard, for people to sit up and pay attention. If we'd tried to sideline her, she would have been difficult. But if we actively encouraged her, I knew she'd get bored. By the third committee meeting, I'm quite sure she'd have high-tailed it back to London.'

Eve couldn't help but smile. She liked Anastasia's practical approach.

'As it happens,' the bursar continued, 'my efforts were unnecessary.'

Eve frowned. 'Because she was killed?'

'No, goodness, I didn't mean that. But because—' She paused a moment, her eyes on the scene outside her window. 'Because she was dying.'

17

Eve caught her breath as she tried to take in the bursar's words. 'I'm sorry?'

'Natalie told me two weeks ago. She'd had a terminal diagnosis. Cancer.' She shook her head. 'Everything that's happened is a tragedy.'

So all the while she'd been winding the coven up, she'd known her time was limited. How must she have felt, having that ultimate full stop ahead? She'd been spirited still. Shown no fear. If she was frustrated at the way Southwood was run, her patience would be tested to the limit. A terminal diagnosis would throw everything into sharp relief. 'Did many people know?'

Anastasia looked at her quickly. 'No one else, as far as I'm aware. Natalie asked me to keep it to myself. You're thinking she might not have been killed if the murderer realised? I'd had the same notion. But there's more. Natalie came to me on Saturday and told me she'd decided to waive her share in the school.'

Eve sat up straighter. 'Why would she do that, if she knew she'd likely die before she came into her inheritance?'

The bursar gave a wry smile. 'I'm no spring chicken, don't forget. I might have beaten her to the afterlife. Given that, I suppose renouncing her share simplified things. But my bet is she did it for emotional satisfaction. To shock the coven a little, and gain her freedom. For her, it was taking control. She'd had the paperwork drawn up ready.'

'She never said a thing at the meeting.'

'I think she enjoyed seeing everyone squirm one last time. And squirm we did.'

Eve could imagine Natalie delighting in it. 'Did the others find out she was waiving her share before she died?'

Anastasia's look was knowing, once again. 'I WhatsApped them immediately. Natalie wanted the paperwork signed before she went back to London. They each popped in to add their signatures after the parents left. It wouldn't normally be such a rigmarole, but Natalie is the last legal beneficiary on our side. Her share will pass to Ada now. That little girl will have a lot of responsibility one day.'

The information confirmed Eve's hunch. If Martin and Lucia had killed Natalie, Ada's inheritance and the school's welfare wasn't their motive, assuming all this was true. She'd pass the information to Greg, just to be sure. Natalie's terminal diagnosis sat there like a stone in her throat. To be faced with such awful news then killed in cold blood was horrific.

She forced her mind back to recent events. 'No one talked about Natalie waiving her rights at the drinks on Saturday.'

'I'm afraid that was on your account. We'd agreed to keep quiet until Martin had drafted a letter to the parents. Between ourselves, they'd already started to write in with their concerns about Natalie taking over at Southwood.' She raised an eyebrow. 'Anticipating my demise, clearly! The ones who're really engaged have been following the scandal about Natalie in the papers. And even before that they didn't like it. Her talk show's not their cup of tea. Martin wanted to manage the news so that it would appear we'd taken action – intervened in some way.' She shook her head. 'Not wholly honest, I'm afraid, but good PR. Bridget suggested it.'

Eve remembered Eliza's words at drinks on Saturday night. *Oh believe me, Natalie already has plenty of influence. And nothing's going to change that.* She'd said that knowing Natalie wouldn't inherit. Whatever control she'd had over Eliza, relinquishing her share hadn't ended it.

'Did you like Natalie?'

The bursar put her head on one side. 'I liked her drive, but I didn't approve of her television show. I think it made her cruel. Her producer encouraged her to be as combative and manipulative as possible.'

'Do you know if she ever regretted her work?'

'She never said so. She seemed consumed by it.'

'I saw she was down to play the lead in a school production of *Grease* at a theatre in Ipswich. It made me wonder if she'd wanted to act.'

Anastasia's brow furrowed. 'That's funny. I don't remember it.'

'I can see from the reviews that an understudy took over. I don't know why Natalie pulled out.'

'When was this?'

Eve checked her notes. 'She would have been sixteen.'

The lines in the bursar's brow cleared. 'I had to have some time off around then due to ill health. It must have been while I was away, so I don't know the background. I could contact the drama teacher who was here then if you'd like? Ask her about it? Shall I give her your email address?'

'That would be really helpful. Thank you.'

'But I'd say she was settled in her talk-show role. And addicted to it. I'm afraid it fed her mean streak.'

But Eve thought her instinct to hurt had started earlier. Sparked by her dad's decision to send her away, perhaps, as her

ex-husband thought. Then compounded by Eliza, who'd probably treated her just as badly as she had Viv. She reminded
Anastasia of the love poem Natalie had read out.

'That was cruel, but it was part of a pitched battle between
them. I gather Natalie produced a piece of creative writing
which Eliza found preposterous. She annotated it and made
photocopies to share with the class. They discussed how hope-
less Natalie was in front of her.' Anastasia raised her eyes to
heaven. 'She might have expected some kind of retaliation. And
her crush on Anthony wasn't news to anyone; she was always
following him around. Everyone fell for him. He was tremendously good-looking and the nicest man you could hope to meet.
He didn't take the poem badly. He felt very sorry for Eliza and
worried about it for a long time afterwards.'

Eve didn't imagine that had helped. Pity as well as humiliation. But all the same, she could see the bursar's point. Eliza's
approach to discipline was appalling. 'Haven't any of the
parents complained about Eliza's methods?'

'She's changed her ways now; we intervened before it got to
that stage. Bridget had a word.'

Told off by the wife of the man she'd fallen for. Once again,
Eve wondered that the woman had chosen to stay at Southwood. But if Natalie had been blackmailing her, she might have
lacked the money to retire. Was she free now? It would be an
excellent motive for murder.

'She relapsed a while later,' Anastasia went on, 'but was
warned again and I've heard of no problems since.'

The relapse must have occurred while Viv was under her
so-called care.

'So yes,' Anastasia continued, 'although Natalie was cruel to
Eliza, there were extenuating circumstances. And Natalie was
having a difficult time. Her mother had died a few years earlier,
and her father coped by shutting down – keeping everyone at a
distance, including his daughter. Natalie had always kicked

against authority, but it was worse during that period. I took her to task over it, and we frequently sparred over other things too. But that meant we didn't hold anything back. I knew where I was with her. I suppose I became something of a stand-in mother.'

'I guess you must know whether she was happy?'

Anastasia sat back in her chair. 'I'm not sure I'd call it happiness, but she was fully engaged at work, as I said. Got a kick out of every scandalous revelation. Always wanted to up the ante, shock her audiences more each time. It seemed to give her life meaning. I found that sad.'

'Were you worried when she invited people from Southwood to go on her show? She must have been after some juicy inside secrets.'

Anastasia laughed. 'I don't think we're *that* exciting. What would people say?'

Eve imagined the bursar watched the staff and students carefully, but she wouldn't see everything. She doubted she could really be that confident.

'And how was Natalie's private life? I was reading about Gavin Vale.'

The twinkle and laughter left Anastasia's eyes. 'Natalie was about to divorce him.'

Eve took a sharp breath. 'Did he know?'

Once again, Anastasia's look told Eve she'd read her mind. 'I remember Viv mentioning your involvement in murder investigations,' she said. 'You're right – it's a crucial question, if Gavin's down to inherit. I don't know how she left her money, or if she'd told him she was filing for divorce. She hadn't had it out with him when she came to see me a couple of weeks ago.' She shuddered. 'She showed me a hateful note he'd left her, accusing her of infidelity. Threatening her and calling her all the names under the sun.' She shook her head. 'The police are bound to look into him. I've told them what I've told you and I assume they'll find his note amongst Natalie's belongings. She said she was keeping it with her for safety. She might want it as evidence.'

To use against him in the divorce? Or to broadcast on television perhaps? Gavin Vale could have come to Southwood to kill her and retrieve the note. Eve felt a renewed sense of anticipation about interviewing him later, but a pang of trepidation along with it.

'I don't know if he has an alibi,' Anastasia was frowning, 'but I could imagine him acting on his threats. Even before the papers dredged up evidence of the supposed affair with Calvin Wright, he seemed to hate her. I'm not sure why they married. But whatever Natalie did, he had no right to threaten her.'

'Absolutely.' It was all wrong, though he was probably hurt and upset. He might not have meant what he said. Or he might be a killer. Eve took stock. The bursar had raised her previous role in police investigations – it cleared the way for her to ask some more direct questions.

'Do the police know what the killer used as a weapon? Could it have been something in the hidden room?'

The bursar shook her head. 'They say it was a blunt instrument. A hammer perhaps. There was nothing like that kept there.'

The killer must have brought it with them then. Images of Natalie's crushed skull filled Eve's mind again. She took a deep breath and tried to focus on what they'd witnessed at the library.

'Anastasia, did it occur to you that the silhouette we saw, the night Natalie died, might not have been her, but someone who wanted to blur the time of death and give themselves an alibi?'

The bursar put her hand to her brow. 'I must confess it hadn't, but now you mention it, I see it's possible.'

'It was just weird. What we saw looked like a secret assignation, yet the woman we took for Natalie stood so close to the window that her outline was clearly visible. And she chose a time when we were due to walk through the quad to meet for drinks.'

She frowned. 'That's true.'

'If it was Natalie, I'm wondering who she was with. And if it wasn't, then there are two people to identify.' And one of them was likely a killer.

'I'd already been wondering about the man, of course,' Anastasia said. 'Not Martin. The gait was wrong.' Then she paused, shook her head quickly and gave a bark of a laugh. 'I'd have discounted him anyway, on other grounds.' At last she gave a large shrug. 'I wonder about our stand-in gardener. I've heard whispers that he and Natalie were spotted together in a lonely part of the grounds.'

Eve felt the blood rush to her cheeks.

'And if the silhouette wasn't Natalie, it could have been anyone, dressed up.' The bursar frowned. 'The man could still have been the gardener, I suppose. If he had cause to meet Natalie in secret, he could have had some reason for wanting her dead.'

18

Eve had some spare time before she was due to interview Scarlett. She went outside and looked over at the tower with the hidden room at its top. White-overalled CSIs were swarming in and out of the doorway there, busy, like ants. Students, crossing the site between lessons, watched them from a distance with wide eyes. Eve couldn't approach the tower of course, but she could estimate the distance between it and the library by eye and check her timings. Her guess had been right: it would have taken Natalie five minutes to walk there, even if she'd hurried. If the silhouette had been her, she couldn't have died before 9.38 p.m. And assuming the killer was amongst the key players, only Scarlett, Eliza or Gavin Vale could be guilty.

As Eve crossed Old Quad, the chill wind bit and she pulled her chocolate-brown coat more tightly around her. If only she knew the exact time of death. Either way, she had to make this next interview count.

She was still five minutes early. It always happened. She allowed too much time – she hated being caught on the back foot.

She went and knocked on Scarlett's door anyway. Maybe

the girl was waiting for her. She might be glad to get the talk out of the way.

She heard a hurried rustling inside the room, as though Scarlett was tidying something away. When she opened the door half a minute later, she looked flushed.

'Come in.' She stood back and Eve entered her room.

Her bedroom wasn't much smarter than the one Eve had been given. Once again, she thought of the fees.

'I wonder when these rooms were last updated,' she said aloud. It might break the ice.

'I know.' Scarlett almost laughed, though she seemed self-conscious. 'But apparently a lot of the parents objected when Anastasia suggested an upgrade.'

Eve raised an eyebrow.

'Most of them have an old-fashioned, spare the rod, spoil the child attitude. They think nice furniture and en suites will make us soft and entitled.'

Eve tried to imagine being packed off to a place like this by a parent who was willing to pay to make sure you weren't too comfortable.

Scarlett shivered. 'Maybe they're right about the rooms. They've left me with a strong desire to make my own way, whatever it takes, and get out of this dump. Perhaps that counts as fostering independence.'

For a head girl, she was very disenchanted. Her determination to push for her goals seemed all the more powerful.

'Does the coven know what you think?'

'It's hardly worth the bother now, telling them. I'll be out of here soon, making my way in television.' She stroked her long red hair absently. It didn't seem to have crossed her mind to speak up for the sake of the younger students she was meant to represent.

Eve imagined her as the library silhouette. She wouldn't

even need a wig to look like Natalie. She could just use curling tongs.

'Why ruffle feathers?' Scarlett added. 'It makes sense to get along with people to get ahead.'

'I guess it does.' Eve felt a flicker of disapproval. The approach meant Scarlett was neglecting her job. And it was just plain false, anyway. Then again, Eve was making herself pleasant to Scarlett to access information. 'You seemed to be getting on with Natalie by the time she died.'

'She was always very good to me.'

Eve took a deep breath. 'I'm sorry, Scarlett, but I know that's not true. I wasn't listening on purpose, but I heard you in the bathroom. You were applauding Natalie's rebelliousness, just after the coven meeting, but her response was cruel.' The words had stuck in Eve's head. It was horrible to repeat them, but she needed a truthful reaction from Scarlett. Justice, and Robin's future, might depend on it. 'She told you that you sounded like a creep. And that if you really believed in rebellion you'd hardly be head girl. She was disgusted at the idea you might have anything in common.'

Scarlett flushed, but Eve ploughed on. It was too important not to. 'She was laughing at you. I was shocked at how hateful she was.'

The head girl's mouth half opened, but whatever she'd been going to say died on her lips. Eve's words had almost got her to talk, but not quite.

'I saw you follow her across the quad on Friday evening, when she was chatting to Lucia Leverett. You took care to keep out of sight.'

'I needed to speak with her in private.'

To Eve, her behaviour had seemed stalkerish. 'She'd already told you to stop pestering her. You appeared to be listening in.'

'I wasn't. I didn't hear what they said. I went away and caught Natalie later.'

'It seems extraordinary that you were acting like best friends the following day.'

'Natalie was a celebrity. She must have got fed up with people following her around. She'd have thought I was just like the rest. But when we talked, she realised I wasn't.'

'And suddenly she liked you?'

Scarlett looked down into her lap.

'When did you first get to know her?' Eve couldn't work out what had brought them together. 'Was it when you became head girl?

She nodded. 'I wrote to her at that point.' She faltered.

Eve sensed she wished she hadn't said it. 'Why was that?'

'I was interested in the media and the careers teacher said we should "mine our contacts". As part of the managing committee, we were almost connected.'

'I see. And Natalie replied?'

Scarlett was back to looking at her lap again. 'Not then. But she explained on Founders' Day that she would have. She was just busy.'

Why the change in attitude? 'She wasn't prepared to chat when you spoke to her in the bathroom.'

There was a long pause. 'Maybe she was tired from her journey. In a better mood later on.'

'Did you discuss going on her show?'

Scarlett looked up quickly. 'As a co-presenter? Of course not. I wasn't expecting miracles.'

Why did she think Eve meant as a co-presenter? Eve could only imagine Natalie had mentioned it, but that was just plain odd. Scarlett had no experience and Natalie worked alone.

'I was thinking of as a guest.'

'Oh, goodness no!' She seemed genuinely shocked. 'I wouldn't have agreed to that. I knew what she was like with her interviewees. But she was kind to me.'

'It must be hard,' Eve said. 'You saw her just before she died. What did you talk about when you went to her room?'

Scarlett twisted her fingers together. 'She offered to introduce me to her media contacts. It was so generous. She gave me their details, but she was going to write letters of introduction. Only she never got that far, of course...' After a moment, she took a ragged breath and Eve realised she was fighting tears. She had a feeling it was missed opportunities she was mourning, not Natalie. Her own ambitions and desires seemed topmost in her mind, despite the horror of yesterday. It didn't say much for her character. And had she really believed the talk-show host would open doors for her? Eve just didn't see it. But none of that added up to a motive for murder, unless Natalie had dangled the prospect of help in front of Scarlett, then changed her mind. But there was no evidence for that, and Scarlett would have to have been livid enough to find a blunt instrument and follow Natalie to kill her in cold blood. It didn't feel right.

'I'd love to talk to anyone else who saw her that night. Do you know if she was planning to meet someone after you?' If it was her in the library, she might have mentioned an appointment, but it was a long shot. Eve doubted Natalie would have shared personal information, despite the apparent new-found friendship.

Scarlett examined her cuticles. 'She didn't mention anyone.' Then her eyes met Eve's. 'But of course, we all know Eliza Gregory was hanging around the guest block.'

19

After Eve left Scarlett, she took a walk around the outer perimeter of the school, along country lanes and through woods. Her plan to sneak in at night and follow Anastasia played in her mind. The gates would be locked. She'd need a way in. When she saw a weak spot in the school boundary, she told herself she was just looking. Not committing to anything. But when she got home, she called Viv to talk it over. By the time she hung up, she knew the die was cast.

She was glad to see an email come in from Natalie's property-developer ex: husband number one. It ought to act as a distraction. But it turned out the message had been sent on his behalf, not by him direct. It was loud and clear: he didn't want to contribute to the obituary. No explanation or comment.

After what she'd heard from Natalie's third husband, Eve wasn't entirely surprised. She shivered. What would Gavin Vale have had in store if Natalie had lived? And how much did he know about his predecessors?

She'd find out more that afternoon.

. . .

After lunch, Eve picked Robin up just outside Saxford. She drove north to Greenside House, Natalie Somerson's palatial country home.

Robin was quiet and she turned to glance at him quickly. 'Are you okay? Were you back at Southwood this morning?'

He took a deep breath. 'Yes, but when I finished, the bursar asked to speak with me. The school thinks it's best if I hand over to the under gardeners now. She says they'll manage until Frank's back on his feet.'

'Heck. I'm sorry, Robin. I mean, I know you don't need the work, but...'

'I know.' He rubbed his jaw. 'It feels weird. They know I'm under suspicion, but it's more than that. They actually think I might be guilty. Still,' he grinned for a moment, 'it'll be good to get back to an even pattern of work. I've been cramming my regulars in at odd hours.' But then his smiled faded.

She could guess what he was thinking. His usual clients might think he was guilty too. She felt a nip of anxiety in her stomach. She'd had the same worry.

There was a pause.

'Is something else wrong?' She glimpsed him nod as she turned to take the road towards Ipswich and the wide, cold blue skies ahead.

'I've lost my ring. The one that belonged to my dad.'

Robin had taken to wearing it. With his parents dead and home mostly cut off, Eve guessed it must be a comfort to have it to hang on to. Like a talisman.

'I had it this morning. I took it off as usual before I started gardening and left it in the shed but when I got back it was gone.'

'Someone took it?'

'I'm not sure. I found a cat in there, and the door was ajar. It's possible the catch was loose. There were a couple of things knocked over on the bench, close to where I'd left the ring. As if the cat might have leaped up. But I searched and there was no sign of it.'

'Did you report it?'

'I mentioned it to the bursar during the sacking conversation. She came and helped me look but she couldn't find it either. The shed's quite close to the main gate and there's no proper security there. It's not impossible someone came in. They could have checked the shed for tools and found my ring.'

'Maybe.' Eve was sure he didn't believe it, and she didn't either. Had they got a light-fingered student on their hands, or was it something more complicated than that?

They drove on in silence but then Robin spoke. 'How did Gavin Vale sound when he invited you over?'

Her thoughts shifted to the interview ahead. 'Eager. He double-checked the article would be in *Icon*. After that, he offered me photos to go alongside the obituary. Judging from his tone, I guess he'll want to feature in them.'

Maybe he missed the old days when he and his band had been headline news. She thought of the reports she'd read about him. He still attended the right parties and got himself talked about. If he inherited Natalie's place, he'd be able to throw some of his own.

At last they entered the grounds of Greenside House, a huge cedar tree occupying a sweeping lawn to their left, a majestic oak beyond it. More parkland and mature trees lay to either side of the Victorian pile.

'Coverage okay?'

Eve glanced at her phone and nodded.

'Right. Let's open a call now. Any problems and I'll find a way in.'

Once that was sorted, Eve dropped Robin off before they neared the house. He planned to walk amongst the trees, rather than let Vale see him waiting in the car. He was already the centre of attention with the police; there was no point in advertising his presence.

Eve knocked on the door.

20

Gavin Vale welcomed Eve to Greenside House himself, casual in a dark grey flannel shirt, black jeans and Chelsea ankle boots. He was smiling, but it didn't reach his eyes.

'Come in!' He stood back and directed her with his right hand, the movement almost a bow. He was attractive, with his laughter lines, wavy greying hair and deep brown eyes. Eve could see why Natalie had fallen for him, but if her third husband's words were anything to go by, their relationship wouldn't have been stable. And things had been volatile on Vale's side too. Thoughts of the threatening letter he'd sent put her on high alert.

'I read about your band,' she said.

For a second his smile looked more natural. 'We're making a comeback. Played a rather good gig last night and the reviews are excellent.'

Last night? After a police interview presumably, in the immediate aftermath of Natalie's murder.

He sighed. 'I know what you're thinking. It seems unimaginable to go on stage after what happened, but the venue had sold out. We couldn't just walk away.' He hesitated. 'Besides, I needed an outlet for my feelings. The press talked about what an emotional performance it was.'

It sounded like something he'd just come up with.

'Were you gigging the night before as well? It would be harrowing, knowing you were on stage with all that energy and buzz while Natalie was attacked.'

Vale gave her a knowing look. 'As a matter of fact, I wasn't. I was with an old friend.'

Old friends weren't great, as alibis went.

'Can I get you a drink?' He'd guided them through a hall with a grand staircase and into a vast sitting room with a large open fire, occasional tables and three couches. He was standing by a collection of decanters filled with spirits.

'Just a soda water, thanks.'

He filled a cut-glass tumbler for her, before pouring himself a sizeable Scotch.

'Please take a seat. Ask me all you need to know and then I'll give you the grand tour. I'd be glad to be in the photos for the article.'

The publicity would help with the band's comeback. 'I'll get *Icon*'s photographer to call you to arrange a time. When did you and Natalie meet?'

Vale told her about a smoky celebrity party in a basement flat in Kensington and went into some fairly graphic detail about the goings-on there. Eve would resort to an obituary writers' euphemism. 'Bohemian' ought to do it.

'That was three months before we married. There was no need to wait. It was clear we were two of a kind.'

Yet Natalie hadn't struck Eve as the romantic sort. Eve had the impression she'd become more armour-plated and cynical each time she married. The rush to wed recently seemed strange.

'How much did you see of each other, day to day? Was it

difficult with you both working antisocial hours?' Eve wanted to steer the talk to the current state of their marriage.

'Oh, for sure.' Vale leaned back in his seat and took a swig of his whisky. 'With homes here and in London, we were like ships that passed in the night.'

'Did you worry it might be a problem? After all, Natalie had three divorces under her belt. Some people might have been daunted. Especially given the way Natalie treated her exes.' It wasn't all in the public domain, but surely there must have been rumours.

Vale's gaze shifted to the carpet. 'I wouldn't have married her if I didn't think we could make a go of it.'

He hadn't been scared to start with, Eve guessed, but something told her fear had crept up on him in the end. 'You bought this place together?' Eve knew they hadn't.

Vale raised an eyebrow. 'Natalie had it before we married.'

'How did you cope, seeing so little of each other?'

He shrugged. 'We were both free spirits. There was nothing possessive about our relationship.'

Eve thought of the note Natalie had shown Anastasia. 'Not jealous types?'

He laughed, but it sounded forced. 'Not at all. After that first party it was clear we both enjoyed... adventure.'

His tone made her cringe. 'But you decided to marry?' Eve tried not to look around the luxurious room they occupied. She could see why Vale might have wanted to make it legal, but what about Natalie?

'We both liked having someone there for the long haul. For lazy breakfasts in bed on country weekends, or public dinner engagements.' He threw back his head for a moment then faced Eve head on. 'Natalie didn't like to be seen alone, and although hook-ups are easy to come by, you don't take them to a media dinner at the Savoy. Besides, Natalie loved to be gossiped about. You can't create a stir with your affairs if you're single.'

His words flowed, as though he'd been prepared for her question. That said, it made a horrible sort of sense.

'So you each saw other people? The affair with Calvin Wright was genuine?'

He nodded, but his jaw was taut. 'Natalie would want you to know – would want to be written up that way. For my own part, I think it's part of a healthy marriage. With variety, you stay keen.'

It was hard not to react, knowing he was lying. 'You were happy together, then?'

'Absolutely!' Vale threw out his arms in an expansive gesture, but his eyes told another story. Eve could see the interview was a strain. She wondered if Natalie had told him she wanted a divorce. Either way, he must have known it was a danger.

Vale gave Eve a few anecdotes about wild nights out in London, and gatecrashing a smart party, where they'd caused a scene. She hated to admit it, but it would go down well with Portia Coldwell and *Icon*. It was the stuff that sold magazines.

'Now, let me show you round.'

He led her through a grand dining room with deep blue walls and lamps with red shades, then on through a second sitting room, and up to several vast bedrooms with views over the park.

She imagined the sort of shots *Icon*'s photographer would take, each with Vale in them. She'd be tempted to have him edited out later, but his presence told a story. He was still there, enjoying the house Natalie had bought. He'd won. Or so it seemed.

'Could I use your bathroom before I leave?'

'Of course.' He showed her the downstairs cloakroom.

Inside, Eve caught her breath. On a shelf, next to the loo, sat a photo in a silver frame. Eliza Gregory. Just under it, still in the framed area, was a typed caption.

DON'T BE A LOSER

It made Eve shiver. Had Natalie looked at that image and repeated that mantra? Did she have a photo just like it in her London flat? One in her handbag? What kind of person did that? She got that they'd clashed, but this was obsessive. It made her wonder if there was more to discover about their relationship.

When she'd finished, she asked Vale about the photograph.

He seemed distracted. 'Oh, some teacher she hated at school. She bore a grudge.'

'Well, thanks so much for seeing me.' They were outside the house now, on the front drive.

She saw Vale relax as she prepared to ask her final question. The bombshell. 'Before I go, I heard you wrote to Natalie shortly before she died.'

His mouth half-opened. 'What do you mean?'

'A note, telling her how furious you were with her for having an affair. Threatening her.' She wondered if he'd known she was dying but wasn't sure it made a difference. He might have been so angry that he'd wanted emotional satisfaction there and then.

'You—' His face contorted as he realised she'd strung him along. 'You haven't been honest with me.'

She refused to feel guilty, under the circumstances. 'You don't deny it then? You wished her harm in that letter, and now she's dead.' She wouldn't have pushed if she hadn't known Robin was close at hand.

His face darkened now. He was literally livid. But his aggression was turned inward – he was clutching clenched fists to his chest. 'You don't know what she was like.'

Nothing justified threats of violence, but Eve wanted to hear his story. Speaking to Duncan Ross had convinced her there'd be way more to the marriage than Vale was letting on.

'Perhaps you'd like to tell me. If you do, I can make sure the article in *Icon* reflects the real woman. I don't have to quote you or go into specifics if you'd rather I didn't.'

She held her breath as Vale's chest rose and fell.

At last, he spoke. 'I don't inherit this place, you know. She's left all her money to a cats' home. Every penny. And she never even owned a cat. I'm only here until the paperwork goes through. Not that it came as a shock. She told me a week or two back. I can still see the look in her eye.'

When she got her diagnosis maybe. Or on receipt of his threatening letter. 'So the photos for *Icon* will be for show?'

'It's best to walk the walk. If her bequest doesn't make the papers maybe people will assume I decided to move out.'

Best of luck with that. The cats' home was bound to release the news: they'd want the publicity. 'What was she really like when you first met?'

'Funny, sexy, adventurous. Famous. A couple of friends warned me she was poison, but I took no notice. She suggested marriage and I thought I was in love. We signed a prenup, but I told myself that was standard. And she gave me a monthly allowance. Her earnings eclipsed mine. At the time it seemed like innocent generosity. You might be wondering what she got out of it.' He put his hand over his face. 'Contacts, is the answer. She got exposés on three of my friends in the first six months of our marriage. I was still in touch with some big names, and I made the mistake of trusting her once we'd tied the knot. I thought I was telling her things off the record.'

'But it became clear you weren't?'

He nodded. 'Even then, I tried to ignore it. Told myself it wasn't happening. I liked my new life.'

Eve could imagine. Natalie had got him where she wanted.

'I think divorce would have come next,' Vale said at last. 'Old mates had started to avoid me, and I'd stopped talking. I was no longer any use to her. Not worth the monthly fee. She was ready to move on to the next sucker. And another one after that.'

He'd anticipated a future Natalie would never have had. He hadn't known about her illness then. Perhaps she'd wanted to deny him the satisfaction. But he'd been right that divorce was on the cards. Natalie had wanted to press ahead with that, even though she was dying.

Eve felt the cold ripples of information sink in. She'd bought him, used him and finished with him. What she'd told Duncan Ross was true. She'd learned from her first three marriages, though her take-home message had been governed by her own warped viewpoint. She'd moved on. Changed her approach. Gone into the fourth purely as a business arrangement, never putting her heart on the line. It was appalling and sad at the same time.

'I shouldn't have lost it and sent her that note,' Vale said, rubbing his chin. 'It gave her ammunition. But I'd never have killed her. She was funding me – at least for a little while longer.'

It was true, Vale wouldn't gain financially by her death, but emotionally was another matter.

'A worthwhile interview,' Robin said drily as he got into her car, partway down the drive.

'You said it.' As Eve pulled out onto the main road, she told him about the photo of Eliza Gregory in the bathroom.

'That's extreme. Conclusions?'

'Vale could see how Natalie would treat him if he ever crossed her, now or after they'd broken up. He might have been scared. She'd imagined slights in the past, if what Duncan Ross says is true. I could see Vale killing her – either from hatred, or like a person with a fear of spiders, crushing one to make sure it never crawled out from behind the skirting board again.' And she could imagine him going to the school prepared, with a murder weapon. It didn't have to have been him in the library. Maybe he'd seen Natalie from a distance, making out with another man, and it had spurred him on. How to get proof was another matter.

21

That evening, Eve was in Elizabeth's Cottage, making preparations. She forced herself to carry on, though she was queasy with nerves and questioning her plans. When she'd called Viv earlier, her friend had been determined to join her on her mission to follow Anastasia. She'd wanted to break in alongside Eve, but that was a step too far. Eve had made her promise to wait outside the grounds instead. She'd considered keeping an open call to her, just as she had with Robin, but decided against it. Viv was too likely to blurt something or absent-mindedly put on a CD, inadvertently revealing Eve's presence. Even quiet noises from her phone could give her away in the dead of night. Instead, Eve had a text ready to send, asking Viv to call the police. She'd use it if necessary and Viv knew to raise a riot at Southwood's gates if she was summoned.

Gus looked at her with his head on one side, his eyes anxious, and she felt guilty.

'It's not ideal,' she said as she pulled on a pair of black jeans, a black top and jumper. 'But I need to know where Anastasia goes at night. If I get found out it will look bad, but not as awful as if I went with Robin and we both got caught. And I can't risk letting Viv in with me.' She didn't do stealth.

Gus gave a low whine and put his head against her leg. He knew she was tense and she was making him miserable. But she couldn't get the knowledge any other way.

'I don't think it's that dangerous,' she said aloud. 'Anastasia wasn't hiding when I saw her. And if the library silhouette was Natalie, she's got a cast-iron alibi for her murder. Equally, if someone created the silhouette to blur the time of death, Anastasia's out of it, unless she's in league with two other people. It doesn't seem likely. She's fiercely independent.'

But deep down, Eve still didn't trust the bursar quite enough to ask her about her midnight wanderings, rather than following her. Southwood was a close-knit community. What if she was protecting someone?

Eve pulled on a black beanie and checked her appearance in the mirror. It was a pretty good outfit for trailing someone after dark. She added a padded black jacket and gym shoes and finally left the house at midnight. Viv appeared by Eve's car, her red-orange hair gleaming in the glow of the street lamp. She was carrying several bars of chocolate.

'Just in case it's a long wait. You should have some too. It'll give you strength before you go.'

'Ugh. I couldn't.'

'Are you sure this is a good idea?'

'Not entirely...'

Eve parked in a back lane near Southwood and left Viv with her mobile on her lap. She only hoped she didn't fall asleep and miss her text.

The weak spot in the school's defences was further down the lane, where there was no space to park. If a car came Eve would be spotted in an instant, hopefully before the driver mowed her down. She edged along the perimeter of the school: a double-layer hornbeam hedge, with wire mesh at its centre.

There was no moon, and every so often she stumbled over a tuft of grass or a root. She scanned the trees as she went, and listened for any sign of movement on the other side. Every rustle made her jump, but the sounds were too quiet to be human.

Her mind slid to Robin. He'd be furious if he knew what she was up to.

At last, she came to the spot she'd been making for: a patch where an old hornbeam tree outside the mesh had been replaced with a newer one. It left a gap, big enough for Eve to squeeze through.

Tucked in her hidey-hole, she could just see the school buildings through the mesh. Nerves made her feel hot one minute and shivery the next. Anastasia probably wasn't the killer, but someone was. And everyone would be on high alert, after what had happened.

Using the tree next to her, she managed to hoist herself up. To get over the mesh she needed to push her toes into its holes. The gaps were barely big enough, but her gym shoes were flexible with rubber soles. Just as she pushed up, her foot slipped. She flung out a hand and grabbed the hornbeam beyond the mesh and scrabbled with her feet, her heart pounding.

If anyone was close by, they'd have heard her. She tried to catch her breath as she stabilised herself and waited, listening.

More rustles, but only those of mice or other night-time creatures.

She had another go, and managed to get one leg over the fence, then the other. The hornbeams pressed in close, their leaves rustling with every move. Gradually she eased herself down behind the inner hedge, crouching low, looking at the school.

She was behind the cookery classrooms she and Viv had used. At least they were unlikely to be occupied at one in the morning. In theory, she should be able to risk pushing through the hedge now. Thank goodness Southwood didn't have guard dogs. She took a deep shaky breath and, keeping as low as possible, shoved through the branches, which poked her as she went.

A quick glance behind left her palms clammy. If she needed a fast getaway she'd be sunk. From this side, the hedge all looked the same. One long expanse of russet-leaved, densely packed trees. She found a white tissue in her pocket and put it under a stone to mark the point where she'd entered. But how long would it take her to find it in the dark and make it back to the lane? Her legs felt like jelly.

If she wanted to see anything, she needed to enter Great Quad. It was where Anastasia's rooms were, and Eve had seen her take the route twice. If the bursar appeared, she'd need to stick like glue to the quad's outer edge and creep after her.

She found a side passageway to reach her destination, then picked a place to lie low, close to the buildings, deep in shadow, hardly daring to breathe.

Ahead and to her right was the main passageway that led to Old Quad, with the hidden room in its corner. There was a second route through as well: the smaller passage Anastasia had taken, two nights running. Had she visited Old Quad, or somewhere beyond?

Eve's heart rate ramped up. Moving from one quad to the other would be the riskiest part of the proceedings. She could leave the quad altogether and go round the outside, but the chances of missing Anastasia then were huge.

She crouched there, her mouth dry. What if Anastasia was simply an insomniac who took a nightly walk? Would Eve follow her around the quads and back to her quarters for nothing?

Would she even come? She might not sleep badly every night.

But at that moment, she caught movement. A gowned figure was just visible, emerging from the accommodation block in

Great Quad. Making for the narrow passageway. The same one Anastasia had used. It was darker tonight, and Eve couldn't be certain it was her.

Her chest tightened and her throat constricted as she stared after them. The figure looked the right height and build for the bursar. The stride was right. And the long gown. It must be her.

Eve waited until she'd disappeared into the tunnel before daring to follow, but then she moved quickly. She mustn't lose her. Once the bursar reached Old Quad she might slip into a staircase and go to someone's room. Scarlett's quarters were there, and the guest rooms too.

Eve took a deep breath as she entered the main tunnel. There was nowhere to hide if Anastasia doubled back, but it was essential to keep up.

At last she emerged in Old Quad. Anastasia was still ahead of her, walking purposefully. Eve turned left and skirted the buildings again. She was halfway along her route when she thought she heard something behind her. The sound of a small pebble being kicked along the flagstones? She turned to look, but everything was in deep, inky shadow. The small shrubs planted along the edges of the buildings made it hard to see.

She carried on, glancing over her shoulder periodically, but heard nothing more.

Anastasia was ahead of her and entering the tunnel that would take her out beyond the quads. Eve risked hastening again to catch up. Moments later, she could see the bursar walking between the tennis courts and around a playing field, head down.

Eve could see it was her now. Once again, she waited. She'd be out in the open when she followed. The bursar was too close. Only when she'd entered the woods did Eve hurry after her. She'd just have to hope Anastasia was intent on her mission and didn't look back.

At the edge of the trees, Eve paused to check over her

shoulder and this time she thought she caught movement. A shift in the shadows along the hedge beyond the courts. Had someone taken a detour to continue following her and the bursar? But it was breezy. It might just be foliage, shifting in the gloom. Eve could give up. Turn around. But if she was being followed, she'd still be spotted. If someone was a danger to her, that would be true even if she turned back. And she'd leave without information.

Once again, Robin filled her head. What he'd think if she came to grief. How awful it would be if she couldn't explain. But how desperate she was to solve the murder.

Inside the wood, the lane curved round, so that she couldn't see Anastasia. She hoped she'd continued ahead and not gone off through the trees. Eve walked on, feeling less and less sure of her mission, but at last, she saw a building on the other side of the wood. Gravestones next to it. A lychgate. The school chapel. Eve remembered seeing it on the map now.

She still couldn't spot Anastasia, but as she approached the building's arched windows with their stained glass, she saw a faint glow inside.

The outer door to the church was ajar. Eve peered over her shoulder, up the lane towards the nearest perimeter fence and back towards the woods. Nothing.

Anastasia must have entered the chapel moments earlier. She wouldn't dash straight out again. Hopefully.

Eve crept up the pathway and into the porch. The inner door wasn't quite closed, and beyond, Eve could hear the bursar talking. Who was she meeting with? Eve couldn't see. And why choose the chapel?

She stood there, straining to hear the words. The wind blew an order of service off a shelf, and outside came the sound of a footstep.

22

Eve could hardly breathe. She felt as though something heavy was pressing on her chest. There was nothing she could do. If she waited in the porch, Anastasia and the person she was meeting might discover her. But if she crept back into the churchyard, the person outside might block her path.

For a moment she stood, shaking, undecided. But only one scenario was a certainty. She chose the churchyard, exiting the porch with her head down, like a thief in the night. As she slipped back into the open, she risked a look around her.

She could have sworn she'd heard footsteps, but everything seemed still and quiet.

And then she looked up and saw a tiny flash from somewhere ahead, through the dense dark trees by the perimeter fence.

Someone signalling? To her, or to Anastasia? She was torn. To go ahead, or to turn and run. But then the light winked again, and a faint glow shone from her jacket pocket. Turning her phone so she could see the screen, she saw she'd had a text.

Guess who? I'm behind the yew trees by the perimeter fence.
Suggest you join me.

Robin. It must have been him she'd heard outside. She felt
her cheeks flush, the relief mixed with awkwardness. She
walked towards the thick foliage where she'd spotted the tiny
flash of light.

At last, she was close enough to see the glint of his eyes.

'We can watch from here.' Robin's voice was so low she was
picking up on the smallest of vibrations. 'See what happens
next.'

She wanted to apologise. To explain why she'd risked
coming alone – argue her case. But it wasn't the time for a whispered conversation.

They stood, perfectly still, and watched. Every minute felt
like ten. After what seemed like hours, Eve shifted slightly and
realised how stiff she'd got.

The cold was seeping into her bones by the time Anastasia
appeared. She looked over her shoulder as she left and closed
the door behind her. She couldn't be up to anything too secret.
She didn't seem at all worried about being seen.

Eve and Robin's eyes met for a moment.

The bursar strode back towards the school buildings, her
shoulders relaxed.

All was quiet at the chapel. Eve stared at the porch, but no
one appeared. She realised she'd been holding her breath and
took a lungful of air. What could Anastasia's companion be
doing in there?

As the time wore on, Eve shifted from foot to foot to try to
keep warm, but still no one came out. At last, Robin turned
to her.

'I'll take a look inside.'

She shook her head. 'I'll do it. You can still wade in if there's
a problem, but I don't like to think what'll happen if one of the

staff is in there and reports you to Palmer. If it's me, he'll put it down to my "busybody" nature... But I can loiter at the door while I look. I'm pretty well disguised. I'll use my torch app, then run for it. I doubt they'll catch me and they won't see my face if they're dazzled by the light.'

'That sounds like a horrible idea.'

'But you know it makes sense.'

He held her for a moment. 'All right. If you have to run, run here and I'll give you a leg-up over that gateway.' He pointed behind him. 'It must be old – it's permanently locked – but it's climbable.'

How the heck had she missed it when she'd looked for a way in?

She nodded, swallowed, and made her way towards the chapel, glancing over her shoulder as she went. Everything was still. The chapel seemed to be in total darkness now.

At last, she reached the porch, then the inner door. She put her hand on the latch and turned it quickly, wanting to take whoever it was by surprise. The creak she made sounded loud in the quiet of the night.

As she pushed the door open, she shone her torch inside, ready to dazzle whoever looked up.

But there was nobody there. Eve's breath caught somewhere in her upper chest. Anastasia had been talking to someone. If they were hiding, something had spooked them. She must be a threat to them – which meant they were a threat to *her*.

She stood in the doorway, her weight on one foot, tensed and ready to backtrack. But if she didn't push for the truth, Robin remained in danger. Finding the killer couldn't wait.

Holding her breath, she used an ancient iron doorstop to force the heavy chapel door open so she could bolt for it unimpeded if she needed to.

She walked to the nave and began a journey towards the

altar, taking it slowly, sweeping the torch left and right, checking for anyone hiding amongst the pews.

No one.

She bent down as she went, to look underneath. If someone had flattened themselves on the floor she could have missed them. But there was nothing. Just dust, tiles and a dropped tissue. It was eerily quiet.

She walked on, checking the choir stalls on either side of the chapel. Empty. As she went, she darted glances over her shoulder. For anyone trying to run. Or trying to sneak up on her.

There was a side chapel, but that was deserted too. The smell of polish and incense hung in the air.

The last possibility was the vestry, its dark door hiding what was beyond. She walked closer, listening, but there was nothing she could detect. She put her hand on the doorknob, planning her escape route, the direction she'd run, how quickly she could be out in the open air.

She'd been quiet as she approached the door. She might take them by surprise. She'd be ready to react quickly.

In one fluid movement she turned the knob and thrust the door open.

Empty. She almost laughed with the release of pent-up tension. She checked that room thoroughly too, behind the door, under the desk.

At last, she was satisfied.

As she walked out of the chapel, pushing the stop out of the way and closing the door behind her, she felt a mix of relief and confusion. What a perplexing wild goose chase.

23

Eve found Robin again and explained. Not that she had a proper explanation. He raised an eyebrow and pointed towards the perimeter. 'Shall we?'

The iron gate was welded shut but Robin gave her a leg-up as promised, then followed her over. Beyond were soft leylandii, cut low. Much easier to navigate than the hornbeams.

As she landed, he put his finger to his lips and led the way through the forgiving hedge. Up ahead was a covered swimming pool and a patio with a table and chairs set on it. And beyond that, a rather nice modern detached house.

She followed Robin as he edged his way along the dwelling's back boundary, after which they squeezed through another hedge and out into a lane beyond.

'Handy,' Eve said, her teeth chattering. 'Thanks.' She gave him a look, then lowered her eyes. 'I'm sorry. I would have told you normally, but the idea of you coming and getting caught was frightening. Viv was on standby though.'

'I know. I found her doing a sudoku.' He handed her a chocolate bar. 'She gave me one of these, but I reckon you might need it more urgently.'

'How did you know we'd be here?'

'I was worried. I was out for a late walk and noticed your car was gone from the village green.'

Eve guessed he wasn't sleeping well. She wasn't surprised.

'Viv's house was in darkness too,' he went on, 'and that's not normal.' He shrugged at her look. 'I'm an ex-cop. I notice these things. Anyway, I rang her, and she spilled the beans. I would have called you, but I had a nasty feeling you might be up to something delicate.'

She gave him a rueful look. 'I can't believe you had us sneaking through someone's back garden.'

'It seemed like the lesser risk.'

She was sure he was right. 'Would you have tried to stop me if you'd arrived earlier?'

He nodded. 'You're too precious. Please don't hold out on me again, Eve.'

'I don't intend to. Honestly.'

From his look she could tell he hadn't missed her careful choice of words. He sighed.

'I need to cut back and find Viv so I can drive her home.'

'I'll come with you. Drop me off at my van?'

She nodded. 'The least I can do, under the circumstances.'

She was still shivering and Robin put an arm around her as they walked. 'So what was Anastasia doing in the chapel, do you think? Praying?'

'Could be. She's lost a niece and she's probably worried about the effect of Natalie's murder on the school.'

'And what about the hooded figure?'

Eve's chest tightened. 'What do you mean?'

'I thought you'd seen them. You looked behind you once, just after I'd spotted them.'

'I thought I heard something, but later I convinced myself it was you.' She saw his raised eyebrow. 'Sorry. I should have guessed it wasn't.' He could creep around more quietly than anyone she knew. 'What did they do when I went into the porch?'

'Watched from a distance. I was ready to step in if they became a threat, but I was too late to stop them seeing you. Given that, I thought watching and waiting might be informative. They crept back towards the school after the bursar left.'

'It could have been someone after answers, like us. They might have spotted Anastasia's late-night wanderings and decided to follow her.'

'Or they could be the killer. They were certainly careful to keep their identity secret. You have to take care, Eve. They'll be wondering what you're up to. If they guess you're investigating, you could be in danger.'

Eve hoped to goodness the darkness and her turned up collar had been enough to disguise her.

When Eve got up the following morning, she found Gus guarding a note on her doormat. He glanced up at her, as though for approval. She bent to ruffle his fur, then picked up the bit of paper which was folded in four.

Inside there were two typed sentences:

NO SIGN OF BLACKMAIL. TERMINAL DIAGNOSIS CONFIRMED.

Eve crouched there for a moment, shivering in the draught that came under the door, then went to make coffee. Her eyes felt gritty and her mind fuzzy after her long night.

'It has to be from Greg,' she said, over her shoulder to Gus. 'He can't help Robin directly, but I told Olivia Dawkins I thought Natalie might have been blackmailing someone. He must have checked her bank account and found no regular deposits.' She frowned as she reached for a cup. Maybe her victim sent cash and she spent it by degrees. She presumed the police couldn't check if any of the suspects made regular cash withdrawals. It was useful to have Natalie's illness confirmed too, not that she'd doubted Anastasia.

Eve felt a spark of hope, knowing Greg Boles was secretly looking out for Robin.

The warm feeling left her when she went to the village store after breakfast for more milk and a newspaper.

'Ah, Eve dear!' Moira, the storekeeper, leaned over the counter, her plum lipstick and auburn hair shining in the over-head light. 'You're just the person. I had Deidre Lennox in earlier. She was asking about the dreadful business at South-wood School. What a thing to have happened at such a respectable establishment.'

'It would be very upsetting, wherever it took place.' Eve thought of Eliza Gregory's behaviour towards the students. Not respectable in her book.

'Well, of course!' Moira gave a deep sigh, but Eve could see the promise of gossip was more than enough to offset the horror of Natalie's murder. 'I said to Deidre, Eve will know more. You were there, after all, and everyone knows how observant you are.'

'Viv was there as well.' Eve would like to share Moira's attention if possible.

'Oh, yes, but she hasn't got your track record. So tell me, do you have any idea who might be responsible? To hit someone over the head like that, so brutally... It must be a man, of course.'

As Eve counted to ten, she heard the door open behind her and the old-fashioned bell jangle. A brief glance told her it was her neighbours from Haunted Lane, Sylvia and Daphne. Salts of the earth. She could speak freely. 'I don't think we should discount Natalie's female contacts.'

Moira beamed over Eve's shoulder to welcome the newcomers, then ploughed on. 'Still, a man does seem more likely. I don't like to speak ill of anyone, of course, but people are talking about Robin Yardley.'

Eve felt a shot of adrenaline quicken her breathing. She mustn't give herself away.

'I know he's been in the village a long time now,' Moira went on, 'but we've never really got to the bottom of what he did before he came here, have we? And now I've heard that he and Natalie Somerson were spotted together in a secluded part of the school grounds! That strikes me as very interesting. Perhaps she knew him before he came to Saxford, and he killed her to stop her talking about it. Or maybe he made advances towards her and she threatened to report him.' She shook her head. 'These strong, silent types can be very dangerous. I've seen it on the news, and—'

'Muckraking again, Moira!' The words were said with a cackle.

It was Sylvia who'd spoken. She and her partner were amongst the few who knew Eve and Robin were together, though, like Viv, they weren't aware of his police background. Eve glanced at them. Daphne was blushing at Sylvia's words, but she looked a good deal more upset than her.

'Robin's a dear,' she said quietly.

'He's no more likely to batter someone over the head than the vicar is.' Sylvia laughed again.

Moira flushed as Eve paid for her goods and flashed her neighbours a grateful smile.

Outside, she collected Gus, unlooping his leash from the dog hooks, and marched across the village green towards home. Tears pricked her eyes. Sylvia and Daphne were dear friends. They'd defend her and Robin to the hilt, and it touched her, but others wouldn't be so kind.

Sylvia's response was the most reassuring. She hadn't even taken Moira's words seriously. But she was strong and independent. What would the other villagers say when they heard the storekeeper's gossip?

'We have to sort this out, Gus,' she said, walking more quickly. 'And fast.'

24

As Eve approached Monty's kitchen that morning, ready to work a shift, she heard Viv's mother-in-law Sabina's voice. It wasn't just her hectoring tone that set Eve's teeth on edge. She was talking about Robin too. Eve marched straight in. It was best to tackle Sabina head on. The only way to treat a bully.

Viv's eyes met hers as she entered and took off her coat. She bit her lip and mouthed 'sorry'.

Sabina turned and fixed Eve with her cold-eyed stare. 'Ah, Eve. I knew you'd want my input for Natalie's obituary. I thought we might as well get it over with. I've had quite enough of interviews already. To think the police asked for my where-abouts when the murder took place. And the looks they exchanged when I explained I was alone at home with Edward! They seemed to imply that we couldn't be trusted. I had to get Detective Inspector Palmer involved.'

He'd have been putty in her hands. He judged suspects by house size and influence. That said, she couldn't see Sabina as the killer. It would be unthinkable to her. Low, messy and grubby. And though Natalie had been an irritant, Sabina hadn't had to deal with her as often as those at Southwood. Eve tried to keep her voice calm. 'I'm meant to be working.'

Sabina rolled her eyes. 'Aren't you in charge of who works when? You can rejig your shift, can't you?'

Eve was tempted to refuse on principle. Plus, she was exhausted; she wouldn't be firing on all cylinders. But she'd rather get it over with too. Sabina was a friend of Eliza's with an old connection to the school. She might know more about the head of sixth form's relationship with Natalie than anyone else. Whether Eliza was guilty, even. Getting her to give up her secrets wouldn't be easy, but she was keen to try. She turned to Viv. 'Do you mind?'

'Not at all. You can sit in here for privacy. I'll just get on. I won't disturb you.'

Eve almost smiled, despite the situation. She knew Viv wanted to listen in. On the upside, it would save Eve relaying it all afterwards.

Sabina looked at the chairs and table they'd been offered in the kitchen and her lips narrowed. She pulled out the seat gingerly. Eve had the distinct impression she thought it might be sticky and felt insulted on her own and Viv's account.

'How well did you know Natalie?' she asked as she sat down.

'Too well for my liking.' Sabina pushed the nail of her fore-finger into the flesh of her thumb as if she was squashing an imaginary bug. 'I was on the disciplinary committee when she was a student. We had to come up with new punishments specifically for her misdemeanours: standing on the battlements wall, climbing over the perimeter fence and staying out overnight.'

Viv give Eve a meaningful look. 'I can't believe anyone would climb over the perimeter fence.'

Eve bent over her notepad so they wouldn't lock eyes again.

'That was the least of it,' Sabina replied. 'She stole, then *sold* a vase left to the school by Emily Fox, her own ancestor, if you please.'

'Were the police brought in?'

Sabina twitched suddenly in her chair as though Eve had tasered her. 'Certainly not. It was an internal matter. But as you can see, she had no sense of decorum.'

'It was all swept under the carpet?'

Viv's mother-in-law looked at her narrowly. 'She was grounded. Denied privileges. It was properly dealt with.'

Eve wondered why Natalie had done it. Had she upped the ante to try to get expelled? Maybe she'd seen it as the only way to exercise some control over her destiny.

'You must have been glad when she left Southwood.' And Natalie would have been too, by the sound of it.

'Undoubtedly. I thought we'd never see hide nor hair of her after that, but she visited. At first it was just every six months or so.'

'I gather she met Eliza when she came back.'

Sabina drew herself up. 'Who told you that?'

'I did.' Viv sounded unrepentant. In her place, Eve might have been tempted to keep quiet.

'Your tittle-tattle is hardly helpful at a time like this,' Sabina said. 'What Eliza suffered at Natalie's hands is diabolical. Thank goodness it's over.'

'But surely she wasn't still suffering because of her?' Eve met Sabina's eye. Or was she? Had Natalie been a blackmailer and Eliza her victim, despite Greg Boles' lack of evidence?

Sabina blinked and Eve let the silence stretch.

'Natalie reminded her of the poem she wrote on Founders' Day,' she said at last.

'But there's more, isn't there? You were referring to something ongoing.'

Sabina's lips thinned. She knew she'd been caught. At last, she sighed, irritably. 'I've never got the full details out of her.

Just hints.' She sounded honest. Annoyed at not knowing more.

'But you know Natalie still bothered her.'

She waved a hand. 'You're putting words in my mouth. None of us relished her regular visits to Southwood.'

'Natalie still saw Eliza every six months?'

'More often, lately,' Sabina said. 'She's been in and out every month or so on some pretext or another.'

Eve could hear the irritation and puzzlement in her voice. Why had she been? Near the end, it was clearer. She'd had marriage troubles and probably health worries too, leading up to that final dreadful diagnosis. It was natural that she'd turn to Anastasia. But before that?

'What did she do, when she visited?'

'Made her presence felt in the coven. Brought presents for Martin and Lucia's children and had little chats with him about running the school. I think Eliza wondered if the conversations were about her.'

'What did she imagine they were saying?'

Sabina gave a quick sigh. 'She's never been totally frank. But whatever happened between her and Natalie, I can assure you Eliza won't have been at fault. If they came up before a jury, I'm sure it would be Natalie who got the sentence.'

The mention of a jury made Eve pause. 'Eliza hinted the secret talks might relate to something criminal?' Natalie could have ended up in court for blackmail, if she was guilty of that, but what about the head of sixth form?

'I was speaking figuratively.' Sabina had stopped meeting Eve's gaze for a moment but raised her eyes again to add: 'I don't know any more.'

That last bit might be true, but the image had been specific. If all Eliza had done was hint, Eve couldn't help feeling that Sabina had remembered her words and unthinkingly repeated them. If Eve was right, the head of sixth form had imagined standing in a courtroom.

'Everything's gone downhill thanks to Anastasia's interference.' Sabina pushed her hands down flat on the table, her silk scarf quivering as she spoke. It seemed like a transparent attempt to change the subject. 'She should never have championed a head teacher from outside the founding families for a start. Bridget Leverett wasn't up to the job. I can't think why she made such a fuss about keeping her. She didn't run things like a true descendant would have. It's in the blood. And to push for a male head teacher after that! Martin's a descendant of a founder, of course, through his father, but to pick a male role model for Southwood's students. It's preposterous.

'Well, I must go. I can't spend any more time talking about Natalie. She was a disgrace to the school, but people will associate her with her sleazy television show, not Southwood, thank heaven. Your article must focus on that, Eve.'

As she got up and swept out of the room, Viv handed Eve a plateful of chocolate brownies. 'Quick. Take one before irritation makes you self-combust. And then we need to talk.'

Five minutes after the medicinal brownie, Eve was beating butter, ready to make some spiced apple cakes.

'So what did you make of Sabina's tirade?' Viv was melting butter and sugar for a batch of apricot flapjacks.

'Interesting.' Eve let her thoughts fall into place as she added granulated and soft brown sugar to her mix. 'I wonder if Eliza did something extra to hurt Natalie, beyond showing her up in front of the class. Something criminal. I sense Sabina's being honest when she says she doesn't know the details – she looked frustrated. But she clearly has the impression Eliza's worries are over now Natalie's dead. I still wonder if Natalie was blackmailing her.'

'Eliza has a top motive, then.'

'Potentially. I wonder why Natalie visited Southwood more frequently in the run-up to her death. If she was getting money out of Eliza, she wouldn't need to see her every month to keep that going. Even if Eliza paid her in cash, she could send it by post. My guess is there's another reason, which also led her to accept the role of Founders' Day Champion. She was certainly worming her way in. Sabina says she brought presents for Martin and Lucia's daughters. That sounds kind on the face of it, but maybe Lucia didn't like her getting too close. She voted against her.' Eve wouldn't want someone like Natalie cosying up to her kids, and they were adults. 'And Sabina gave the impression she was trying to influence school policy too.' What had she been up to?

Eve added an egg direct to her mixture. No shell!

'Get you!' Viv said, pushing her blue hairnet up as it threatened to come down over her eyes. 'I thought it would never happen!'

'It was time.' Eve tried to hide her pride as she added another couple of eggs. She'd found you had to believe as you cracked them. It meant you'd do it firmly enough and all would be well. 'Going back to Natalie, the idea of her influencing school policy is interesting. Everyone says she wasn't remotely interested in Southwood, and that she hated the place from when she was a child. Maybe her diagnosis focused her mind; made her realise she'd like to make a difference. But perhaps she was acting for personal reasons. To get Eliza sacked, or Scarlett removed as head girl.'

'You think she'd do that to Scarlett, even though they seemed like best buddies by the time she died?'

'She was hateful towards her to start with, don't forget. As for the best buddies act, I can't believe she'd genuinely changed her mind. I'd say something external caused that superficial change of heart. And if that's the case, things could have soured again just as quickly.' She sighed. 'But this is all speculation. Scarlett's opportunity's clear enough, and she was shifty as heck about meeting with Natalie the night she died, but I still don't have a motive for her.'

'Very frustrating.'

Eve reached for the apple juice. 'Eliza and Gavin Vale are more solid suspects. And then there are the others, but if any of *them* are guilty, and dressed up as Natalie to fake an alibi, they must have an accomplice.'

'And Anastasia would have needed two.'

'Right.'

'Eliza and Scarlett could have worked together.'

'They could.' It was hard to imagine, though. Eliza's voice had dripped with disdain as she'd talked about the head girl. 'Someone could have worked with Natalie's husband, but that doesn't seem likely. How would he know who to trust?'

Viv nodded as she stirred dried apricot into her oat mixture. 'And the others don't have motives?'

'Not that I've discovered, now we know Natalie had renounced her share in the school. But it's early days. And after last night, I've got more queries. Anastasia talking to herself in the chapel is one thing. She could have been praying or just making sense of recent events in a quiet, calm place. But I'd like to know who followed us both.'

'The creepy hooded figure. I'm so glad you got out of there okay. What do you think they were after?'

Eve shrugged. 'Clues, perhaps, like me.' But she remembered Robin's warning. 'Or it could be the killer, wanting to know if I or Anastasia are onto anything.'

The thought of someone flitting through the night in her wake left her shivering. Had she been recognised? Would she be watched now?

'So, what's your plan?'

'I'm off to interview Eliza this afternoon. I want to push her.

She seems so raw; I'm hoping she'll give away more about
Natalie.' They'd each goaded the other. She wanted to know
how far that had gone. And it made sense to focus on her. She
was Eve's top suspect. 'And Lucia Leverett's agreed to see me
afterwards, assuming nothing crops up with a student. I want to
ask about her heart-to-heart with Natalie.' She closed her eyes
for a moment. 'I'll be watching everyone I meet. If someone saw
me last night, I might come face to face with them today.'

25

It was Lucia who showed Eve into Eliza Gregory's office, a corner room with windows facing in two directions. All the better to see miscreant sixth formers through.

Eve was met with the smell of wax polish and the sight of Eliza shutting the window.

'Goodness, Eliza, this looks wonderful.' Lucia looked surprised but pleased, her kind eyes losing their worried look for a moment. 'And it's lovely and fresh in here.'

Eliza put her shoulders back. 'I thought an airing was in order, though it's too cold to keep the window open for long.'

'But you've been sorting out too.'

The head of sixth form nodded. 'About time, I daresay, though obviously I knew it would need doing.'

Lucia's brow furrowed. 'I'm sorry, I—'

'You've not spoken to Martin?'

'No, I've been with a student.'

'When are you not?'

Lucia flushed. 'It's my job. I was about to find Martin now.' She turned to Eve. 'I'll be in the staff room when you're ready.'

Eliza motioned Eve to a chair and raised her eyes. 'She'll be there unless there's an emergency. The girls are far too reliant on her. She's so eager to provide a listening ear that they'll never learn to be self-sufficient.'

'She seems very dedicated.' Eve imagined a head of pastoral care would have their work cut out, especially with someone like Eliza on the staff.

The woman took a seat behind her desk now. She seemed different somehow. Was it her hair? Everything about her looked... looser. Her shoulders less stiff, her mouth less pursed.

'I can imagine what you've heard about me and Natalie,' Eliza said. 'We had our battles. She wasn't my sort. Not Southwood's sort. But my reasons for not wanting her here weren't personal.'

Eve found that very hard to believe. Not *only* personal perhaps. 'Why did you object, then?'

'She was a dangerous person. She found things that were whole and broke them. Look at her talk show. It was her hobby, her passion. Anastasia says it's because she lost her mother, but I think she was born that way – kicking against everyone for the thrill of it. Knowing she could get what she wanted. She delighted in winning.'

'That must have been hard to take.'

She nodded. 'It most certainly was.'

'In which case, I don't imagine the way she humiliated you when she was a student was an isolated event. You must have wanted to fight back. I know I would have.' And then it would have been Natalie's turn again.

Eliza frowned. 'What are you implying?'

'I know you made Natalie feel a fool in front of her class. And then she humiliated you in front of the school. Things were escalating. I'm just wondering what happened next.'

'If you're suggesting I killed her, decades later, to get my revenge—'

'I'm not. I'm trying to understand your relationship to

inform my obituary. If the battle between you was ongoing and she held a grudge, it shows her character. I'm interested in what happened directly after that Founders' Day when she read out your poem. Did you keep the battle going? And what did Natalie do next?'

Eliza blanched. All the former tension was back. She seemed to search Eve's eyes. 'What makes you think something happened?'

She was testing Eve. Wanted to know how much she knew, Eve was sure of it. There was something to unearth. The thing Sabina had been unable to get out of her. 'If I'd been you, I'd have been livid. I'd have wanted to have it out with Natalie at the very least.'

'Responding was part of my job. Not to "have it out" with her as you so vulgarly put it, but to discipline her if she misbehaved. The fact that it was personal was irrelevant.'

Eve tried to imagine what had happened next. Had Eliza gone to Natalie for the umpteenth time to ground her or give her detention? Eve pictured Natalie sneering at her, goading her. 'How far would she have to have gone before she got expelled?'

'We very rarely expel anyone from Southwood. It would be a sign of failure.'

And Eve imagined it would be even less common to push a descendant of one of the founders out. Especially one who was motherless. Eliza had been stuck with her. The strain must have been immense – for both of them.

Eve wanted her to relax again. She was more likely to slip up that way. She got her onto less contentious memories of Natalie. Acting in school productions, winning a debating society trophy.

'She was always a good talker,' Eliza said. 'And it didn't make any difference which side of an argument she was asked to address.'

'She could see both sides?'

But Eliza shook her head. 'She was amoral. Didn't care. It's as I said before, she only minded about winning. Her passion came from that, not from conviction.'

It all fitted with what Eve had seen. But maybe she'd been taught that caring was dangerous, because whatever your feelings, you couldn't control life.

'And what about her acting?' Eve referred to the time when she'd been down to play Sandy in *Grease*.

Eliza frowned. 'Yes. I do remember. She wasn't up to scratch. Everyone agreed.'

Odd. Surely that would have been discovered earlier, before the programmes were prepared? 'Wasn't up to scratch' sounded subjective, and 'everyone agreed' came across as defensive. Eve wondered how big a part Eliza had played in getting Natalie dumped. She was looking forward to the drama teacher's input to help her judge the background.

'Do you know if she had boyfriends, back in her school days?'

Eliza's eyes popped slightly. 'Not here within the walls of Southwood, obviously, but on excursions and at a local ball I saw enough.' She twitched suddenly and met Eve's eye. 'I trust you won't put that in your obituary.'

Eve shook her head. 'No, but what you're telling me is useful. It gives me an idea of what she was like as a whole. I can convey that in a general way.'

'Good.' Once again, Eliza relaxed back in her chair. 'I wouldn't want the boys concerned to think I'd been gossiping. Some of them are well known now.'

'And there's the school's reputation too.'

But Eliza waved her hand. 'I've spent my whole life trying to protect that. I'm tired now.'

At that moment, there was a knock on the door.

'Oh, sorry to disturb you, Miss Gregory.' A young woman

hovered in the doorway, glancing at the head of sixth form anxiously. 'It's just the post.' She put a handwritten letter down on Eliza's desk. Eve noted the writing: italics, bold and characterful, written in fountain pen.

'Don't worry, Jackie. Thank you.'

Eve noticed Jackie's shoulders relax at the reply. She hadn't been expecting it. And she sniffed the air as she left. The scent of polish was clearly unusual. Eve assumed it was normally only the cleaners who bothered.

Eliza glanced at the letter momentarily. She was waiting for Eve to go. 'If there's nothing more?'

Eve hesitated. She'd been told in confidence that Natalie was dying, and depending on the motive for her murder, it might not make a difference. If she'd been killed in a fit of passion, or because of something time sensitive, it would be irrelevant. But what about that overheard conversation? The one which had sounded like blackmail. If Eliza had been Natalie's victim, she might have killed because of it. But that became less likely if the head of sixth form knew Natalie's blackmailing days were numbered.

'Just one last thing. I heard Natalie was ill before she died. Seriously ill.'

She watched Eliza's expression. She looked confused, then dismissive. 'Oh, I'm quite sure we'd have known all about it if she had been. She loved attention.'

Eve was pretty certain Eliza hadn't known. And that she'd misread Natalie. She might have loved attention, but she was fiercely self-sufficient. Had made herself that way.

Eve got up to see herself out. 'Thank you for talking to me.'

She hadn't quite closed the door when she heard Eliza gasp. A moment later came a sob that turned into a howl. Jackie was still just outside and pushed past Eve through the door. Eve had turned too, automatically. Eliza sounded ill.

'Are you all right, Miss Gregory?' She stood between Eve and the room, blocking her view.

Eliza made a choking sound, but a moment later she spoke, the words grating from her. 'Get out!'

Jackie closed the door, her cheeks flushing.

26

Eve's mind was full of Eliza's outburst as she knocked on the door of Southwood's staff common room to look for Lucia.

The head of pastoral care was there as promised. She glanced up from some paperwork, then got to her feet.

Over to her right, Anastasia was talking to Martin and his mother, Bridget. 'A memorial service would be appropriate. Done quietly, to show respect, and done quickly to draw a line under what's happened.'

Martin looked ashen, his eyes wide. Lucia had been smiling at Eve, but now she went still, her focus suddenly on her husband.

'I'm sure Martin can make his own decisions,' Bridget said tartly.

Eve was fairly sure Bridget didn't like Anastasia, which was interesting. The bursar said she'd pushed for Bridget to be appointed head. And Sabina had said the same thing. She'd questioned her judgement, choosing a non-descendant. If Anastasia had fought Bridget's corner, you'd think Bridget would cut her more slack. But maybe Anastasia's position as part-owner of Southwood had introduced tensions. She'd had the power to veto plans made by the coven. Bridget might have felt her headship meant a lot of work and very little power.

Lucia was at Eve's side now. 'Shall we?' She gestured towards the door.

Eve followed her to a room with a coffee machine, a box of tissues and comfortable chairs. There was a desk, but it was tucked away in a corner. The woman followed Eve's gaze. 'When students are having a difficult time, they don't tend to confide if things are too formal. I make them a hot chocolate, or a coffee for the older ones, and we sit down as equals.'

'It must be a challenging job.' Eve imagined her, absorbing everyone's worries and secrets. 'But rewarding too, I guess.'

Lucia nodded, her wavy dark bob falling over her eyes. 'I love it. But it makes me feel guilty sometimes.'

Eve raised an eyebrow.

'I haven't always been there for Martin when he's needed me. I used to think, he's an adult, he can take care of himself. But marriage is meant to be a partnership. And I hate it if my daughters need me and I'm tied up with a student.' She took a deep breath. 'Bridget is always there to help, of course, when Mimi isn't around.'

'But?' Eve took the coffee Lucia poured her and the seat she motioned her to.

'It's not the same as having my own mum here. I really would relax then.'

'Is she local? Can she visit?'

Lucia shook her head, her eyes bleak. 'All the way up in Scotland.'

She looked as though she could do with a shoulder to cry on as much as her students. 'It's hard, isn't it? My parents are over in Seattle.'

'Oh, of course – that's far worse.' Lucia instantly sat up straighter.

'It amounts to the same thing. If you rarely get the chance to meet.'

She'd pulled herself together. 'True. But I have Anastasia as well as Bridget. She's more objective. I can confide in her without her passing judgement. I know Martin talks to her too, secretly.' She smiled and shook her head. 'I think it's partly her practical character and partly her office. It was his father's for years and Anastasia has kept a lot of Anthony's stuff. It all feels familiar to Martin.'

Eve wondered if Bridget knew they relied on Anastasia. Maybe she was jealous. It almost sounded like the bursar had taken Anthony's place, not just his role and office.

'What kind of problems do you find, being head teacher's wife?' Eve was curious, though it was off-topic.

Lucia gave a small smile. 'Many and varied. This is our home, we live above the shop, so to speak. We always have to be on our best behaviour. I can't relax. And problems crop up at all hours. Especially in my role, but sometimes for Martin too. And then there are difficulties you might not think of. Half the school has a crush on him, just as they did on his father. I asked Bridget how she coped. She and Anthony were in a similar position, with senior roles.'

'What did she say?'

Lucia hesitated. 'Between ourselves, she told me I had to deal with my lot, just as she had. I was disappointed – I thought we might bond over shared experiences.'

'I'm sorry.' But Eve wasn't surprised. Bridget wasn't the touchy-feely sort. After a moment, she changed the subject. 'I'd love to ask Martin for his memories of Natalie too.'

Lucia seemed to withdraw into herself, contracting a fraction physically, like an animal. For a moment Eve saw a familiar emotion in her eyes. Fear. 'You're very focused on us all, here at Southwood. I thought you'd want to spend more time in London, looking at Natalie's life there.'

Eve took a deep breath. She'd expected them to wonder, but not so quickly. 'I'm investigating that too. I've got an appointment with her producer tomorrow. And I've contacted her ex-husbands, and the current one too, Gavin Vale. But Natalie's life was so closely linked with Southwood, and the school's such an interesting backdrop. I know *Icon*'s readers will be interested. That's why I'd love to speak to Martin.'

But Lucia had been at the coven meeting when Viv had mentioned her past involvement in murder investigations. She still looked wary. 'He's very busy.'

Eve didn't want to back down, so she stayed silent.

A second later, Lucia added, 'But of course, I can ask him for you. Anyway' – she shook herself – 'you want my memories of Natalie now.'

'I was interested to see you talking together, the evening before Founders' Day.' Eve watched Lucia carefully. 'You looked quite close.'

Lucia double took. 'I didn't know anyone was watching.'

'I was with Viv, clearing up our equipment inside a class-room. We'd switched off the light to avoid her mother-in-law spotting us. We were checking for her when I saw you through the window.'

Lucia laughed. Eve had hoped she might.

'Sabina's a formidable woman. Not that I should comment, obviously. But as for me and Natalie, we weren't close.' Her tone was firm. 'I'm used to having heart-to-hearts with the students, don't forget. It's automatic.' She looked down at her lap for a moment. 'If someone comes to me with a problem, I don't turn them away. But what they tell me is confidential, of course.'

'So Natalie had worries, before she died?' Had she told Lucia about her illness?

Lucia met her eye now. 'She was on the verge of making a

decision that would have led to disaster. In talking to her, I steered her away from that.'

Eve had the impression Lucia was telling the truth, yet it didn't seem to fit with what she'd seen. It looked like she'd been the one confiding. It had been Natalie who'd had her arm around Lucia. And what was the disastrous decision Lucia mentioned? Eve knew it was no good to push. The head of pastoral care would be used to keeping confidences.

Was there any chance it related to Scarlett, and the head girl had taken action to stop Natalie? Eve still wasn't sure whether she'd deliberately listened in that night, or simply trailed after Natalie, hoping for a chance to talk.

She tried to piece together the main facts. What had happened that would fit with Lucia's words but also with what Eve had seen? All she knew was that the following day, Natalie had cornered Martin and told him off. *She told me all about it,* she'd said. *It's heartless of you! How could you treat her so badly?*

'Why did you vote against Natalie as Founders' Day Champion?'

'The students need strong role models – people they can emulate. Natalie simply wasn't suitable. She didn't have a moral compass. I was worried about the effect of having her here.'

'I gather she used to bring your children presents when she came to visit. It sounded like a kind gesture.'

'She was good at winning people over. And at reducing other people's influence. It pleased her. I didn't want the girls to accept the gifts, but they didn't understand. I suspect it was intended to drive a wedge between us.'

Eve imagined how powerless she must have felt. The more she'd tried to come between them and Natalie, the more of an unreasonable stick-in-the-mud she must have seemed. It didn't seem a strong enough motive for murder, though. 'What did Martin think?'

'That I was worrying too much. The girls liked the presents

and Natalie would be gone in the morning. But she always came back.'

Until now.

After the interview was over, Lucia escorted her back to the staff common room, so she could collect her things.

Inside, they found Martin clutching at his hair, and Anastasia with a hand on his shoulder, trying to calm him down.

'She's asked to see me later. Maybe I can get to the bottom of all this.'

'What's happened?' Lucia asked, as Eve got her coat.

'Eliza.' Martin shook his head. 'She handed her notice in this afternoon. All well and good. Not before time.'

Lucia glanced at Eve. It wasn't a conversation for her ears, but Martin was too upset to care.

'But now she's withdrawn it again. And she's furious about something. I heard her crying after she'd been in here. I don't know what the devil's going on.'

27

Anastasia caught up with Eve as she walked down a corridor towards the main entrance.

'We're going to have a memorial service for Natalie.'

She'd got her way then, despite Bridget's objections. But to Eve the arguments for going ahead quickly seemed sensible. The students must be shocked and upset. Bringing everyone together and acknowledging what had happened had to be part of the healing process. She nodded. 'That's good. I'd like to attend, if it's possible. I'm sure Viv would too.'

'That was my reason for catching you. It will be tomorrow morning. It's mostly aimed at the students and teachers. I'm sorry it's not more notice for you.'

'Of course. I understand.' The schedule for Monty's was clear in her head. The lovely Lars, beloved of Saxford mums, daughters and others besides, was down to work a full day. Tammy was doing a stint between her college lectures, and they could call on their new girl, Allie, who was always after extra hours. Her art course left her free on Wednesdays. 'We should be able to make it.' It would feel right to be there, but useful too. The more she saw of Natalie's contacts, the better.

That evening, Eve made her way to Robin's home again, cutting through Blind Eye Wood, Gus dashing ahead of her. The air was cold and crisp, an early hint of winter as autumn marched on. The leaves rustling under their feet meant their approach was far from silent, but the noise of a cracking twig behind them was louder. Eve caught her breath and jerked round. Gus turned too, with a quick, short bark. Eve stared between the trees, straining to see into the shadows. It might just be a creature. But it would have to be a large one to make such a crack.

A person? Another innocent walker in the woods? But they didn't appear or shout hello. Was she being followed?

Whoever it was, she didn't want them seeing her enter Robin's garden. She slipped her phone into silent mode and stood stock-still, watching and waiting. Gus's instinct seemed to be telling him the same thing.

After ten minutes of silence, Eve risked carrying on. She went more carefully than she had been, but still the leaves crackled under her feet.

The moment Robin opened the door he seemed to know something was up. There was no ritual on the step as Gus mobbed him and Eve waited for her hug. Instead, they dashed inside.

'Are you okay?' His voice was hushed as he closed the door behind them and locked it.

'I'm not sure.' She shivered as he held her. 'I heard some-thing in the woods. A twig cracking.' She explained how they'd waited to make sure the coast was clear.

'Thanks.' He beckoned to her, then headed up the dark, steep stairs, with Eve and Gus on his heels.

Gus seemed to feel the nervous tension. He was quivering a little as Eve bent to pat him when they reached the tiny landing.

Robin made for his box room – he used it as a study – and walked towards the desk by the window without turning on a light. A moment later he had a pair of binoculars to his eyes, scanning the woodland beyond his back garden. His body was a tense block next to her, every muscle rigid.

Eve and Gus waited in silence.

It was several minutes before he spoke. 'I think I've got him. He's a way off now.' He let out a long breath and his shoulders went down. 'Hopefully your patience paid off. I doubt he knows you're here.'

But his reaction made Eve more anxious. 'You think he was following me, then?'

'Or keeping an eye on who visits me.' Robin's tone was sober. 'I can't be a hundred per cent certain, but I think it's the same guy I saw earlier today on my way back from a job.'

Eve felt goosebumps on her arms. 'You think it's to do with Natalie's murder? An undercover cop maybe?'

But Robin shook his head. 'I wish I thought the local police had the resources to tail a suspect. No. I'm worried Natalie managed to place me before she died. Perhaps she mentioned it to her producer or a friend. My history would make me an appealing chat-show guest. I wonder if word's got out.'

Eve swallowed. 'So this is one of your old enemies? Someone who knew you as Robert Kelly?' The thought of Robin, isolated in his tiny cottage, stalked by someone who wished him dead, sent her heart dropping. She gripped his hand tightly.

He managed a smile. 'I hope I'm mistaken. I reported the first guy to Greg. I'll text him an update now. He knows my contact on the London force. I just have to trust him. And keep my eyes and ears open.' He touched her cheek. 'We might have to be more careful about how we meet.'

She'd known it was a danger, the moment Natalie said, so playfully, that she remembered his face. If he thought he was putting her in danger, he'd stop seeing her altogether. Losing him was unthinkable.

They walked down the steep stairs, Robin's steps slow, even Gus subdued. Her dachshund would be bereft too, if they were forced apart. And he wouldn't know why. The thought made her ridiculously emotional.

The curtains were drawn in the kitchen.

'We can shut it out for now,' Robin said. 'Along with the night. Tell me about your day.'

Eve closed her eyes for a moment and tried to focus on the information he wanted. 'I spoke to Sabina at Monty's. She defended Eliza to the hilt, while making her sound guilty as heck. She said Natalie had been making her life a misery up until the end, and all that's stopped now.'

Robin gave a half-smile that made Eve feel a little better. 'If that's how she helps friends, I'd hate to be her enemy.'

'Quite. But it got worse. She said something like: "Whatever happened between her and Natalie, I can assure you Eliza won't have been at fault. If they came up before a jury, I'm sure it would be Natalie who got the sentence." Sabina claimed not to know the details, and she sounded honest, but her words were so specific, I wondered if she was quoting Eliza. Maybe she's guilty of something criminal – or serious at least. It could have allowed Natalie to blackmail her, though I got an anonymous note saying there's no evidence to support that.' She explained the circumstances.

'Good old Greg.' Robin was uncorking a bottle of red. He had some onions and oregano sizzling in a pan. It already smelled amazing. Eve hadn't realised how hungry she was.

She nodded. 'Definitely. On another topic, Sabina gave the impression Natalie was trying to influence school policy. She'd visited more often lately – had meetings with Martin. She could have been trying to get Eliza the sack, or remove Scarlett as head girl, perhaps. I still don't buy the way Natalie moved from despising her to being best friends forever. I'm sure there was more to their relationship. Possibly more than Scarlett understood.'

Robin poured them glasses of Malbec.

'I need to dig deeper.' She told him about the memorial service the following day. 'That should be good for observing them as a group. Another weird thing happened too.'

Robin raised an eyebrow as he and Eve chinked glasses.

Eve explained about the meeting she'd had with Eliza, and her extreme reaction to the letter which had been delivered at the end of her visit.

'What on earth was that all about?'

'I don't know exactly, but it seemed to have a profound effect. It turns out she'd handed in her notice just before we met, but she'd withdrawn it again by late afternoon. I'd say the letter writer is responsible for that. The timing's too much of a coincidence. My theory is that Natalie knew something about Eliza which controlled her. I'd guess Eliza was paying hush money and had to keep working to keep it up. Then Natalie died, and Eliza thought it was all over. She was free. Until the letter arrived. Now I'm wondering if Natalie bequeathed her knowledge to a contact and they've written to tell Eliza she's not off the hook.'

'If you're right, Eliza had a strong motive for murder, and if she's guilty, it was all for nothing.'

Eve nodded.

'And if Natalie was in the library, Eliza could have killed her after that. She had the opportunity. But for the sake of argument, what about an accomplice, if Eliza killed her earlier, then put on a wig and pretended to be her?'

Eve took a deep breath. 'I still don't know. But when I spoke to Lucia, I said I'd like to interview Martin and she looked scared. It was only for a second, but something's bothering her.'

'Did she let anything else slip?'

'When I asked about her heart-to-heart with Natalie, she

claimed it was Natalie who was in trouble.' Eve explained the details. 'It's making me question my conclusion that Natalie had taken Lucia's side in an argument with Martin. Maybe she was talking about someone else.' The words circled in her head again. *She told me all about it. It's heartless of you!* 'Scarlett perhaps? I wondered if the secret conversation in the quad might have given her a motive for murder. She was close enough to listen in. But none of it quite fits. Natalie's outburst in the library puts Martin in the hot seat, not Scarlett or anyone else. And killing Natalie wouldn't kill the secret when Lucia knew too. Though she's a lot more tactful, of course.

'Eliza and Gavin Vale are still my top suspects, but there's so much I don't know.'

Eve was interrupted by a knock at Robin's front door. Loud, imperious.

They all jumped, and Gus let out a bark.

Robin stayed still for a split second. 'Might be best for you to hide upstairs,' he said in an undertone. 'But you stay here with me.' He patted Gus. 'There's no hiding you now the visitor's heard you bark.' He pointed under the kitchen table and against all the odds, Gus went. Eve's breath shortened as Robin pressed her glass into her hand and she crept upstairs.

She was in his bedroom, the door closed, when she heard the front door creak as Robin opened up.

28

As Eve crouched shivering in Robin's bedroom, all her thoughts were of the man who'd been watching him. Her heart was thudding, her phone out in case she needed to call for help. But as she sat there, the rumble of the newcomer's voice filtered through the floor. It was familiar.

Detective Inspector Palmer. The realisation gave her a fresh jolt: a wave of relief that it wasn't the stranger in the woods, mixed with fear that the head of Natalie's murder investigation was there to interview Robin. He'd already talked to the police and Palmer didn't like working late. They must have something fresh.

Carefully, she lowered herself to the floor and lay with her ear to the carpet. The rumble became more distinct. She pressed closer still, the twists of fibre pushing into her skin. And now she could hear the words.

'... dog?' That was Palmer. *Heck.* He must have noticed Gus – though if he stayed under the table she hoped the inspector wouldn't recognise him.

'Looking after her for a friend.' Robin sounded natural. How did he do it?

'... wanted to speak to you. We have some new information.'
There was a long pause. Palmer did that when he wanted to
unnerve people. At least it wouldn't work on a former cop who
knew the tactics. 'We've been talking to Natalie Somerson's
producer. He had some very interesting things to say about your
relationship with the deceased.'

'My relationship?' Robin didn't sound ruffled. 'We spoke
once or twice during her stay at Southwood, but on each occa-
sion, she approached me. We were never alone together in
private. We didn't have a relationship.'

Eve's adrenaline was going on Robin's behalf. She could
feel her heart beat, her chest pressed against the floor. Almost
worried they would hear it down below. Robin must be tense
too, underneath it all.

'I'm talking about the dynamic between you. About your
past.'

That long pause again. How much did Palmer know?

'I'm sorry.' Robin – as unhurried as before. 'I don't follow.'

'The producer said, and I quote, "She mentioned some
lackey at Southwood".' Indignation bubbled in Eve's chest. 'The
stand-in for the head gardener. Said he'd make a huge story if
she could coax him on for an interview. But she said the guy
was being difficult. He clearly wanted to keep his past secret.
She said she could understand why.'

Silence.

'I'm sure you can see why we're curious, Mr Yardley. If it is
Mr Yardley? My team have been having some problems
researching your history.'

'I'm sorry to take up their time.' His tone was dry.

'I'm not here to play games!' Palmer had gone for an age-old
tactic – the sudden raised voice, the slap of the hand on the
table. Eve heard that too. And Gus barking.

'Thank goodness,' Robin said. 'I'd hate to have to delay
supper to provide you with an evening of light entertainment.'

Eve imagined Palmer turning the colour of beetroot soup. Just a little cream stirred in...

'Apparently, Ms Somerson didn't tell her producer your secret.' Palmer's voice was quiet now – dangerously so. Eve had to strain to hear. 'She said he'd have to wait. Teased him with it. Said she'd taken a while to remember where she knew you from. She implied the news would bump up their ratings and hit the papers.'

'I didn't need to kill her to avoid going on TV. A simple refusal would have done the trick.'

It made Palmer sound ridiculous, but they all knew it wasn't that straightforward.

'That wouldn't stop her sharing your secret.'

'True, but I still wouldn't kill over it.'

'I'm not convinced of that.'

There was another long pause. 'You're right. I wasn't born Robin Yardley.'

She felt the breath go out of her. She could tell by his tone that he was going to come clean. But what about the police at the station? Could they be trusted? Robin's old enemies were an organised crime network and their corrupt police contacts. Who knew how far that network went? What if the London officers had links in Suffolk?

'I'm former Detective Inspector Robert Kelly. I was forced to leave the Metropolitan Police when I uncovered high-level corruption.' He told Palmer the story. 'If you call this number you can speak to my contact there. I still help with undercover work related to the network I discovered.'

Palmer hit the table again. She heard the slam and visualised his meaty, pudgy fist coming down on the old familiar wood. Gus whined but Eve doubted Palmer would focus on one small dachshund. He was too irate with Robin.

'Why the blazes didn't you tell me?'

'Is that a serious question? My life has been on the line for over ten years because of the dishonest police I crossed. I've no idea how wide their network is. I've kept my identity secret with approval from my former colleagues.'

'This doesn't mean you're off the hook! I believe you'd have told us from the beginning if this was all you had to hide.' *All?* 'I think you kept quiet because Ms Somerson had a hold over you. You've built yourself a comfy new life here, with unsuspecting villagers employing you as their gardener. You don't want to lose that. You know being on the side of law and order doesn't guarantee security. Who's to say you didn't take things into your own hands this time? Copy your corrupt contacts and kill your way out of trouble?'

Eve tried to find it funny. The man had no brains, no brains at all. But she was hot all over.

'We'll be investigating further.'

A moment later, Eve heard the front door slam.

Back downstairs, her eyes met Robin's.

'I'm all but certain the man you heard in the woods is looking for me because word's got out. From what Palmer says, Natalie remembered the truth before she was killed. She could have told someone, even if she kept it from her producer. Or maybe he's been digging since; she must have made him curious.'

The possible consequences flashed through Eve's mind. If he knew the full story, he wouldn't want to reveal it casually to Palmer. He'd save it up to sensationalise on TV. It didn't bear thinking about.

Robin took her hand. 'It means I had nothing to lose by opening up to Palmer. But my contact in London will make it clear what will happen if he tells the villagers – or anyone on the force who doesn't need to know. He's got my back.'

'You're sure Palmer will call him?'

'Not in the least, but I'll let him know what's happened. He'll make contact himself if Palmer doesn't.' He took a great breath. 'Palmer will keep quiet if he values his job. And he can't prove I'm guilty when I'm not. Hang on to that thought.'

But Eve was worried. Palmer was known for cutting corners, and his prejudiced views. And he'd left angry and determined. The need to find Natalie's murderer was so pressing she could hardly breathe.

29

On Wednesday morning, Eve and Viv stood with Lucia in the staff common room at Southwood. Everyone wore black. Eve had picked the shirtdress and jacket she always wore to funerals, with some knee-length black boots. Viv's autumn-orange hair provided a splash of colour, but seeing her in a dark formal trouser suit was enough to make Eve uncomfortable. It was so unusual compared with her standard tie-dye tops and jeans.

Lucia seemed tense too – not that it was surprising, under the circumstances. She was tapping her fingers against her thigh, over and over, her expression distracted. She was well turned out though, in a midi-wrap dress, her pale face beautiful.

Behind her, her husband Martin was chewing his lip, exchanging words with Anastasia and his mother. His and Lucia's daughters stood close to him, Ada leaning against his side. The four-year-old co-owner of Southwood. *What a weird thought.* His hand rested protectively on her shoulder.

Scarlett arrived at that moment, a little breathless. She gave a sniff as she entered the room but the emotion sounded fake.

'Talk about overdoing it,' Viv muttered in an undertone as

Lucia checked her mobile. 'Dark glasses? You'd think she'd lost her best friend.'

Scarlett wore lipstick to match her name too. The impression she hoped to make was clearly topmost in her mind, only she'd been torn, thought Eve, between wanting to look like a model, in case any photos made it onto social media, or to look genuinely grief-stricken.

Anastasia and Bridget glanced at her. Eve could see the bursar's suppressed eye-roll and the former head's irritation.

'I won't let you leave until you've blotted that lipstick, Scarlett,' Bridget said.

Scarlett's cheeks went almost as red as the offending lips. 'But I—'

'She's right, you know.' As Anastasia spoke, Bridget shifted away from her, as though she didn't want her backing.

Scarlett huffed, losing all dignity, and pulled a tissue from a box on the table to do as she was told.

Did that mean she had no tissues? She couldn't have been tearful when she left her room, or she'd have remembered to bring some.

'Let's make a start,' Anastasia said. 'We can't wait any longer for Eliza. She has a perfect right not to attend if she doesn't want to.'

Lucia hesitated. 'Do go on ahead.'

Anastasia, Martin and their group did so, but Eve hung back. Viv shot her a glance, her eyebrows raised, and Eve shot one back. She hoped it conveyed, *You go ahead if you want to but I want to know what Lucia is going to do next.* Judging by Viv's response, it had fallen short, but she hung back too, and didn't protest.

Lucia was looking at her phone again.

'Are you okay?' Eve asked.

The head of pastoral care took a deep breath. 'It's true that

Eliza's under no obligation to come. But I feel it sets a bad example to the girls if she stays away. We ought to be teaching them that it's good to forgive and forget. If Eliza can't manage that, even when Natalie's dead, it seems—' She stopped abruptly. 'I think people will wonder why.' Eve guessed Lucia was wondering herself. 'And besides, if someone hurts you and you cling on to it, it's only you that suffers. Better to make peace and let it go.'

It sounded like sensible advice, if the other person let you. Eve had a feeling that wasn't the case here.

'I think I'll just knock on Eliza's door on the way over to the chapel,' Lucia said. 'Do feel free to go on ahead.'

Once again, Eve and Viv's eyes met. Viv's eyes said *no way*, loud and clear, mirroring Eve's thoughts perfectly.

'We're happy to walk with you.'

The three of them crossed Great Quad towards one of the accommodation buildings.

'Eliza's suite is just through here.' Lucia opened an arched oak door and they followed her down a shadowy corridor.

'She's got her door open,' Lucia said, as Eve saw daylight spilling into the corridor. 'Maybe she was planning to come after all, and was simply delayed.'

But when they got level with the open door, they saw it wasn't Eliza inside, but one of the housekeeping staff, wearing a blue tabard emblazoned with the Southwood crest. She turned towards Lucia as she entered the room, duster in hand.

Eve followed Lucia in. Eliza's bed was made, though the housekeeper might have done that. On the head of sixth form's bedside table, Eve saw an unopened box of sleeping tablets and a part-used blister pack of the same brand next to it. Omoxidol. She wondered if Eliza had suffered bad nights all these years because of Natalie's attentions. Or maybe it was the job that disturbed her. Even if she'd been paying Natalie hush money, you'd think she could have found work elsewhere.

'I've not seen her,' the housekeeper was saying. 'No reply when I knocked, so I came in and started work.'

'Not to worry,' Lucia said. 'We'll probably find her at the chapel.'

But Eve could see a black outfit on a hanger on the back of Eliza's door. For whatever reason, she hadn't changed into the dress.

Viv followed Eve's gaze and her lips parted slightly.

Lucia led them out into the quad again, through the main walkway and Old Quad, then on towards the chapel. It took Eve back to tailing Anastasia and the question of who'd followed them both.

Once they arrived, Eve and Viv filed into a pew reserved for senior staff and waited as Lucia, Martin, Anastasia and Bridget exchanged words with other members of staff, and Lucia comforted a couple of students. They looked anxious rather than sad. Eve wondered which of the people present genuinely mourned Natalie. Martin and Lucia's daughters looked tearful. Of course, it sounded as though Natalie had aimed a charm offensive at them. Anastasia was the first to spot their distress. Eve watched as she stepped towards them, but Bridget saw her move and inserted herself in the narrowing gap, drawing them into her arms rather stiffly.

When the group finally filed into the pews, Anastasia ended up next to Eve. Eve felt her chest tighten. Did the bursar have any inkling she'd been followed on Monday evening? Somehow, being in the chapel with her, side by side, made it feel more likely she'd guess, though Eve knew that made no sense.

'It's a beautiful building.'

'I've always liked it,' Anastasia said. 'Not that I'm remotely religious,' she added in a stage whisper, 'something I have to keep quiet around here.'

She hadn't been praying here, then. Just talking to herself.

Eve had a feeling she'd do the same, if she were the bursar. A lot of people leaned on Anastasia, but she had no one. She needed a Gus.

As the service started, Martin and Lucia shifted closer together in the row in front. Their daughters were on either side of them, each pulled in by the protective arm of a parent. As Martin turned towards his wife, Eve saw his eyes were damp, his jaw taut.

For a second, Lucia leaned her head on his shoulder, and he inclined his head towards hers. Anastasia was looking at them, sympathy in her eyes. Bridget was next to one of her grand-daughters, but she looked straight ahead.

After the service, the entire school went for refreshments in the refectory, back at the front of the site. The day was excep-tionally mild for early November, and the doors were open so people could take their plates into the gardens.

'The girls will scatter to the four winds, of course,' Anastasia said with a laugh.

'It's unseemly, after what's happened.' Bridget pursed her lips.

But Eve didn't blame them. They'd be back in the classroom before long. They'd want the chance to let off steam after the service, and enjoy the fine weather, come to that. It would be different if they'd known Natalie well.

'I honestly think fresh air's the thing on a day like today,' Lucia was saying. 'When I'm counselling the students I always include getting outside in my advice. Having nature around you is healing.'

Bridget gave Lucia a slightly withering look but Eve agreed wholeheartedly.

Anastasia was looking around her. 'Eliza never did come.'

Lucia explained their trip to her suite. 'I suppose Natalie reminding everyone about the love poem can't have helped.'

'I don't like being reminded either,' Bridget said tartly.

'Of course not. I'm sorry.'

'It must have been difficult for Dad.' Martin turned to Bridget. 'Did he talk to you about it? What he felt?'

'Never. I have no idea whether it bothered him or not.' Her tone was dry and short.

'He always was a perfect gentleman,' Lucia said.

'Oh yes.' Bridget took a rather juddery breath. 'Always stuck to protocol. Just like Southwood, he placed a strong emphasis on etiquette.'

Anastasia had been right about the pupils. They were gradually fanning out across the lawns.

'Do you think we should call them back?' Martin said, his eyes anxious.

'Maybe give them ten minutes,' Lucia replied. 'This whole business has been an appalling shock.'

Martin nodded, and Lucia took his hand and squeezed it.

'You can see how we were treated,' Viv muttered, taking a slice of ginger cake from a passing waitress. 'Ten minutes' freedom was a rare treat. In fact, if we—'

But she was interrupted by a scream, coming from somewhere to their right, beyond the trees.

Lucia was immediately on her toes. 'Where did that come from? Towards the lake?'

'I think so.' Anastasia was frowning, moving as she answered, heading off at speed with Lucia and Martin.

'We should stay here,' Bridget said to her granddaughters. 'Can't have everyone running off like hares, can we?'

The girls looked uncertain.

Eve walked quickly across the grass in the direction the others had taken, with Viv at her heels. The screaming had stopped, but she could hear crying, which rose in pitch, then subsided, only to take off again a moment later.

Anastasia and Lucia were each comforting Southwood students, turning them away from the lake.

And beyond them, Eve could see a body, face down in the shallows. Wet dress, straggled hair, deathly pale skin.

She guessed before she looked who she'd see. Here was the reason Eliza Gregory had failed to make the memorial service.

30

Eve felt guilt tug at her insides, the result of the selfish fear that hit her almost as quickly as the horror at finding Eliza's body. Was this murder or suicide? And if Eliza had been killed, when had that been? It was bound to be overnight. No one would risk bringing her to the lake during the day.

If only she'd stayed with Robin. In the end he'd walked her back under cover of darkness, figuring it was safer than leaving it until morning. Not that Palmer would count her as a reliable alibi. He'd probably put her down as an accomplice...

She thought of the meeting she'd had with Eliza just the day before. However she'd died, it was a terrible end and Eliza had been in a state of misery beforehand.

She and Viv turned away from the scene and Eve focused her attention on their surroundings. There was no sign of a tussle that she could see: no patches of mud where the turf had been scuffed by someone manhandling a body, no cracked branches. If someone had brought Eliza there to kill her, Eve guessed she hadn't struggled on the way. Yet she couldn't imagine anyone dragging a dead weight without leaving a sign either. But if two people were in league...

Viv put a supportive arm around her shoulders. 'Don't look now. I'm afraid that moron Palmer has arrived already.'

They sat in awkward silence, waiting to be interviewed. A burly officer was pacing the hall, which was being used as a waiting room. The police had commandeered the library as their headquarters, and classrooms for interviews. Each time anyone spoke the police officer fixed them with his beady eye and they shut up again.

At last, Eve was called in to a high-ceilinged room, where watery sunshine filtered through leaded windows. Dust motes caught in the light as Detective Sergeant Greg Boles invited her to take a seat. She found herself blushing. It was so weird to be interviewed by the man married to Robin's cousin. Someone who knew exactly who he really was and how close she was to him. It felt like play-acting, something Eve had never enjoyed.

'Your name?'

She gave it, though he knew it well. Out of the corner of her eye she saw DI Palmer walk past the classroom window, Anastasia Twite by his side.

As soon as his shadow had gone, Greg leaned forward slightly. 'Eve, I hope you understand why I can't confide in Robin like I normally do. And I hope he does.'

Eve nodded. 'It might be a long while back, but he hasn't forgotten what it was like to be a cop.'

Greg's shoulders relaxed. He hesitated, then took a deep breath. 'I shouldn't be saying this, but it looks like Eliza Gregory's death was suicide. I hate to see what Robin's been going through. We might be coming out the other side.'

Eve hardly dared breathe. 'I guess it makes sense. I always thought Eliza had an excellent motive for Natalie, but I had no proof. And she left the drinks in the staff common room at ten.' It was within the window Eve had been asked to account for.

She wouldn't have needed an accomplice if she'd killed Natalie then, and the silhouette in the library had been genuine. 'Did she leave a note?'

Greg had already taken a risk, confiding in her. It was unfair to ask him to carry on, but Eve had to try. The more she knew, the better she could help.

At last, he nodded and referred to his notebook. '"Dear Headmaster, I need to write to explain about Natalie. It's true I lashed out, but she was awful to me and I hated her. The poem was the final straw..." The handwriting was messy but it matches other samples in her office. She didn't write any more. We think that's when she went off to the lake.'

So the reminder of the poem had tipped her over the edge. She'd known Natalie's habits – where she liked to hang out as a pupil. She'd found her there and killed her. And then last night, guilt and the mysterious letter, relating to some other misdeed perhaps, had made her take that tragic final step.

It seemed entirely plausible. Eliza had thought she was free of Natalie's influence after her death, but the letter had brought her world crashing down. She was no longer retiring. Stuck at Southwood, presumably to earn enough money to pay off some contact of Natalie's.

The sergeant's eyes met hers. 'Did Robin tell you what happened last night with Palmer?'

Eve nodded. Better not explain she'd listened in.

'I'll keep an ear to the ground at the station. Palmer knows he can't pass the information on. If I get any hint it's got out...'

'Thanks, Greg.'

He nodded. 'So, tell me about your interactions with Eliza Gregory.'

He wrote notes as Eve explained about the handwritten letter she'd seen delivered and its effect. He promised they'd look out for it, but if it was damaging, she guessed Eliza would have destroyed it. She hadn't mentioned it in her note.

Eventually, they got on to Eve's account of her arrival at Southwood that morning. Eve recalled Lucia's concern at Eliza's absence, and following the head of pastoral care to Eliza's rooms. She mentioned the quantity of sleeping tablets she'd seen, next to the dead woman's bed. Omoxidol.

'It made me think she'd been sleeping badly for some time. I guessed they must be on repeat prescription, the way she had a spare box lined up like that. Though I'm not sure most doctors would keep dishing them out these days.'

Greg's hand had paused over his pad. 'Omoxidol, you said?'

Eve nodded. She could see the unease in his eyes. New lines on his forehead.

She felt her stomach tense. 'What is it?'

'I shouldn't be telling you this, but there was a half-empty jar of pills found on Ms Gregory's desk. It looks as though she'd taken some, along with some brandy. Maybe to blur her feelings, take the edge off things before she went to the lake.'

'A jar?' Not a blister pack like she'd seen.

He nodded. 'Rivarol. A different brand of sleeping tablets.'

Eve leaned forward and put her head in her hands. She could imagine what he was thinking.

'It doesn't mean she didn't take her own life,' Greg said.

But if Eliza had a whole bundle of prescription pills in her bedroom, why get hold of a separate brand to take before she walked to the lake?

And anyway, why go to the lake at all? She could have locked her office door and stayed there.

'She still wrote what looks like a confession, Eve.'

As she left the classroom, the words 'what looks like' reverberated in her head.

31

There wasn't much of the day left by the time Eve was cleared to leave Southwood. Viv was still waiting to be interviewed, so she got a taxi home. She was just being mobbed by Gus on her doorstep when her friend texted to say she'd finally finished.

Got Olivia Dawkins. Result! Cross Keys tonight 7 p.m. for debrief.

Eve texted back.

Thanks for asking so nicely.

Her phone sounded again a moment later:

You know you love me really. Yours, Watson

After that she called Robin. She felt desolate. 'My observations about Eliza's room made Greg question his thinking.'

She could hear his soft laughter down the line. *'You can stop helping now.'*

She tried to laugh too, but it wouldn't come. Her stomach knotted tight.

'Joking apart, the CSIs will have found the pills you saw by now anyway. Besides, I want justice for Natalie and Eliza and I know you do too. Ignoring the evidence won't help. Anything else strike you as odd about what Greg said?'

Eve sighed. 'The note, to be honest.' She explained the contents. 'If you're going to write a confession, why trail off partway through like that? It seems odd. I wonder if she thought she might come back to it.

'I need to find out exactly what went on with Natalie. Try and work out which of her connections might have sent that letter. But even if Eliza was killed, it doesn't have to mean she was innocent of Natalie's murder. She'd started to write a confession, after all.'

At seven o'clock that night, Eve stood at the bar in the Cross Keys pub. She'd lost Gus already – he was over in a corner, scampering giddily around the pub schnauzer, Hetty. You'd think they hadn't met in months. Toby, Hetty's owner, was pouring Eve a glass of Pinot Grigio and laughing at their antics.

'I hope Jo doesn't come through. Nothing should get in the way of true love.'

Jo was Toby's sister-in-law, and the pub's fearsome cook. Her meals were amongst the best Eve had tasted, but she had very definite ideas about how the pub should be run. Gallivanting canines were a no-no, as was modern technology at dinner. Jo reminded Eve of her schooldays far more than visiting Southwood had. She had the ability to make her heart race if she was breaking the rules.

Viv had appeared at Eve's side and requested a Chardonnay. They both ordered food. Eve had been eying up the pan-fried chicken breast on bacon mash for some time...

'I heard you were at the memorial service at Southwood today,' Toby said as he poured Viv's drink.

Viv nodded. 'I can't believe there's been another death. Though Eliza Gregory was a poisonous character. I expect they'll come out with all the usual platitudes, but she won't be sorely missed by me.'

'I'm assuming you didn't say that to DC Dawkins,' Eve said, as they turned to walk towards their table. She'd lowered her voice. You never knew who might be listening in a small village.

Viv shrugged. 'I did, actually. I told her what she did to me when I was at school. Best for them to know the truth.'

'You have an alibi for last night, I hope?'

Viv stuck her tongue out. 'No, but rumour has it she took her own life.' Suddenly, her look was sober. 'I know I said I won't miss her, but I still hate the thought of her being in such torment. I wonder if she was ever happy?'

Eve's chest felt heavy at the thought. She was worried the answer might be no. But before she could reply, Viv's face fell and in an instant, she disappeared under the table.

Eve only had time to glance over her shoulder before Sabina and her husband Edward appeared at her side.

'Wasn't Vivien here a moment ago?' Sabina was leaning on Edward, her face drawn. 'Wait a moment, didn't I just see...' She flicked the tablecloth up and Viv's face – now rather red – appeared.

'Sabina! I just dropped my phone. One moment.' Viv struggled back to a sitting position with as much dignity as she could manage.

'Please.' Eve stood to pull over two chairs from a neighbouring table. 'Take a seat.'

'We won't stop.' Sabina's cold eyes rested on Viv. 'After

what's happened, we couldn't face supper alone at the hall this evening, but we want a quiet dinner for two.'

'I understand. I'm so sorry for your loss.'

Viv rolled her eyes. Eve knew she thought she was laying it on too thick, but Sabina had probably been Eliza's closest friend. Eve sensed they'd been bound by shared convictions, rather than affection, but losing her would still be a shock.

'I know your reputation, Eve.' Sabina spoke with the utmost disapproval. 'I respect Inspector Palmer, and I trust he'll do his job, but there are rumours that Eliza took her own life. She had many a cross to bear but I don't believe it.'

'Why is that?'

Sabina drew herself up. 'I don't know the details, but there was something going on with Scarlett Holland. Eliza was too upstanding to gossip, but whatever it was, I'm convinced it mattered. She was a strong champion of justice; I simply don't believe she'd have chosen death before she'd seen the matter through.'

'And you think you'd know about it, if she had?'

Sabina was turning away already. 'From what Eliza hinted, I'm certain.'

32

'Talk about cryptic,' Viv said as her in-laws retreated.

'Absolutely. For such a stickler for high standards, Eliza seemed to drop an awful lot of hints about private matters.' Eve wondered if she'd enjoyed being the one in the know. And the one to sit in judgement. 'Still, from what Sabina said, it looks like Scarlett might have had a motive for Eliza.'

'But still none for Natalie?'

Eve sighed. 'Nothing confirmed, but we know their relationship developed in an odd way. And she could have killed Natalie any time after supper on Saturday.'

'True. Thanks for inviting my in-laws to sit with us, by the way. Just as well they wanted a private dinner. If we'd had them all evening, I might never have forgiven you.'

'I had to think on my feet when you dived under the table and left me alone with them.'

Jo appeared with their food. Beyond her, Eve saw Gus and Hetty were standing to attention, like two dogs who never did anything wrong.

'I hope you two aren't going to bicker as you eat.' Jo's sharp ears must have caught the tail end of their conversation. She gave them each a piercing look, like a mother with two recalcitrant toddlers. 'I won't have you getting indigestion then blaming it on my food.'

Viv sniffed her fish pie. 'All thoughts of our tiff have been pushed from my mind.'

Jo raised a suspicious eyebrow.

'What she said,' Eve added.

The cook shook her head. 'You're both getting far too cheeky for my liking.' But Eve saw a smile cross her lips as she turned towards the kitchen.

'Right,' Viv said, pulling a notepad out of her bag, 'let's get down to business.'

Eve liked the combination of eating and work. Food helped her think.

'Do you think Eliza was killed?'

'I'm afraid so.' Eve explained about the pills found in her office, passing it off as rumour. 'If she wanted to take her own life, I can't think of any reason not to use the tablets in her bedroom. They're clearly her regular brand. So maybe her killer got hold of the other ones, crushed them into a drink to get her woozy, then left them behind to fool the police. They could have walked her down to the lake when her defences were low, ready to finish her off.'

'Why drown her, rather than let the pills do the work?'

Eve had wondered about that. 'It might have been hard to get Eliza to take enough to kill her, whereas mixing a smaller amount in her drink was less likely to be noticeable. I guess it would have been sufficient to make her easy to control. There were no signs she put up a fight on her way to the lake.'

Viv shook her head. 'I can't believe your analytical brain was still functioning at a time like that. Still, good work.'

'Thanks. But even if Eliza was pretty far gone, she can't have been totally out of it. There were no signs of a body being dragged. And I heard whispers that she wrote a note.'

'Wow – you have got good gossip.'

'It mustn't go any further. I don't know if it's true. Swear?'

Viv swore, so Eve told her what Greg Boles had said about the contents.

'Blimey. That sounds pretty damning.'

'It does – on the face of it. She could have killed Natalie then been killed.'

Viv nodded. 'So if Eliza was killed, then we come to who by, and why?'

Eve frowned. 'If she murdered Natalie, perhaps that was earlier in the evening and she had an accomplice after all: the other library silhouette. That person might have suspected she wanted to confess and found her halfway through writing her note. I hear she hadn't named anyone. The letter would have given them the chance to kill her and get off scot-free.'

Viv shivered.

'If she didn't murder Natalie then the confession's hard to explain. Leaving that aside, maybe she chanced on the truth. But if so, I don't know why she wouldn't go to the police. I can't honestly imagine her being fond enough of anyone at the school to protect them. And I'd guess keeping quiet would have gone against her principles. Unless the killer had a hold over her.'

Viv made more notes.

'Scarlett already had the widest opportunity for Natalie, and now Sabina's implying she and Eliza might have had a run-in. She's got to be worth considering.'

Eve imagined Eliza draped over Scarlett – being supported by her as she made her way to the lake. If Scarlett had done something to upset Eliza, she might have come to beg forgiveness. But would Eliza have agreed to sit down and have an alcoholic drink with a sixth former? Eve doubted it. Then again, maybe she'd been drinking already, when Scarlett arrived. She'd certainly been upset by the letter she'd received. That scenario was more likely. Then Scarlett could have slipped some of the

powdered pills into an existing drink. But the head girl's motive
for Natalie was still nothing more than the vaguest speculation.

'Other than her, there's Martin, Lucia, Anastasia or Bridget.
I could see Eliza sitting down for a stiff drink with any of them.
But Bridget's too stocky to be one of the library silhouettes and
Anastasia couldn't have been. And could any of them have
forced her to write that confession?'

'And their motives for Natalie?'

Eve shook her head. 'Nothing convincing, but I don't know
it all yet. Martin's the most suspicious. I need to find out who
Natalie was talking about when she cornered him in the library.

'And then finally there's—' But Eve broke off as she spoke.

'What?' Viv hissed.

'I was going to say there's Natalie's widower, Gavin Vale.'
Eve was still reeling from a huge double take. 'And that he
seems less likely, now Eliza's been killed. It's not as though he's
local. But he's here. That's him, up at the bar now.'

Eve decided to get herself another drink and took a place
next to Gavin Vale.

Natalie's widower turned away as soon as he saw her. He
moved across the pub at speed, but she caught him.

'Mr Vale? Gavin?'

'What are you doing here?' He'd been intent on removing
himself, and he still looked poised to run. More edgy than when
she'd seen him last.

'Meeting a friend.' She'd given him her card but it only had
her mobile number, not her address. 'And you?'

'I've been staying here.' The pub had rooms to let over the
bar. 'The police weren't making any progress. I thought it best
to keep an eye on things.'

'They've been focused on you?' Eve guessed that was his
motivation for coming. It couldn't be love of Natalie after what
he'd told her.

He paused a moment, then nodded. 'It was that stupid

letter I wrote. But I'm going home tomorrow. It looks like Eliza Gregory was guilty. Of course, it makes sense. I knew they were old enemies. I had that photograph looking at me every day as a reminder.'

Eve remembered it, with its *Don't be a loser* caption.

'Have you visited the school since you arrived?'

'I went to talk to the head yesterday.'

Eve's heart rate increased a little. He could have hidden – stayed on site. Killed Eliza if she'd guessed his guilt. He must have hated Natalie for what she'd done. And there was something else she needed to check.

'Gavin, I believe you wrote to Eliza on Natalie's behalf, just before she died.' In reality, she couldn't imagine Natalie nominating him as her stand-in, but she needed to be sure.

His frown of confusion said it all. 'Why on earth would I do that?'

She was saved from replying by his mobile ringing. He excused himself, then disappeared through the door that led to the bedrooms.

Toby looked thoughtful as she returned to the bar and ordered her drink. 'I didn't realise he was a close connection of Natalie's.'

'Her husband. Have you seen much of him?'

Toby nodded. 'He was in here all yesterday evening, asking questions about the murder, getting the gossip from the locals.'

Wanting answers, like her, or anxious and guilty, checking how much people knew?

'But wait, he was here yesterday evening?'

Toby nodded. 'He went out during the day, but he was back by six or so.'

'Did he stay in the bar?'

He frowned a moment. 'Yes. Had dinner, and carried on quizzing people who came in. He was here until closing time. Then he went upstairs.'

So he couldn't have hidden at Southwood after his meeting with Martin.

'Any chance he could have sneaked out after last orders?'

Toby paused polishing the glass he held. 'None. I'd have seen him. And if he waited until we were in bed, Hetty would have barked.'

'Good point. Thanks.'

He nodded. 'Nice to be part of the team.'

Eve reported back to Viv the moment she'd sat down. 'Him being here makes him look suspicious, but in fact, I think he's out of it.'

That evening, Eve noticed Natalie's actor friend, Calvin Wright, was trending on Twitter. She clicked to see what was up.

A series of Calvin's acting contacts had featured on the *Natalie Somerson Show* that evening, apparently – interviewed by the temporary presenter. All had tales of how the actor had stolen their parts, wives, girlfriends and opportunities. Played dirty in every way you could imagine.

Five minutes later, Eve received a text from Gavin Vale.

Did you see Natalie's show? Must have been in the works for months. It's as I said, she formed relationships when she wanted something. In Wright's case, it was a story. He sounds like a git, but I almost feel sorry for him.

33

The following morning, Eve woke to a second anonymous note on her doormat.

ELIZA GREGORY'S DEATH BEING TREATED AS SUSPICIOUS.
ANNOUNCEMENT TO BE MADE THIS AFTERNOON.

She'd known it was coming, but it still struck her in the gut. It was kind of Greg to warn her.

She sat at the dining-room table and tried to concentrate on prepping her questions for Natalie's producer. It was all the more essential to focus. She took Gus for a walk along the estuary path afterwards; the smell of mud and saltwater steadied her.

An hour later, she was sitting in Monty's, opposite Dirk Acton, much to Viv's delight. She was supposed to be baking, but intrigue kept drawing her out.

Eve and Dirk had a pot of Assam tea and a plate of cinnamon teacakes in front of them. Eve was conscious of Viv leaning casually against the kitchen door frame as she poured.

'Thanks so much for seeing me. I'm sorry for your loss. I gather you and Natalie went back a long way.'

He nodded. 'We worked together early in her career. It was me who first put her in front of the camera. She was quite a find.'

That was one way of putting it. But Eve needed to keep an open mind. Acton had probably known Natalie better than most people. His viewpoint was important.

'You're visiting Southwood too, while you're here?'

Dirk's dark eyes met hers. He was attractive in a smooth sort of way which instantly made Eve mistrust him. His suit was immaculate, his dark grey hair perfectly styled.

'That's right. It's horrible to visit under these circumstances, but Natalie's viewers will want to understand what happened to her. And this latest death of her old teacher has only raised more questions. Fans would think it odd if we didn't cover it. Her stand-in on screen will do the piece, but I'm here to nail down the details.'

He smiled and raised his teacup to hers in a mock toast. 'Thanks for this. It's a welcome break before I start work. I heard a lot about the staff at Southwood from Natalie.' He shook his head. 'The coven. What a name for the top team!'

It would play well with their audience, Eve guessed. Everyone loved a peek into a cliquey closed environment. How fortunate for Dirk that he could add a couple of murders to spice up the mix. Eve tried to wipe the lemon-sucking expression off her face and give him her best fake smile. 'They're an unusual lot.'

'They sound it.'

Eve sipped her tea. 'So, she talked to you about Southwood?'

He nodded. 'It was a constant theme over the years. She was always a rebel; it was clear she hadn't fitted in. When the school exercised its iron grip she got ruthless.'

And her hatred had stuck inside her, never loosening its hold. That fitted with the photo of Eliza that Natalie had kept in her bathroom. There had to be something extra behind such a long-lasting and deep animosity. The teacher's mental cruelty must have made an indelible mark, but keeping the picture was extreme. And certainly self-destructive. It would have reinforced the hard knot of anger inside Natalie – a constant reminder.

'You knew she was down to inherit a half share in the place?' Eve picked up her cinnamon cake.

'Absolutely.'

'I suppose she might have tried to reform it.'

He laughed. 'I don't think that was on the agenda. It would be more like her to burn it down. She didn't believe in that style of education. She told me she was planning to renounce her share.'

'I'd heard that too. Yet she visited Southwood a lot.'

He smiled again. 'For her own ends, I'm sure.'

'You think she came to make trouble?'

'She held some sway. And she always had a malicious sparkle in her eye when she was planning a trip there. And when she came back again. Trouble for someone.'

'She never told you what went on?'

He shook his head, his eyes twinkling. Eve sensed he was pleased he'd got her curious. Of course, he made his living drip-feeding gossip to get people hooked.

'Did Natalie ever mention individual staff or students by name?'

Dirk leaned back in his chair as Viv approached their table. Eve gave her a warning look.

'Can I get you another pot of tea?' Viv said, with her most innocent smile.

'We're fine. Thank you.' Eve focused on Dirk.

'She talked about most of them, I think.' He chuckled.

'Natalie said her aunt was the only one she could talk to. And she talked about "catching up with Martin, Lucia and their lovely children". She always referred to them like that. I doubt she was fond of them really. And then she'd say, "and last and in every way least, dear Eliza".'

'What had she told you about their relationship?'

'That Eliza ruined her life. Or tried to. Before Natalie got interested in talk shows, she'd wanted to be an actress. She had a good voice too, and the drama teacher cast her in a show at some big local theatre.'

Eve remembered the programme she'd found online. 'Sandy, in *Grease*?'

He raised an eyebrow. 'That's right. I'd forgotten. Anyway, this Eliza woman went to watch the dress rehearsal and went ballistic, apparently. Slagged Natalie off in front of everyone there. Said she wasn't putting in the effort and couldn't hold a note, and her acting was wooden. Natalie always said the drama teacher didn't agree, but Eliza pulled rank and they ended up using an understudy right at the last minute.' He shook his head. 'She never forgot it. There was a talent scout at the performance and the understudy ended up with a part in some BBC children's drama – can't remember what. Natalie was convinced that would have been her, but for Eliza. It would have been her big break.'

Eve's skin prickled. This could explain the depth of Natalie's grudge. She felt her English teacher had changed her life, and maybe she had. Out of pure bile, perhaps, if the drama teacher disagreed. Eve was still waiting to hear from her. She'd chase via Anastasia if necessary. 'She'd have preferred acting?'

Acton shrugged. 'From what she said. But she was the perfect host. It would have been a waste. One thing I can say, Natalie could definitely sing. All that about her not holding a note had to be rubbish.'

The picture of Natalie and Eliza's relationship was

becoming clearer. Eve guessed Natalie must have tried to break into acting again later, if she was keen. Auditioned, but never got her break. So much was down to luck and timing. The unanswered question must always have been there: would she have succeeded if Eliza hadn't interfered? Eve could understand Eliza's feelings, but she was an adult. Did she have to punish Natalie in that way?

'Did Natalie ever mention a girl called Scarlett?'

He frowned. 'Scarlett? That's a memorable name.' He sipped his tea. 'No. Doesn't ring any bells.'

Eve hesitated for a moment. She wanted to ask about Robin too. She wondered if Dirk had tried to find out more after Natalie mentioned him. 'What about other staff? Not the teachers, I don't mean, but support staff working on site?'

Dirk's look sharpened and his eyes narrowed. 'Why do you ask? Have you been speaking to someone?'

Eve raised an eyebrow. 'Not at all. I'm just trying to find as many people as possible who knew Natalie.'

'I see.' His laugh was uneasy now. 'Well, the answer's no.'

She knew he was lying – Natalie had mentioned Robin at least. Palmer had made that clear. But there wasn't much she could do to force the information out of him.

'Did Natalie ever talk to you about her mum and dad? And what life was like at her first school? I gather she boarded from the age of seven.'

His shoulders went down and he relaxed back in his chair. 'It was tough, by all accounts. She had a chip on her shoulder. No bad thing, perhaps. It made her driven. She told me it was her dad's decision to send her away. He was looking for an excuse, according to her. Her mum wasn't well, so he was the primary carer. She said he was always on her case. Then one day she was playing a game. He'd already told her to do it more quietly. Twice. When he had to tell her a third time, he said enough was enough. He was sending her away to school to learn some discipline. Just like that.'

Why had he gone to such lengths? There were plenty of ways to be firm without resorting to banishment. Once again, the mist cleared a little. Such a sudden and major decision must have left Natalie reeling. She could never be certain of anything. Life and people must have seemed random and unpredictable. Was that why she'd kept classmates at arm's length? Because she'd learned not to rely on anyone, even her nearest and supposedly dearest? Had she kicked at the world because the world had kicked her first? Maybe she'd decided that's how things worked.

Eve thought again of the letter that had been sent to Eliza. The possibility that Natalie might have bequeathed some kind of damaging secret about her former teacher to a friend so that they could continue to blackmail her. Might Dirk be the one who'd taken the baton? She'd clearly confided in him. Or was there someone she was missing? It was time to get cunning. Maybe she could ask and rule him in or out at the same time...

34

Eve watched Dirk Acton closely. 'Can you think of anyone else I should talk to? Anyone who knew Natalie well? What about her personal assistant on the show, for instance?'

The producer's brow furrowed. 'Kitty? You're welcome to contact her.'

'Thanks.' She turned to a fresh page in her notepad and pushed it and a pen across the table to him. 'If you could give me her full name and number.'

He shrugged and leaned forward to oblige. 'Sure. But I don't think they socialised outside work.'

And Eve didn't think Kitty was the person she was after. Not after seeing Dirk Acton's distinctive italic handwriting. He'd addressed the letter to Eliza Gregory. There was no doubt about it.

He stood up, but Eve wasn't finished.

'Before you go, I'd like to ask you about the letter you sent to Eliza Gregory before her death.'

Acton went still but he couldn't hide his feelings entirely. There was annoyance and surprise in his eyes. He must be wondering how she knew.

'I saw her receive it. The handwriting on the envelope was yours. It's very distinctive. Natalie was blackmailing Eliza before she was murdered. You took over. I know that much.' It was best to go in strong. She had no idea of the details, but Acton was the sort to wriggle out of answering if she didn't bluff. 'I want to know what Natalie had on Eliza.'

He gave a forced laugh, but sat back down, his eyes darting quickly around the teashop. Anxious in case anyone had heard, Eve was sure.

'You're dreaming. This is fantasy.'

'I don't think so.' She fixed him with her gaze. 'It seems likely Eliza Gregory took her own life after receiving your letter.' He'd know better by that afternoon, but it was now that counted. 'Imagine the publicity if that gets out.' She had to try to get the truth from him.

He hesitated, chewing his cheek.

Eve could imagine what was going through his head. Now Eliza was dead, he was probably working out what else he could do with the information he had. Serve up the details on TV perhaps, depending on how juicy they were. He wouldn't want to tell her and lose exclusive rights to the information. Any more than he'd want to admit to blackmail.

'If you share the details with me, I won't tell anyone you sent the letter which triggered Eliza Gregory's death.'

She felt her stomach quiver. He might not be in the running for murderer, but bargaining like this could still be dangerous. It felt wrong too, the lying. But at least she wouldn't really be protecting someone who'd pushed Eliza over the edge. And she needed answers to get at the truth and save Robin.

Acton let out an irritable huff. 'Oh, all right. But it's not what I'd call blackmail. I don't get any money out of it. I agreed to do it when Natalie told me she was dying.' He watched her eyes. 'You knew about that too?' He shook his head ruefully as she nodded.

'Here.' He woke up his phone, called up a photo and turned it so Eve could see. 'This is a copy of the letter that was in the envelope. Natalie wrote it herself. I wanted a record.'

Eve drew his phone to her and read Natalie's words.

My dear Eliza,

I might be dead and gone but you're still being watched. If you hand in your notice at Southwood it will be noted and our little secret won't be secret any more. Congratulations. You get to carry on teaching into old age. I hope you die with students' laughter ringing in your ears.

Your ever-present Natalie.

'She was forcing Eliza to stay at Southwood?'

Acton nodded. 'The perfect revenge. She knew how much the woman hated her work. She asked me to carry on sending the letters she'd written annually. Forever. If she left, or even if the school went under, I was allowed to publicise the secret Natalie had kept.'

'And what was that secret?'

Acton took up his phone again and navigated to another image. 'Scroll through the next three and you'll see. The three after that explain what went on and when.'

The first image was of a blurred, teenage Natalie in an ornate mirror, with a gash down her cheek, blood dripping from the wound. A much younger Eliza, caught in the corner of the picture, her eyes wild with fury, hair awry.

The second must have been taken as Eliza drew back, spittle in the corner of her mouth, her hand held up in an attempt to block the photographer's view.

The third – more blurred than the others – showed Eliza in flight towards the camera, her hand outstretched as though to grab it. Eve saw the old-fashioned ring on her middle finger, with its chunky stone. The sort that might cause a gash if it came in contact with a cheek.

But not if Eliza had slapped Natalie. Only if she'd hit her with her fist.

The three images after that presumably showed the reverse sides of the photos. Each was numbered and dated 4 November 1985. The first included a note:

> *This photo shows my injuries at the hand of Eliza Gregory,*
> *currently the head of sixth form at the prestigious Southwood*
> *School. The other photos convey how Miss Gregory lost*
> *control. She attempted to snatch my camera, but I managed to*
> *get away.*

Natalie would have been in her final year of school back then. Furious at the way Eliza Gregory had treated her. Determined to make her suffer. She felt Eliza had altered the course of her life, and it was in her nature to hit back.

'If the letter contributed to Ms Gregory's death in any way then I'm deeply sorry.' Eve didn't believe him. 'But I owed it to Natalie to follow her wishes.'

And he'd probably insist he owed it to himself to publicise it all on his TV show too. He had the evidence on his phone after all; she wondered if he was planning to face Martin Leverett with it. Ask him to comment.

'People will guess you had a hand in the blackmail if you put the information out there. An administrator at the school saw Eliza receive your letter. They'll know someone took over from Natalie after she died, even if I say nothing.' All the pieces would fit together, once people understood the background.

The irritable look was back. 'I'll think about that.'

She only hoped it stopped him making it public.

He stood again. 'It's been educational, meeting you. Just as well I've got time for lunch at the pub before I head to the school. I could use a drink.'

Eve watched him walk towards Monty's door. Outside, he crossed the village green and disappeared inside the Cross Keys.

She turned to see Viv had been watching too.

'It's time to unpick what he said.' Viv's tone was firm. 'I'm ready for a spot more Watsoning.'

35

'So,' Viv asked. 'Was Dirk Acton useful?'

'Yes. Very. But he still hasn't told me everything.' Thoughts of him secretly working on Robin's story filled her mind. Natalie had tantalised him with partial details, according to Palmer. He was bound to dig, if he hadn't already. 'I need to find out more. The moment he comes out of the Cross Keys, I want to follow him to Southwood.'

Viv tutted. 'You're not going to have an adventure without me, are you? I hate it when that happens. Redeem yourself by telling all. I'll sit with you now and take my lunch break.' She smiled at Lovely Lars, who was serving, and he nodded and gave her a thumbs up.

'I'll bring you both tea and cheese scones in a moment.'

'Love that boy,' Viv said, as they took seats in the window. Eve could monitor Acton's movements nicely from there. She filled Viv in, which took a good five minutes. By the time she'd finished, they had food and drinks in front of them.

'Natalie invented a punishment to last a lifetime,' Eve concluded. 'I'd assumed Eliza carried on working to pay black-mail money, but I knew Natalie didn't need it. She just wanted

Eliza to suffer. She realised how much she hated her job; ensuring she died in harness was the ultimate revenge.'

Eve remembered Natalie's words to Eliza at the coven meeting. *You epitomise everything I associate with the school. I'm so glad you're still here, carrying on into your dotage.* No wonder the head of sixth form had almost lost control. Natalie had been goading her, knowing she couldn't retire or retaliate.

As for Eliza's attack – it had been appalling and vicious. It must have been traumatic for Natalie. But she'd had a camera with her and been ready to use it, well before the days of smartphones, when everyone had one in their pocket. Eve pictured the ornate mirror in the photos. Wherever their fight had occurred it hadn't been in Natalie's room. Eve had a feeling she'd anticipated what might happen and been ready to capture it. Maybe she'd been goading Eliza ever since the woman had robbed her of her role in the musical.

'Where does it leave us?' Viv asked.

Eve put her head in her hands. 'With the sands shifting.'

'Please don't talk in riddles.'

'I'm just thinking about the confession Eliza wrote, the night she died. She could have been referring to injuring Natalie all those years ago. She said the poem was the final straw. Originally, I thought she meant the way Natalie had reminded everyone of it on Saturday, but that's not actually what she said. And she talked about lashing out. That would fit with her losing control when she was face to face with Natalie, back in the day – not tracking her down with a murder weapon in hand.'

'Blimey. You're right. And the date on the photos would fit.'

Eve nodded. 'I expect Eliza attacked Natalie just after she'd recited the poem on Founders' Day. And as soon as that punch was thrown, Natalie had her. Total control, forever. It might not have worked on another person. After all these years, and with Natalie dead, there'd be no police enquiry. But Eliza was always belittling everyone else's behaviour. Meting out justice to school children for minor misdemeanours. It would have shown her to be an utter hypocrite. And Natalie was in a position to publicise her wrongdoing far and wide, before or after her death. She was an expert in destroying people, just as Acton must be. Eliza's face would have been known nationally. People lap up scandal, especially when it relates to an elite institution like Southwood.'

'Yes.' Viv sipped her tea. 'Letting it go public would have been unthinkable for Eliza. If you hadn't told me about the suspicious pills in her office, I'd definitely have assumed Natalie's arrangement had pushed her over the edge.'

'Me too.' Eve sighed. 'Even though I'm sure she was murdered, I don't see how it might relate to her and Natalie's past. I suppose the timing could be chance, but it's a heck of a coincidence. She was writing about their history the night she died. And she'd only just received the letter Dirk Acton sent.'

'So Natalie's coercion and her death have to be connected?'

'I think so. Maybe the killer knew about Eliza hitting Natalie. They could have coaxed her into writing her confession to Martin, to make it look like she was guilty of murder and intending to take her own life.'

'Does that mean Martin's out of it?'

Eve paused for thought. 'I'm afraid not. Because another scenario is that she was writing it in desperation, of her own accord, when her killer came to find her. Maybe she hoped Martin would keep her on, but allow her extended leave. Some kind of workaround to fool Dirk Acton, who was keeping watch.'

'That would fit.'

'It would have cost her a lot to admit the truth, but I imagine she was at breaking point. If Martin walked in on her and saw the letter, it would have given him the chance he needed. A sympathetic hand on her shoulder. Telling her he understood, pouring her a drink. Slipping the powder in.'

Viv shuddered. 'But why would he kill her unless she was a danger to him? It's like you said yesterday, she'd have gone to the police if she'd known he was guilty.'

'Yes, I'm sure she would have. It's not as though Martin was family. And we don't have a good motive for him to have killed Natalie either. Just as well I'm due to interview him this afternoon. But not for a while yet. I've got enough time to tail Dirk Acton.'

Their eyes drifted across the green to where the producer had emerged in the pub doorway.

'I still consider it most unsatisfactory that you're going without me. Report back soonest, won't you?' Viv followed Eve towards the door.

'As if I'd get the choice.'

Viv laughed.

Outside, Eve went straight to her car. She was willing to bet Dirk Acton knew way more than he was admitting, and not just about Robin. He was a driven man – every bit as ruthless and ambitious as his late colleague, Eve imagined. If Natalie had confided in him, he might have a hunch who'd killed her. And she could see him keeping it secret. Controlling the release of information was his stock in trade. She wanted to follow him – see as many of his interactions as she could.

36

It was handy that Eve was due to speak with Martin Leverett that afternoon. She had an excuse to be at Southwood, and could always say she'd arrived early. The interview itself would be a delicate one. She wanted to know about Natalie's attempts to influence school policy, which shouldn't be too difficult to bring up, but also why she'd been so furious with Martin on Founders' Day, which was a lot more sensitive.

But for now, she focused on Natalie's producer. She wanted to see who he met and whether he homed in on anyone in particular. She bit her lip as she drove north-west. She guessed the school reception would direct Acton to someone official first – Martin probably. She'd have to watch carefully to see if he sneaked off undercover after that. It was lucky she had plenty of time before her own appointment with the headmaster.

As she travelled up the long lane towards the school, she could see the navy Audi ahead. She slowed her pace to avoid him spotting her. On the upside, he was unlikely to know what car she drove. She didn't feel too conspicuous.

As Acton entered the grounds, Eve's view of the Audi was blocked by the hornbeam hedge, then partially obscured by trees. She pulled over and took out her phone, pretending to take a call as a car behind her overtook.

Up ahead, she could just see the second car – a Volvo – pull up at the front of the school, close to the main entrance. Interestingly, Acton had parked further away, well to the right.

Why give himself the extra walk? He didn't strike her as a man to waste time. Eve's Mini Clubman was crawling along now. She wanted Acton to get out before she caught him up, so she could exit her car without being seen as he entered the school. But Acton wasn't shifting. She peered through the trees, straining to catch sight of any movement.

At last, the visitor in the Volvo went through the main entrance towards reception. It was only then that Acton moved, and it wasn't in same direction. Eve was glad she'd slowed right down. The producer glanced over his shoulder as he let himself out of his car, but he couldn't have seen her. He didn't stop. Instead of heading for the main entrance, he made for the side of the school.

Eve put her foot on the accelerator again. What did it mean? He seemed to know his way around rather well for someone who'd never visited before.

She parked some distance from Acton, away from the main entrance too. If he was going in unannounced, she needed to follow suit. She paused a moment, thinking, then opened her glove compartment, took out the beanie she kept there and pulled it on. Her pixie crop was one of the most distinctive things about her. Wearing the hat might help her go incognito. For a second, she wondered what the heck she was doing. The police were still on site, using the library as their incident room. She didn't fancy Palmer's reaction if he caught her. But finding out the truth was simply too important.

A moment later, she'd checked over her shoulder, just as Acton had done, and peered around the side of the school to see if it was safe to follow. He was ahead of her, perfectly visible, though he was taking precautions – ducking each time he passed a window. Two could play at that game, and she was shorter than him. She could avoid the windows more easily, and dive behind one of the shrubs next to the walls if she needed to. It had to be worth the risk to see where he was going. As she passed a classroom to her left, she heard the muffled sound of a teacher's voice.

Eve kept her eyes on Acton, hardly blinking. He could turn at any moment and she needed to predict when he might. He'd see her for sure, otherwise.

As she went, she saw him pull out his mobile and glance at it. You could find plans of the school layout on its website. That might explain his unhesitating progress. But he must be operating in secret for a reason – it would be a lot easier to announce himself and have someone show him round.

Suddenly, Eve was on high alert. Acton had slowed. There was an infinitesimal pause before he turned. Eve just made it behind a shrub in time, her heart hammering. This was crazy. She wasn't scared of him but if she blew it, she'd never know what he was up to.

He might just be on a fishing expedition, scouting for information that would shock his viewers, but Eve didn't think so. He could spend days hanging around without striking gold.

More likely he had a specific mission.

He'd skirted Great Quad, and was faced with one of the routes to the interior of the school buildings. He paused, craning round to check for anyone who might challenge him.

In a second, he'd crossed the danger point and was working his way round the outside of Old Quad.

Eve tiptoed forward and checked the walkway too, holding her breath before she also made it without being spotted.

She shivered. Was he going beyond the school buildings? To the chapel perhaps? Nothing else lay beyond apart from the playing fields and tennis courts.

She was horribly exposed as they left the buildings behind. There was no cover. She pulled out her mobile. If he turned, she'd turn away from him and pretend to chat. With her collar turned up and the hat covering her hair, she hoped he wouldn't recognise her.

He was heading along a path through the trees. For a moment, Eve was convinced she'd got it right about him making for the chapel. But at the last minute, he turned towards a dense thicket of holly and disappeared.

Eve crept forward cautiously and skirted the thicket. If Acton emerged and headed back towards the school, she'd remain well hidden. Behind her was the hornbeam hedge. She tried to control her breathing – it seemed so loud he might hear her. But she ought to be quite safe. Acton had no reason to head that way.

'Great to meet you.' The producer spoke in a warm, smooth undertone. 'I was so pleased you got in touch.'

Eve held her breath.

'I was worried you'd think I was being too pushy.' The slightly breathy bubbly voice carried.

So Acton did know about Scarlett after all.

37

'I like pushy,' Acton said to Scarlett. 'Shrinking violets don't do well in our business. Seems you've got the right qualities.'

'Oh, thank you so much.' She was practically purring.

'I'm curious though. How did you get my number?'

There was a pause. 'I told you.' The head girl's voice was full of bravado, but Eve could hear the note of uncertainty too. 'Natalie gave it to me before she died. She suggested I contact you direct.'

'Now, now, Scarlett. Like I said, I admire people who take the initiative, but I don't want lies.'

'I—' She stopped, then started again. 'I don't know what you mean.'

'Well, think about it.' Acton laughed. 'Natalie wouldn't have done that. She was already acting as go-between when she died.'

'She'd mentioned me?'

'Of course. She called me the day of her murder. She was very keen to have you on the show.'

'But not as an interviewee,' Scarlett said quickly. 'That was what she said.'

'No, no, of course not.' Acton's voice was soothing; it had the opposite effect on Eve, making her heart rate ramp up. 'Natalie planned to have you on alongside her and another guest. You could put some questions, join in the general chat. It would get your face known.'

'It sounds amazing. And you still want to have me on?'

'I'd like to know where you got my number. It's the reason I wanted to see you in person. That and to judge your screen presence. I want the truth.'

The head girl was hesitating. 'I-I'm afraid I peeked in Natalie's address book and copied it down.'

'That's more believable.' There was a pause. 'It's okay.'

Eve could hear Scarlett's breathing, jagged, as though she was fighting tears.

'I told you. I like a person who takes the initiative. You can't always get ahead when you play by the rules. And yes, we still want to have you on. Natalie's stand-in and I will look after you. We must set a date and do a rehearsal or two.'

'Wow. I can't believe it.'

'Well, it's all real. Natalie told me she'd taken to you. She wanted to help. It's tragic that she can't do that now, but I view it as my duty to see her plans through. We'll sort out a date.'

'When?'

'Next week.'

'That soon?' Scarlett breathed out the words.

'We can tie it in with the piece about poor Natalie and her tutor.'

'Oh.' Her voice quavered.

'Problem?'

'No. No, not at all.'

'Speak soon, then.'

He was acting so keen. His side of the conversation had ulterior motive written all over it. Eve shifted position so she could peer round the holly trees. Acton was walking swiftly back along the path towards the school. She guessed he'd go and talk to someone official now. He'd want information, just as he said.

Eve glanced at her watch. She still had an hour before her appointment with Martin Leverett. Maybe Acton would slip in before her.

After Natalie's producer disappeared, Scarlett emerged from the trees. Eve couldn't just let her go.

'Scarlett.'

The girl jumped visibly.

'I'm sorry to startle you. I arrived early for an appointment with the headmaster. I thought I'd take a walk in the grounds to pass the time and I couldn't help spotting you with Dirk Acton.'

Her brow furrowed. 'You know Dirk?'

'I interviewed him just before he came here. Scarlett, we need to talk. He told me he'd never heard of you.'

'You heard what we spoke about?'

Eve nodded. 'I'm sorry I listened in, but I don't trust him.'

'It's natural that he lied about me.' Scarlett took a deep breath. 'He's bound to keep developments about Natalie's old show secret. He'll be looking for someone to take over permanently. The current stand-in's not contracted yet.'

Was that what Scarlett thought this was? An opportunity for her, an eighteen-year-old student, to try out for the part?

'Scarlett, listen to me. How did you really get his number? Copying it down makes no sense if Natalie had already offered to help you. You told us all that she had. Didn't you trust her to follow through?'

'Of course I did. She was lovely to me.'

'She was. On Founders' Day. She was foul before that. What changed? What suddenly put her on your side? Whatever it is, it seems to have got Dirk Acton interested too. Did you steal any other numbers from Natalie?'

Scarlett flinched at the word, but after a moment, she nodded.

'You called them too?'

Another nod.

'And have any of them been as receptive as Acton?'

'Most of them had assistants answering their phones. I'm not sure my message got through.'

'And what happened with Acton?'

'He was eager to talk to me. That makes sense, now I know Natalie had paved the way.'

How could Eve get her to see this was a warning sign? She was only interesting to someone with prior knowledge. What had Natalie told him? She tried to keep her tone measured. 'She must have contacted him after you and she became friends. Something changed her mind about you. What was it?'

Scarlett let out a deep breath. 'I convinced her I wasn't the typical head girl she thought I was. Not such a goody two shoes.'

'And how did you do that?'

She kept quiet.

Eve thought of what Sabina had said in the Cross Keys: that there was something going on with Eliza and Scarlett. Something she'd have wanted to see through. An issue of discipline?

She was running out of ideas. Perhaps a bluff would work.

'I know you were in trouble with Eliza Gregory.'

Scarlett put her hands over her face.

'Did you tell Natalie about that?'

At last, she nodded. 'I thought if she knew I'd stolen the exam papers, she'd realise I'm not so fine and upstanding as I seem. I wanted her to see that I'm more like her. And she did see. The moment I told her I'd cheated she warmed to me. I didn't steal them because I'm no good. I just rebelled like her. Didn't fancy spending all last summer revising.'

That rang true. Scarlett's achievements must be good

enough generally for her to be accepted as head girl, even if her appointment was partly down to her rich dad. Eve imagined Natalie's response would have been pretty hostile, underneath it all. Here was someone she'd instinctively disliked, having it easy for no good reason. Eve felt cross too – she couldn't help herself. She'd have forgiven Scarlett a hundred times over if she'd stolen the exam papers in a panic, worried about how she might fare. Students went through agonies over that kind of anxiety. But to cheat just to stay on top, without expending any effort, while others watched your success from afar and tried to compete... that was beyond the pale as far as Eve was concerned.

'What was Eliza planning to do about your wrongdoing?'

Scarlett gasped. 'Oh my goodness. You think I killed her? No, no, I didn't. Most people seem to think she killed herself anyway. But either way, the truth would never have got out.'

'I heard your father's one of the school's biggest benefactors.'

She shrugged. 'Southwood knows which side its bread is buttered. That's just the way the world works. Always has, always will. Eliza was determined I should be punished – grounded for the whole of next summer term, I don't doubt, and no post-exam celebrations. But my marks would have stood and my place here wasn't threatened. She'd already acknowledged that, though it made her furious. It's not just me. Students don't tend to get publicly shamed. The school sees it as part of the learning process. The punishments can be pretty humiliating, but discipline's an internal matter.'

Just as it had been when Natalie stole school property and sold it on. But would Southwood try to sweep it under the carpet if Scarlett was guilty of a double murder?

'Okay,' Eve said. 'Let's take a step back. Natalie knew you'd cheated at your exams, and that you'd get away more or less scot-free.' She held up her hand when Scarlett started to protest. 'That's how most people would describe the sort of punishment you were expecting.

'Meanwhile, Natalie hated Southwood and everything about it. After you told her, she could see you weren't just head girl, you were protected and cossetted, despite your wrongdoings. And you'd make an excellent bit of TV if she got you to go public.'

'But I wouldn't have.'

'Not willingly.' Eve thought it through, but there was no way to sugar-coat her words. 'Natalie played on your weakness, your desperate keenness to launch a TV career. She told you she'd get you on as some kind of co-presenter. At the age of eighteen. With no experience. And now Dirk Acton is promising the same. He's not bothered what happens to Southwood, of course. He won't get a personal kick out of ruining the school's reputation like Natalie would have. But I'll bet the piece will get good ratings. He can lead in with the scandal of Natalie's death and her feelings towards Southwood, then cut to you live and get Natalie's stand-in to ask you all about your cheating.'

'He said it would be a sort of three-way chat between me, my co-presenter and a guest.'

'I'm afraid I think he's lying. You know what Natalie's show's like, Scarlett. They never have anyone on without a motive. They'll be discussing your cheating in the same breath as Eliza Gregory's death, which I believe will be confirmed as murder. And she had a hold over you. Can you see how it will look?' Acton would be planning a bumper show. He might roll Natalie's blackmail of Eliza into the same story – unless he saw sense.

Scarlett had gone pink.

Eve felt the faintest twinge of sympathy, but it was over-ridden by frustration. 'How did you really get all the numbers from Natalie? Unless she left you on your own with her address book for a good while, I don't see how you copied them without her noticing.'

Scarlett was twisting her hands together.

'Did you steal her address book?' Eve remembered seeing it, beautiful and leather-bound. She'd taken it out when she'd asked Robin for his contact details.

Still Scarlett was silent.

'If we wait here and I call the police, will they find the book in your room?' She had to push. 'They're only in the library. It wouldn't take them long.'

She took out her phone and Scarlett swallowed.

At last, the girl nodded.

'Did you take it the night Natalie died, when you visited her? How is it that she didn't see you?' And then an icy chill spread through Eve's core. 'She wasn't there, was she?'

A small shake of the head.

'But you got in without a problem. You had her key?'

Despite where her thoughts were heading, Eve wasn't scared. Scarlett wasn't armed, and Eve could run if she needed to. The staff and students weren't far away.

After a moment's silence, Scarlett spoke. 'It's not how it looks.'

38

'I can only think of one way you'd have got the key that evening.' Eve stood opposite Scarlett, watching her closely. She might make a dash for it. Eve would catch her but the moment would be lost.

'I didn't have her key!' The girl's eyes were wide, her pitch rising. 'And I didn't kill her!'

Eve waited.

'We were getting on really well. Or I thought we were. She'd promised to have me on her show as a co-presenter.' She closed her eyes for a moment. 'I believed her. I was delighted. I'd never have killed her. But I did go and look for her. We'd chatted in the hidden room, late the night before, after I told her about the cheating. She invited me up. Said it was her special hideaway. So on Founders' Day evening, when I fancied another chat after dinner, I thought I might find her there.'

Goosebumps rose on Eve's arms. 'And you did.'

'Yes!' Her pitch rose further. 'But she was already dead!' Her eyes were wide. 'It was horrific. I ran out of the room and back down the stairs. I couldn't face looking at her, and I was scared. Whoever killed her might have come back.

'But once I got outside, I took some deep breaths and calmed down a bit. I know it sounds bad, but I started to think about what her death meant for me. All my dreams came crashing down. I'd gone from having an offer to try out as a co-presenter on the UK's biggest talk show to having nothing. But I'd seen Natalie's address book. Getting it felt like a way to rescue the situation.'

Eve didn't bother trying to disguise her revulsion. She realised Scarlett hardly knew Natalie, but to chase after her own needs so ruthlessly after witnessing such horror was chilling. Well up on cheating at exams because she couldn't be bothered studying.

'How did you get in to Natalie's room?'

'I broke in. The locks aren't hard to pick – I learned from a video on YouTube last year, when I wanted to play a joke on a first year.'

Poor first year. Eve was so glad she hadn't studied at Southwood.

'Leaving again was easy. The doors lock automatically when you pull them closed. I had no idea Eliza had seen me in the corridor, and I didn't think anyone would miss the address book. Who would ask about it? Most people keep their contacts electronically these days.'

She'd had it all worked out. 'So you've known all this time that Natalie died much earlier than everyone thought.' The silhouette in the library couldn't have been her.

'Yes, but you do see why I couldn't tell.'

It was all Eve could do to contain herself. 'What time was it when you found her body?'

'Around ten to nine.'

A time when none of the staff had alibis, as far as Eve knew. And of course, whatever Scarlett said, she might be guilty herself.

'Did you go to the library, later that evening?'

She looked indignant now. 'No, of course I didn't. It wasn't me!'

But she had motives for both Natalie and Eliza. She might have discovered Natalie was double-crossing her, and worried that Eliza had seen her pick Natalie's lock.

But as Eve thought it through, she realised it didn't fit. If Scarlett had guessed Natalie planned to humiliate her on national television, she wouldn't have fawned over Dirk Acton the way she had.

Eve thought about telling her to go to the police, but she was sure she wouldn't. She'd report their conversation direct to Greg Boles so he could take action.

Scarlett glanced at her watch. 'I'd better go.'

'Will you get in touch with Dirk Acton? Tell him you've changed your mind?'

But even now, Eve could see she hadn't completely convinced her. She was looking at the two sides of the scales: the possibility of a prime-time slot on TV, versus being taken for a ride and forced to confess what she'd done in front of thousands of viewers.

'I'll think about it,' she said, and walked off.

Eve watched her go, her shoulder muscles knotted. There wasn't anything more she could do.

It had started to rain, and she made up her mind to shelter in the chapel while she called Greg Boles to tell him what she'd discovered. She didn't want to see him in the library. If Palmer was there, he'd ask too many questions.

After she'd made the call, she sat waiting for her allotted time to see Martin Leverett. It gave her space to think through the ramifications of Scarlett's confession.

She updated her timeline for the night of Natalie's death on her phone.

6.30 p.m.: The coven, Viv, Natalie & I had drinks in the staff common room, next to the refectory.

7.00 p.m.: We all went into dinner at high table.

8.30 p.m.: Viv and I went to our rooms, with an arrangement to meet again at 9.25 in Great Quad, ready for drinks in the common room. The others could have been anywhere.

8.50 p.m.: Scarlett found Natalie's dead body in the hidden room (if she's telling the truth).

9.05 p.m. approx: Eliza Gregory spotted Scarlett in the corridor outside Natalie's room. Scarlett admits she broke in to steal Natalie's address book. Eliza could have seen her pick the lock. She claimed she wanted to talk to Natalie too, but left when she saw Scarlett.

9.30 p.m.: Viv, Anastasia and I saw a silhouette impersonating Natalie in the library. A second hooded figure stopped at the sight of the imposter, paused in the library porch, then entered. The pair appeared to argue quite violently, before making it up quickly and embracing.

The comings and goings at drinks were irrelevant now, of course. Eve went on to review the suspects. As before, Eliza could have killed Natalie then been killed. She might have thought murder would rid her of her blackmailer. But if so, she'd known Natalie was no longer a threat when she left the common room in a huff. Yet her tone and words didn't fit with that. Plus, Eve couldn't imagine who would have acted out the library scene with her. She seemed unlikely.

As for Scarlett, Eve liked her even less than she had done. But though she had a reason to kill Eliza, Eve didn't buy her motive for Natalie. Even now, she was in awe of the opportunities she'd seemed to offer. And though Scarlett could have killed Eliza, Eve couldn't imagine the head of sixth form going off for a moonlit walk with her. Or Scarlett thrusting her head underwater and holding it there. The head girl was full of big talk, and callous in many ways, but Eve's gut told her that sort of physical ruthlessness would be beyond her.

Bridget and Anastasia were theoretically in the running, but Eve had no motive for them. Beyond that, Bridget was the wrong build to be one of the figures in the library, and Anastasia couldn't have been.

It brought her back to Martin and Lucia. If they'd been the silhouettes in the library, they could have left in time to join Eve, Viv and Anastasia for drinks in the common room.

Their motives still weren't clear, but she could imagine them as the play-acting couple, and there were plenty of questions about them floating in her mind. Their interactions with Natalie were odd.

It was fitting that the interview with Martin was next on her list. Maybe she'd get some answers.

39

At last, Eve walked towards the school's administrative offices to meet the headmaster.

Martin's personal assistant welcomed her.

'I hope he's had a chance to draw breath,' Eve said. 'I gather he was meeting Dirk Acton, Natalie's producer, before me.' It was a guess; the only way she could think of to confirm it.

The PA smiled. 'That's right. But Mr Acton left twenty minutes ago and Martin called for coffee at that point. He'll be ready for you.'

Eve smiled back, but her mind was on the PA's information. It must have been a short meeting. Maybe Martin hadn't liked Acton any better than she had. She wondered if the producer had faced him with evidence of Eliza's violence and Natalie's blackmail.

The PA knocked on his door and walked straight in. Eve was behind her and saw the headmaster jump. He'd been staring out of the window and it took a moment for him to come to. He snapped to attention, glanced quickly down and turned slightly, his back to them, partially blocking their view. But Eve caught sight of the red silk item he was holding – one of his cravats, she thought – just before he stuffed it into his desk drawer, slamming it shut.

'Eve Mallow for you, headmaster,' the woman said. 'I'll bring more coffee.' Martin Leverett looked as though he needed it.

'Please, take a seat,' she added to Eve, pulling out the chair in front of his desk.

'I'm sorry,' he said, blinking at her. 'I had Natalie's producer in here before you. He told me he wanted to pay tribute to her on her show, but it's clear he's hoping for the inside track on her murder. He's decided someone here must know something and I doubt he'll leave us alone until he works out what it is.'

He hadn't bought Eliza as the guilty party, then. Eve wondered if the police had made their planned statement about her death yet. Maybe Acton had seen it before he and Martin spoke.

'He asked for the address of the stand-in gardener we employed,' Martin went on, 'so it won't just be us he pesters.'

Anxiety pulled at Eve's insides. Natalie had remembered where she knew Robin from before she died. How long would it be before Acton unearthed that information too? If he did, there'd be no keeping it private. In some ways it made no odds, with someone already on Robin's tail. But if Acton doorstepped him for an interview the results could be terrible. Slipping quietly away to a new location would be impossible if his face was known nationwide. 'I guess you couldn't pass his details on,' she said at last. It would be against data protection rules.

'Couldn't, and wouldn't anyway, but I don't imagine Acton's the sort of man to let that hold him back.'

He was right. He'd find Robin somehow. As the PA brought the coffee in and set it on Martin's desk, Eve sent Robin a quick text, warning him to watch out.

The PA began to pour their drinks but Martin put out a hand to stop her. 'Thank you. I'll do it.'

As she left, he focused on the coffee pot and cups. Concentrating on the task at hand seemed to steady him.

'So, you want my impressions of Natalie?'

'Please. I gather she visited frequently in the run-up to her death. Lucia mentioned she brought presents for your daughters, and I gather she was interested in school policy too.'

Martin raised an eyebrow. He looked sad. 'She pretended to be.'

'You didn't believe her?'

'I don't now. She renounced her share in Southwood just before she died. She wouldn't have done that if she'd wanted to steer the school's direction.'

'What kind of things did she suggest when she talked to you?'

'Increasing the size of the coven by introducing outside members. Close monitoring of staff involving regular visits by inspectors. Admitting boys.' He took a deep breath. 'In all honesty, I think she was winding us up. We knew she'd hold a lot of sway if she took up her share in the school.'

At last, Natalie had had the prospect of some control over Southwood. Finding out about her illness would have been utterly devastating, but beyond that, it meant the influence she'd looked forward to, for justice or revenge, would never happen. Given that, she could have pulled out of her role as Founders' Day Champion. After the recent scandal, the staff would probably have been glad. Yet she'd turned up as planned. With what motive? That was the question.

'So you thought of her as a mischief-maker, yet you still voted for her as Founders' Day Champion?'

'That's right. Anastasia argued for her. She was convinced she'd get bored if we drew her in – faced her with a load of admin and duties. We hoped she'd become a sleeping partner. As it was, she backed off more thoroughly than any of us expected.'

The way he spoke, Eve was pretty sure he only knew about her waiving her share in the school, not her illness. 'Did you like Natalie?' Eve knew the question would feel blunt. It was intentional.

He paused. 'She was a very compelling character.' After a moment, he added, 'I sometimes liked her.'

There was a hardness in his eyes he couldn't quite hide. 'Her affair just as she started her year-long appointment was hard to forgive.' His knuckles were white as he gripped his coffee cup. 'Terrible for the school's reputation.'

They talked about Natalie's visits to Southwood and her TV show, as Eve built up to her crucial question.

'Martin, please forgive me, but on Founders' Day, I accidentally overheard a conversation between the pair of you.'

He stiffened but didn't respond.

'I was exploring the library, after the speeches. It's such a fascinating room. I found myself in a secluded section where you and she were talking. I couldn't miss her words. She said: "She told me all about it. It's heartless of you! How could you treat her so badly?".'

Still he didn't reply. She had to go for it – keep pushing. There was too much at stake. 'At the time, I had a feeling she was referring to a conversation with Lucia. I'd seen them have a heart-to-heart the evening before. I won't put any of this in my obituary. It just interested me. I got the impression Natalie was quite close to both of you. You were clearly discussing personal matters.'

He shook his head now. 'Before she died, Eliza said you'd be looking into the murder. I remember Viv Montague saying you'd done it before.'

'I end up interviewing the same people as the police. It makes me nervous sometimes.'

He sighed. 'If you're going to dig, I might as well tell you. Natalie's onslaught came out of the blue. You have to believe me, there was no animosity between us.' His eyes met hers. 'But yes, she was referring to something Lucia told her. That I'd been carrying on with the gym mistress here, Sally Rowe.' He frowned. 'It's utter nonsense, of course, but I'd rather tell you than have you think it's something worse.' He shuddered. 'I've spoken to Lucia about it now. She knows it's all a misunderstanding.'

At that moment, there was a knock at the door and Lucia herself appeared. 'Sorry, but it's time for the meeting with Mr Anderson, darling.'

He blinked and looked at his watch. 'Of course. Lucia, come in for a second and close the door, would you?' He waited until they had some privacy. 'Eve overheard Natalie challenge me about Sally Rowe.'

Lucia's cheeks went pink. 'Ah. You explained it was my mistake?'

He nodded.

'I'd never allude to anything like that in the obituary anyway,' Eve said. 'It's got nothing to do with Natalie herself.'

'No, quite,' Martin replied, 'but I'd rather clear the matter up.'

Lucia had a hand to her cheek. 'I should have realised I'd got the wrong end of the stick. So, Mr Anderson?'

He nodded and he and Eve stood up to join Lucia and leave the room.

Eve's mind was spinning. It was possible Martin had slept with the gym mistress, but he and Lucia had decided to put it behind them. Killed Natalie to stop her telling the rest of the coven – or the wider public. But if so, why had Lucia confided in Natalie in the first place? She wasn't the sort to have opened up in a moment of passion. She was calm, measured, and used to keeping secrets. And why tell Eve about it? It made no sense at all. It wasn't even any of her business.

Yet if it was a genuine misunderstanding on Lucia's part as

they claimed, how had she been so mistaken? You'd think she'd have wanted proof before confiding in Natalie, and the fact remained, she was an odd person to choose as a confidante.

And finally, if – as Martin confirmed – it was Lucia's worries over the gym mistress that she'd discussed with Natalie, how did that fit with what Lucia had told Eve? Eve tried to remember her words. She'd said Natalie was on the verge of making a decision that would have led to disaster and that she'd steered her away from that. She'd helped Natalie, not the other way about.

Eve had been convinced she was telling the truth, though it fought with what she'd seen. Yet Martin also sounded honest when he said it was the gym mistress he and Natalie had been discussing. How could both those things be true?

40

Eve called Robin to update him when she got home but had to leave a voicemail with the promise of news. After that, she walked and fed Gus, who was in skittish mood. The wind had got up and that tended to affect him. He leaped this way and that on their way round the village, chasing leaves caught in eddies.

Returning home, she checked online and saw the police statement on Eliza's death had made headline news: DOUBLE MURDER AT EXCLUSIVE SUFFOLK SCHOOL. She closed the page and wrote up her notes, dragging her mind all the way back to Dirk Acton's revelations. She thought again of Jane Parker, who'd taken Natalie's place in the production of *Grease* and ended up on TV. She put her name into IMDb. She'd been acting ever since. Not a household name, but a familiar face. She wasn't as famous as Natalie, but she might be happier. It didn't look as though she lacked work. And Natalie might have imagined she'd have risen higher if she'd got her big break back then. Perhaps the not knowing had eaten away at her. Fed that lifelong hatred of Eliza.

Eve had finished her notes and was halfway through a bowl of spaghetti bolognese when her mobile rang. Robin – at last.

'*We might need a proper chat.*' That sounded ominous. '*Could you meet me by the old mooring block in half an hour?*'

His tone was urgent. It was like the old days, when they were at their most cautious. A remote rendezvous, halfway along the estuary path, in amongst the reeds.

She agreed, and twenty minutes later, she'd pulled on her padded navy jacket. She slipped Gus's leash into her pocket, but they probably wouldn't need it. Haunted Lane was quiet. It only led to two houses and the estuary. Parking was forbidden.

Bright moonlight lit Gus's way as he dashed ahead, up for an extra evening adventure. Occasionally the night got darker, as clouds scudded across the sky, but it remained light enough to see the way. The visibility made Eve nervous. If she could see, she could be *seen*. She glanced over her shoulder, grateful for Gus's presence.

As the dachshund reached the estuary path, he paused and looked back at her, then scampered on again, safe in the knowledge that she was following.

Eve traced his footsteps, turning towards the coast, the sprawling brackish water an inky mass to her left. To her right were fields which separated the path from the village. In between, a damp reedy ditch.

The way seemed deserted. At last, she reached the spot where she'd met Robin countless times before. She pushed her way through vegetation to find the mooring block and saw him, a still silhouette in the night. It made her think of the silhouette in the library. Someone she now knew hadn't been Natalie.

Gus leaped up and Robin fussed him, then pulled Eve into his arms, but only after checking around them carefully and drawing her further from the path.

'Have you seen the guy who was following you again?'

He nodded. 'He was gone during the day yesterday. I went

to several gardens – I'm sure I'd have seen him. But last night he was there in Blind Eye Wood again. And my last client yesterday said someone had been asking about me. The description matched.'

'You're sure it's to do with the old days?'

He nodded. 'There was one guy – always on the periphery. I think it's him. And if I've seen him, it's because he wants to be seen. He's angry enough to try to scare me. But I've still got trustworthy colleagues on the force. He probably doesn't know that. We just need to let Greg and the London team do their work.'

Eve took a deep breath. 'Okay.'

'It's vital we're not seen together. The fact that I haven't been attacked yet makes me worry his plan's not that simple. He might want to hurt someone I love.'

He pulled her close again and held her tight. But even as he hugged her, she felt them being pulled apart by this ghost from his past. Except the spectre hiding in the shadows was all too real.

'I understand.' She swallowed. 'You've got news?'

'You remember the ring I lost while I was working at Southwood?'

She nodded, her head against the rough jacket he wore.

'It's been found. In Natalie's room at the school.'

She took a sharp breath and pulled back to face him. 'Oh no. Robin, I'm so sorry. But you reported it lost at the time, didn't you?'

'Unfortunately, that hasn't helped much. Palmer's already interviewed me. I said someone must have planted it to make me look guilty. I think he was tempted to arrest me then and there, but I pointed out it was odd none of their forensics team had found it when they first searched her room. After that, there was a lot of discussion behind the scenes. I'd guess someone senior pulled rank. It was Olivia Dawkins who told me

I could go. I thought Palmer would have a coronary, he was so angry when I passed him in the corridor.'

'No fresh hunches on who pinched it?'

He shook his head. 'I didn't see anyone go near the shed that day. But I wasn't keeping watch.'

'What made the police go back to the room and check again?'

'They didn't. A cleaner found it and alerted them.'

'Could the cleaner have planted it?'

'She could, but it doesn't seem likely. She was a temp, like me. She only arrived yesterday and there's no hint she'd met Natalie or any of the staff before.'

'And she found it today?'

'That's right. Though it could have been planted any time after I lost it on Monday. The police had already finished searching the room by then.'

'What's Palmer's theory?'

'That I lied about losing it in the shed so as to seem innocent if it turned up somewhere incriminating.'

'But that's stupid. If you'd killed her, you'd just keep quiet about it. It's unlikely anyone at Southwood would recognise it. You took it off each time you gardened.'

'I expect someone put that to Palmer behind the scenes, but you know what he's like. What news your end?'

Eve thought back to the events of the day. 'I spoke to Greg about Scarlett.' She filled him in on her discoveries. 'I'm surprised it wasn't her Palmer hauled in this evening. What I discovered was pretty troubling.'

'I agree. But Palmer will hate her as a suspect – rich, well connected, young, pretty. Greg will have done his best but somehow or other it looks as though they don't buy her as the killer.' He frowned. 'If she dressed up as Natalie to give herself a false alibi, she'd have needed an accomplice. Anyone spring to mind?'

Eve shook her head slowly. 'No. And I'd swear she had no idea Natalie was double-crossing her. She seemed totally taken in by Dirk Acton. Even when I left her, I could tell she hadn't entirely bought my arguments.'

'It seems funny that someone as ruthless as Scarlett could doubt the ruthlessness of others.'

'I know. I think she's so used to getting her own way she can't imagine the tables turning.' Eve sighed. 'I can't believe I haven't managed to work this out yet, Robin. I hate it that you're in this situation.'

He took her hands in his. 'Let's not panic. We both know I didn't do it. And you doubt Scarlett did either? Her motive doesn't stand up?'

She nodded.

'And what about the husband, Gavin Vale?'

'I think he's off the list. There are too many points against him. He was in the pub all evening the day Eliza died. Unless he managed to sneak out later without waking Hetty then he wasn't at Southwood. And I don't see Eliza drinking with him there either. And assuming it's the killer who planted your ring in Natalie's room, he'd have to have sneaked on site to do that too. And have found keys to get into her room, unless he picked the lock like Scarlett did. Plus, he'd need an accomplice to manage the silhouette scene.'

'You're right. It's too much of a stretch. It has to be someone based at the school. At least the police will know they need to re-check the key players' alibis, after your excellent work with Scarlett.' He squeezed her shoulder.

'There's something very odd about the way Martin and Lucia are behaving.' She told him about her conversation with them that day. 'Heck, Robin. I want to know who did this but part of me hopes it wasn't them. What would happen to their daughters? They're very sweet and so young. And Lucia's clearly trusted by the students she looks after. She's always in demand.'

'Maybe it's not them. There's Anastasia, and Martin's mother, too.'

'Yes, but I don't see why either of them would have killed Natalie or Eliza. And neither of them could have been the silhouettes.' Inside, she felt as bleak as the expanse of estuary in front of her. 'I could see Martin and Lucia collaborating.' She pictured them leaning on each other at Natalie's memorial service. 'But I still don't understand why. The reasons I've thought of don't add up. There's something strange going on. I just wish I knew what it was.'

41

Eve found it hard to sleep that night. Robin's situation was so precarious. He and Palmer had argued when he'd interviewed him at home, and clashed again at the station. Palmer would be looking for an excuse to charge him.

The sense of urgency was overwhelming but it made logical thought harder. Panic and strategic planning didn't mix. She knew what she wanted: to talk to Sally Rowe, the gym mistress. She needed to know whether she and Martin had had a relationship. If so, maybe something had tempted Lucia to confide in Natalie, however odd it seemed. Eve could imagine her regretting it, especially if she and Martin had made it up afterwards. He might have told her the affair was over, but if Natalie knew, it wouldn't be. Word would get out.

Eve could imagine them killing Natalie in a moment of desperation, then creating the false alibi in the library.

But marching up to Sally and asking her about the affair wasn't feasible. Even if the gym mistress would talk to her, it wouldn't be wise. Martin or Lucia might get to hear of it and know the way Eve's mind was working.

She needed a way to chat with Sally casually. But time was of the essence and most of Southwood's staff lived on site. She couldn't just bump into the woman on a public street or at the local pub.

After tossing and turning for hours, an idea started to form, but it was a risky one, full of possible pitfalls.

She rang Viv early to share it.

Her friend yawned as she picked up the phone. '*Tell me you have a good reason for calling at this hour.*'

Eve explained what she had in mind, and that she needed Viv's brother's help. Not just his, in fact, but his wife's too.

'*Ooh!*' Viv sounded wide awake now. '*I like it!*'

'Do you think they'd be willing though? I know it's an imposition. But I remember Polly doesn't work on Fridays.' And Simon was his own boss. He ran the local stables.

'*Simon would do anything for you. You know that.*'

'But Polly—'

'*I'll talk to them now,*' Viv said. '*Take no notice of Miss Snootypants.*'

'Mrs.' She and Simon had married that summer.

'*Ugh. Don't remind me. I'll get it all sorted.*'

'Thanks.' She'd rather Viv acted as go-between. It would be easier for Simon to say no than if Eve approached him direct. 'It might be short notice for the school.'

Viv scoffed. '*I should think they'll welcome parents of prospective students with open arms at the moment. I'll have to get Simon to say he's had some gushing recommendations from former pupils. I can give him the names of some of my more swotty contemporaries.*'

'Maybe he can tell them their daughter's only eight, and they're thinking ahead. If they're looking to the future, it'll seem more believable that the murders haven't put them off. They'll be old history by then.'

'*Good plan – I'll tell him. And that will work. Some people*'

*put their offspring down for a place at birth. Child cruelty, I
call it.'*

Eve's mind ran on. 'Then on their way round they need to
claim their mythical child is keen on sport. If they can volunteer
to wander over to the playing fields by themselves to talk to the
gym mistress that would be ideal. I'll hide somewhere nearby.
I'll need to replace Polly for that one bit of the tour. Perhaps she
could sneak into the woods before Sally Rowe sees her. Then,
when I've chatted to Sally, I can make myself scarce again,
leaving Simon and Polly to head back to reception. If anyone
talks about the visit later – which I guess they will – they'll all
remember seeing a couple. Hopefully no one will describe our
physical appearance in detail.' Eve was nothing like Polly. She'd
need to grow several inches, swap her short hair for long blonde
locks, and lose twenty years.

*'Good thinking. There's a good chance they'll be playing
hockey at this time of year. Make for the pitch beyond Old Quad.'*

'Got it.'

What could possibly go wrong? Answers to that filled Eve's
head. But if someone accompanied Polly and Simon to the
playing fields, Eve could abandon her mission. At worst, they
would have a wasted morning. She'd buy them a slap-up meal at
the Cross Keys as a thank you either way. Hopefully Polly
would forgive her. Eventually.

Her other worry was that Sally Rowe might recognise her
from the time she'd spent at Southwood, but they'd had no
direct contact. Only senior staff made it onto high table, thank-
fully. And even if she did make the connection, she had no way
of knowing Eve wasn't married with a school-age child.

'Right,' Viv said. *'I'll text you to confirm it's all on and get
Simon to update you when he arrives.'*

'Thanks, Viv. You're one in a million.'

*'No problem. Though in return you owe me lunch at the
Cross Keys. I must know how it goes.'*

. . .

The plan was simple, but horribly flaky. Eve couldn't quite believe she'd suggested it, but she was getting desperate. When Simon called to say it was all fine and they were booked in for ten thirty, nerves tickled her stomach.

'You're sure you don't mind?'

'*I think it'll be a lark,*' Simon said. '*Beats doing the accounts anyway.*'

'And Polly?'

'*Looked broody when I explained. Which is all to the good. I'd love to have children before I'm too decrepit to help look after them.*' He was closer in age to Eve than Polly.

Eve laughed and told him she'd be in position by the time they reached the school.

She followed a similar process to the one she'd taken when she'd tailed Dirk Acton, only this time advance planning allowed her to park her car away from the school grounds. She used a pedestrian gate – open during daylight hours – to enter the school, then scuttled along the side hedge, well away from the main entrance. Lessons for the day were in full swing, and there was no one around.

After that, she skirted the outer side of Great Quad and Old Quad again. Beyond the buildings, she cut towards the hockey pitch, keeping a careful check around her. When she neared her destination, she stayed back, hidden amongst some trees. Ahead she could hear shouts, and the sound of a ball on wood. Then a cry of dismay, followed by a rousing cheer.

She got shivery, waiting. It was partly the stiff breeze and partly nerves. She was close to the pitch now – near enough to see the girls hurling themselves after the ball, their legs blotchy red from the cold. She felt a moment of gratitude at being an adult, no longer forced to play competitive sports against her will.

Eve was curious to see Sally Rowe, but a proper inspection would have to wait. If she was going to make this work, she needed to get her timing exactly right. At last she saw two figures, walking into the wind, out beyond Old Quad. One of them turned and waved to someone behind them. Good. It seemed whoever had escorted them that far was letting them make their own way to the hockey pitch. Eve wasn't surprised. The weather was uninviting, the member of staff probably busy, and Sally Rowe and her class were in sight. Simon and Polly weren't unattended exactly.

That said, Ms Rowe wasn't focused on them, but on the game in progress. Eve needed Polly to spot that and make herself scarce before the situation changed.

She held her breath, willing Polly to make a break for it. A moment later, she did, heading for the trees to her left. Eve took a deep breath to fortify herself, and strode across the grass to join Simon. As she walked, she checked on Sally and her girls again, but someone had scored, and Rowe had gathered the players into a huddle.

Simon raised an eyebrow and grinned. 'Polly's going to watch from a discreet distance.'

Eve fell in step with him. 'Did she really not mind?'

'She was curious to see the school, especially after the murders. Once I presented it as a nosy day out, she warmed to the idea.'

Eve breathed a sigh of relief. 'Thanks.' She'd worn her smartest coat to try to look like a prospective Southwood parent. It was the same black one she'd worn for the memorial service, with a velvet trimmed collar. She'd wondered about a silk scarf to cheer it up, but it would be too distinctive. She didn't want anything that Sally Rowe might comment on.

She and Simon went and hovered by the hockey pitch. Ms

Rowe issued an instruction to her class and came to join them as play continued.

'You must be Mr and Mrs Maxwell. I got a message to say you were looking around.' She smiled. 'And that your daughter likes sport. That's lovely news. As well as our lessons, we have multiple societies here: everything from lacrosse to gymnastics. What does your daughter enjoy?'

Eve had been prepared for this and leaped in before the woman spotted Simon's furrowed brow. 'Running and long jump.'

'Excellent. And she's eight now, I gather?'

Again, Simon looked helpless.

'That's right. She could come to you at eleven or thirteen. We're not sure of our plans yet.'

'Of course.'

Simon rallied, gamely. Eve knew he'd want to play his part. 'It feels odd, visiting in the wake of the recent tragedies, but we'd had it on our to-do list for a while, hadn't we, darling?'

Eve nodded. 'It's so awful, what's happened. But of course I don't suppose it's related to Southwood. I've only had good reports about the school. I imagine it was personal. Something to do with Natalie's chat show, perhaps. I presume some outsider sneaked on site – a previous interviewee with a grudge maybe. And the poor teacher who was killed knew too much.'

Ms Rowe nodded. 'That's what I think. It's tragic.'

Eve could do with talking to her woman-to-woman now the formalities were out of the way. Luckily, Simon genuinely liked sport. As Eve took over the conversation, he'd begun to follow the game in progress.

Eve backed off a little, indicating that Ms Rowe should follow her.

'I was wondering about life for the girls here,' Eve said, lowering her voice as though she didn't want Simon to hear. 'I didn't feel I could ask the academic staff. A few of them looked a bit forbidding.'

Sally grinned. 'Their bark's worse than their bite. Discipline here is good, but we really care for our girls. What was it you wanted to know?'

'What happens when they get interested in boys? I imagine a single-sex institution increases the girls' confidence – gives them the chance to shine without being shouted down. But they're very isolated here. And in some ways, it's good to get used to interacting with the opposite sex. Or at least, I think so. I went to a co-ed school.'

'I hear you. I did too. But they're not really so cut off. We have interschool matches and socials.' She raised an eyebrow. 'Carefully policed, of course! But I know some of the girls keep in touch with the boys they've met. Messaging's replaced romantic letters. It can be more intense. But if they have a problem, we have our head of pastoral care, Lucia Leverett. And the girls often come to me too.'

There'd been no change in her tone as she mentioned Lucia's name.

'That's good to know. It's nice to hear they have some of the normal teenage experiences.'

Ms Rowe laughed quietly, glancing at Simon, who was still following the match. 'You're more broad-minded than some of the parents.'

Eve shrugged. 'Just my upbringing.' Did other parents seriously want their kids to be cut off from having fun? She leaned forward. 'It must be hard for the staff too. What's it like, living on site? I think I'd find it difficult. And I can't imagine your social life's all that easy.' She knew she was on thin ice. Even if the woman didn't object to her line of questioning, it might not reveal what she wanted.

'Oh, we do all right.' She was still smiling, and her eyes lit up. 'I see my boyfriend at his place. Bringing him here is an absolute no-no, naturally. I wouldn't want to be a bad influence on the girls. But he's only over in Blyworth.'

'That's good.' She grinned back. 'You look happy.'

'Truth to tell, he's just asked me to marry him. Oh, don't worry,' she added, 'I won't give up my work here. They let married staff live off site if they want. I'll be ready to look after your daughter when she joins us.'

Eve felt a stab of guilt and nodded. 'Lovely.'

As Eve and Simon drifted away from the hockey pitch, and Eve slipped off, into the trees, she reviewed what she'd just heard. She couldn't believe Sally Rowe had been having an affair with Martin Leverett, or that anyone might imagine it to be the case. So why had Lucia made the claim?

42

Eve watched through the trees as Polly rejoined Simon, close to the back of Old Quad. She couldn't believe the plan had worked as easily as it had.

As for the results – they were useful, but they left her with more questions. What were Martin and Lucia playing at? She'd been conscious of their secret looks and clutched hands. They were hiding something. Her mind ran back to her interview with Martin the day before. The way he and his wife had talked to her so openly. Then suddenly, she thought back further – to what had happened before that. The way Martin had jumped when his PA had shown her in. The hasty manner in which he'd stuffed his cravat into his desk drawer. Like a child, caught with sweets he'd pinched from the jar. She ought to have focused on that sooner. Maybe it was nothing, but it was odd.

She carried on her way, but the thought bugged her. She was getting nowhere, and the tiniest thing might be significant. She couldn't afford to ignore any oddity. She was running out of ideas.

If only she could get a look inside Martin's desk...

She was creeping along the outside wall of Old Quad when

a bell rang. She was close to a window and heard chairs scraping. A lesson must be over. Soon, the quads would be thronging with students, rushing from one classroom to another. As she reached an archway leading into Great Quad, she could see them scurrying, clutching folders, focused on their friends or the way ahead.

Eve had had an idea, but if taking Polly's place had seemed risky, this was worse. Without giving herself time to fear the ramifications, she walked briskly through to the quad. If she bumped into someone she recognised she could claim she'd lost a scarf the previous day and come back to look for it. But in fact, she only passed students. They accepted her presence without a second glance. It had been like that when she was in school too. Adults were authority figures and seldom questioned. That could be dangerous, but for Eve it was useful. She walked around the quad, holding her head high. It was hard to look confident when it felt like her stomach had been invaded by snakes, but she did her best. She waited until most of the crowds had disappeared back indoors, the stragglers dashing as another bell sounded.

Eve followed the last of them, thanking the girl who held the door open for her. After that she dropped back. Heard chairs scraping again. A teacher's voice in a classroom close by.

She walked down a corridor towards Southwood's administrative hub. She wanted to be near Martin Leverett's office, but not too close. And she needed somewhere to hide – just temporarily.

At last, she found what she was looking for. A store cupboard, close to a fire alarm. Opening the door, she found it was full of A4 paper and exercise books, but there was space to stand in front of the shelves. She paused for a full minute, knowing the disruption she'd be causing. But this was a double murder, and the police thought Robin was guilty. If getting

access to Martin's office brought a killer to justice, it had to be
the right thing to do.

At last, her heart hammering, she smashed the alarm's glass
case. As she heard a teacher raise her voice above the clam-
ouring bell, Eve ducked into the cupboard and closed the door.
She swallowed. The tiny space was pitch dark now. She just
had to wait and hope to goodness she wasn't discovered. She'd
seen the fire assembly point. It was outside the school in the
direction of the lake where Eliza Gregory's body had been
found. The moment it was quiet in the corridor, she must run to
the headmaster's office and hope he'd neglected to lock the door.
There'd be confusion. No one would know if the fire was
genuine. Eve thought there was a good chance she could get
inside, but she'd have to be quick. It wouldn't be long before
someone was dispatched to check the school. They would find
the smashed alarm and realise it was a hoax.

Eve listened at the door. She could hear teachers call, doors
opening and closing. They'd be checking for stray students. She
held her breath, but no one opened the cupboard.

At last, when there was only silence, she ran.

Her footfalls echoed down the corridors as she went, loud
enough to alert anyone remaining. Her breathing was ragged.
But the place was deserted. The evacuation must have worked
like clockwork. Through a window, she could see people filing
towards the assembly point. She cowered back, close to the
opposite wall.

She was thudding up the final approach to the administrative offices when she saw a door open ahead of her.

She halted. Almost fell. A gowned figure. Martin Leverett.
Had he heard her? Would he turn around?

But he plunged through the outer door at the end of the
corridor to join the other staff. He'd taken his time to leave. It
was lucky for her that he'd ended up rushing to catch up with
his colleagues.

It left Eve with a knot of worry. What had he been doing while the rest of the staff vacated the building?

She let herself into the administrative section with shaking hands and made straight for his door. It was as she'd feared. Whatever else he'd done, he'd locked up. Maybe the alarm had jolted him out of a daydream, just as she and his PA had. Perhaps he'd been holding the cravat. Taken time to stuff it into his drawer. Got up to leave and hesitated, deciding to secure the room.

But why would he hide a piece of his clothing?

Eve stood there on the verge of panic, her heart thudding. Had she caused all this chaos for nothing?

But his PA might have a key. Eve skidded to a halt by the woman's desk and checked her top drawer. Bingo. A set of keys, one of which was labelled 'ML's Office'.

She leaped back to his door, fumbling as she tried to get the key into the lock. At last, she had it open, but through the window she could already see a couple of the teachers looking back towards the building. It wouldn't be long before they came to check inside.

Eve's mouth was as dry as sawdust as she went to Martin Leverett's top drawer. If only that wasn't locked too.

It opened.

Inside, Eve found the silk cravat. It was similar to the one she'd seen Martin wear the day she'd attended the meeting of the coven. It was the smell of it that ramped her heart beat up further. It was faint, but unmistakable. Christian Dior's Poison. The fragrance Natalie had worn. A sign that she'd cuddled up to him while he wore the cravat. But as she angled her head so she could see further into the drawer, the contents made her think again.

There, near the back, was a handbag-sized bottle of the perfume. *Heck, he must have bought some and put it on the cravat himself.* Not too much. He wouldn't want the whole room to smell of it. The action spoke of someone who was well and truly hooked. And underneath the cravat was a photograph of the talk-show host. Someone – she assumed Martin – had screwed it up at some stage. A multitude of tiny creases fractured Natalie's face. But it had been smoothed flat again. Bits of the paper were water damaged. Eve was fairly sure someone had cried over it. And finally, she found a piece of pink notepaper, thick, good quality. The strong, sloping writing was familiar. It matched the inscription on the back of Natalie's blackmail photo.

> *Ignore the papers. The affair with Calvin is nonsense. I can't wait to see you again. I told you, you're the one I want. N xxx*

Eve snatched a cautious glance through the window. Staff were on the move. There was no time. She took a quick photo of the drawer's contents, then closed it and backed out, relocking the door, her shallow breathing making her dizzy.

Quivering, she replaced the keys and slammed the PA's drawer shut. She avoided the corridor Martin Leverett had used to leave, running towards the main entrance instead.

Thank goodness the fire assembly point was around the corner from the front door. But she could hear voices. Any one of the teachers might come round to check the building.

Eve ran for it, fighting to control her breath.

43

'You look rattled.' It was lunchtime. Viv sat opposite Eve at their favourite table in the Cross Keys, her head on one side. 'But Simon said the whole thing went like clockwork.'

Eve sipped her St Clements. She needed the sugar. 'It did. I rang to thank him and Polly when I got home. I hate to say it, but Polly liked the school.'

Viv shuddered. 'She would. But don't worry. I'll tell her all about my time there. If they have children, I'm determined they won't go through what I did.'

'You liked it enough to stay.'

'True, but the cookery equipment is past its prime these days. So, tell me what you found out then.'

Eve related her whole visit, from hearing about Sally Rowe's fiancé to smelling Natalie's perfume on Martin's cravat.

'Wow,' Viv breathed, as Eve took a spoonful of her celeriac and pancetta soup.

'I can't quite believe I set the alarm off and searched Martin's desk.' Eve had been questioning herself. 'It was a huge invasion of privacy.' She doubted she'd have done it if Robin's future hadn't been at stake.

Viv waved aside her worries as she took a forkful of risotto. 'Needs must and all that. And look at what you got out of it. Martin's been hiding a massive secret.'

'True. But it's taken me an hour to calm down. Gus had to walk me round Blind Eye Wood while I got my feelings in order.' He was over by the window with Hetty now. They were being unusually well behaved.

'You think Martin was in love with Natalie?' Viv asked, taking a swig of her Coke.

Eve paused for thought. 'I certainly think he felt passionately about her. If he's the one who crushed her photograph, it looks as though his feelings tipped one way then the other. Love and hate. I can imagine Natalie toying with him. She was very attractive, and determined to get her own way.'

Eve spread some butter on her bread roll. She still felt in need of strength.

'So does it help? Might he have killed her?'

'Quite possibly, I'd say. And it does help. Certain things I couldn't fathom are coming together.'

'Such as?'

'When I overheard Natalie slap Martin in the library, I assumed she was reacting to something Lucia had told her, and Martin confirmed that. He said Lucia had confided in Natalie about his supposed affair with the gym mistress. Yet Lucia implied it was Natalie who'd needed help, the night they talked. She said she was on the verge of making a decision that would have led to disaster and she'd steered her away from it. I had a strong sense each of them was telling the truth, but I didn't see how that could be true. There was no sign of an affair between Martin and Sally Rowe, and it looked like Natalie who was providing a listening ear.'

Viv frowned as she swallowed her rice and squash. 'And today solves that?'

'I think so. I suspect Lucia found out Martin had fallen for

Natalie. She voted against her for Founders' Day Champion, naturally. The position meant she'd visit even more often. But that didn't work, so when she arrived, I think Lucia spun her a line about a fictitious affair between Martin and Sally Rowe, to try to drive a wedge between them.'

'So saving Natalie from doing something disastrous was saving her from breaking up Lucia's marriage?'

'It's the only explanation I can find that fits. It seems clear Lucia lied about Martin and Sally Rowe. Why else would she do that? And why confide in a woman she clearly disliked?' So much made sense now. All that time Natalie had spent talking to Martin about school policy. Tucked away in an office together. 'My guess is Natalie believed Lucia, and was furious with Martin for going after someone else. She wanted to be in control, not him. It was essential for her to keep the upper hand. I don't imagine she was in love, but everyone says she liked winning. She wouldn't want Martin to know his behaviour had got to her.'

'So she pretended she was only angry on Lucia's behalf?'

Eve nodded. 'But the slap shows she was livid. She'd have wanted Martin dangling, waiting, hoping for her. Him going off with another woman was more than she could stand.'

'That figures. So, what do you think happened next?'

'There seem to be a number of options. Maybe, despite their argument during Founders' Day, Martin and Natalie made up. He was clearly smitten, and she wanted him to want her. The letter in his drawer proves that. Perhaps Lucia heard him arrange to meet her and knew the story about Sally Rowe hadn't been enough. Natalie had been needling her, worming her way into her household. Giving her children presents to win them over. She must have felt acutely threatened and she didn't know Natalie was dying. Natalie could have hung around for years, trying to break them up, as far as she was concerned. So, perhaps Lucia clubbed her to death in the hidden room.' Eve sipped her drink. 'Or maybe Martin suddenly saw the other side of Natalie and decided to pull back to save his marriage. Only Natalie already had proof of his infidelity and decided to exercise her power. Perhaps she threatened to reveal their relationship to the coven, the whole school, or even on prime-time TV.'

'Blimey. His motive's huge.'

'Potentially. So he could have killed her. Either way, since her death, it's almost as if there's some extra bond between him and Lucia. They were singing from the same hymn sheet when they told me the story about Sally Rowe. And I've seen them clutching each other's hands. It's like they're clinging on for strength.'

'You think one of them knows the other's guilty?'

'And that they set up the scene in the library after Natalie's death.' Eve nodded. 'It looks as though Martin's feelings towards her were very confused. If Lucia killed her, I think it's entirely possible he's forgiven her. He might almost feel relieved. Maybe he sees things more objectively now – realises what he might have lost, and that Lucia and his daughters are more important than Natalie. Though her photo and his cravat show his muddled feelings. Accentuated by guilt maybe. Especially if he did it. If so, I could imagine Lucia standing by him too. Setting up the false alibi would fit. Bits of it were well acted – Martin seeing "Natalie" through the window and starting. Then hesitating in the doorway like a nervous lover. But right from the start it seemed odd that the fake Natalie was standing in the window like a display.'

Viv shivered. 'So what's the plan?'

'I need to challenge Martin. I called him just after I spoke to Simon – said I had a couple of extra questions for Natalie's obituary. He didn't sound keen. I know they all wonder why I'm spending so much time at the school. And they're aware I've contributed to police investigations before. He's definitely jumpy. But I told him I was almost done. That seemed to smooth the way.' She thought of Robin's instructions not to walk into danger. 'At least we'll meet in his office, surrounded by other staff. If I unnerve him, he won't be able to do anything.'

Viv nodded. 'Sounds good. What time are you on?'

'Later this afternoon.'

'Excellent. I've got another job for you first.'

Eve raised an eyebrow.

'Don't be angry, but Sabina, Anastasia and Bridget have joined forces to try to unlock the case.'

'Why would I be angry?'

'Sabina wants you to go round for coffee after lunch to tell them all you know. They know you've been investigating.'

'Heck. This isn't ideal, Viv.'

'I know. Please don't be strict. You know how hard it is to say no to Sabina.' She made an attempt to look contrite. 'I can come with you and hold your hand. And you don't have to tell them anything.'

'They can't know what I've just told you. Bridget's hardly going to let me see Martin again if she knows I think he's guilty.'

'Point taken.'

'Who have they got their eye on?'

Viv grimaced.

'Don't tell me. I can guess.' Robin would be the scapegoat they were all hoping for.

They got up to leave. 'I'll give you a lift,' Viv said. 'Special treat.'

If you liked being driven by someone who seemed averse to looking out of the windscreen...

'It's all right. I'll take my car. I'll need to go back to Southwood after we've finished. I can drop you off then carry on. No point in switching vehicles.'

Viv shrugged. 'Okay.'

As she unlocked her Clubman, Eve saw Viv glance over her shoulder.

'Did you know that guy who sat behind you at the pub?'

'I don't know. If he was behind me, I probably didn't see him.'

'He's just over there now.'

Eve turned in time to see half of a bulky guy with grizzled grey hair climbing into a van. She never saw his face.

'What made you think I might know him?'

'He kept glancing at us. When I caught his eye, he looked away. I thought I'd maybe got an admirer.' She smiled for a moment and glanced in the mirror as she slid into the passenger seat. 'My hair's turning heads this season. But when he went to the bar, I thought maybe it was you he was looking at.'

Eve felt heat rush over her. He couldn't have been giving her the eye. He wouldn't have seen her face until he got to the bar. So what was he up to?

She thought of the man Robin had seen lurking in Blind Eye Wood. A moment later, she wrote down the number plate of the van.

'What are you doing?'

Eve handed her the notepad. 'Can you write a description of what he looked like, and what you saw him do? Best add the time, too.'

Viv looked at her strangely and Eve wondered if she should finally tell her the truth about Robin. But it wasn't the right time.

'It might be related to the case,' she said at last. 'It's best to gather all the information while it's fresh in your mind.'

Viv laughed. 'All right. I know how you love details.'

44

Eve and Viv sat in a sitting room that was just as stiff and forbidding as its owner. Sabina had brought in a tray of tea – pouring it into cups that didn't hold enough to hit the spot. Viv had already spilled half of hers into her saucer, to a look of utter disgust from her mother-in-law.

Bridget Leverett and Anastasia had arrived before them, and were perched on antique sofas. ('Made before they invented comfort,' Viv had said in an almost-whisper as they sat down. Sabina had darted her a warning look.)

Outside, at the back of the house, Eve could see Robin. She knew he did the Montagues' garden but it was somehow still a surprise to find him there. It felt like enemy territory. He wiped his brow, almost as though he could feel the pressure, and pulled off his hat, chucking it behind him somewhere.

'I see you didn't cancel him then.' Bridget Leverett's eyes were on Robin too.

'They say keep your friends close and your enemies closer. I'd rather watch him. He might give something away.'

'It seems a bit strong to call him an enemy,' Anastasia said. 'We don't know he's guilty of anything.'

'Well, you discontinued his employment at Southwood. You must view him in the same light.'

'I didn't like doing it.' The bursar frowned. 'I felt I had to. When something shocking happens, the school has a duty to batten down the hatches. I know it's what the parents would expect, and the police are interested in him. But I didn't like acting in such a knee-jerk way.' She stood up. 'I'm going to go and apologise to him. Explain my reasoning.'

Sabina's lips thinned but Bridget nodded.

'It's no bad thing if he talks to Anastasia. We can't get information sitting in here.'

Eve tried to breathe evenly and pretend not to see Viv, who'd been shooting her sympathetic looks. It was a kind thought, but she was making it rather obvious.

'We should search for clues too,' Sabina said. 'Anastasia's the only one who saw the room where Natalie died. I gather the police have finished with it now. We should go and look.'

Sabina offered Eve a fondant fancy, which was the last thing she felt like. Her stomach was churning. Through the window, she could see Robin nodding to Anastasia. He managed a smile, though Eve imagined he'd prefer to be left alone.

'So, Eve,' Sabina said, as Anastasia reappeared, 'I expect Viv has told you why you're here. We're pooling resources. The longer this goes on, the worse it is for the school. I've lost a friend, and Anastasia a niece. What have you found out?'

She could never join the diplomatic corps. 'I'm still looking into the situation. I haven't reached any firm conclusions.' Her mind was on Martin and Lucia. 'What about you? What ideas have you had?'

'No firm ideas, I'm afraid,' Anastasia said, 'but a possible piece of evidence. I think I was followed on Monday night.'

Eve felt heat rush to her face and her breathing change. She knew Viv was looking at her but didn't dare look back. 'Where were you going?'

She laughed. 'Just on one of my nightly walkabouts. I don't need much sleep and I love Southwood after dark. I tend to stroll around the grounds and think about the day's events. Plan for what's coming next – that type of thing. Sometimes I go into the chapel for some quiet time.'

Eve's mouth had gone dry. She took a sip of tea, trying to eke it out. 'And you saw someone follow you? Or did someone tell you you were followed?' She thought of the additional figure Robin had seen on her tail. Someone in a gown.

'I saw them myself. I don't suppose anyone else was around to witness it.'

Eve had had no inkling she'd been spotted. 'You've no idea who it was?'

She frowned. 'I wondered about a student. They were small, slender.'

Bridget dashed her cup down in its saucer. 'You surely don't think a Southwood girl killed Natalie.'

'I'm not saying this person killed her. But I'd like to know why they followed me.'

'It sounds like a distraction,' Bridget said. 'We should focus on the murderer. The gardener's by far the most likely.'

'We have to face facts, Bridget,' Anastasia said. 'We're not just looking for one person, are we? If Robin Yardley – he has a name, you know – is guilty, he had an accomplice. The man or woman who pretended to be Natalie in the library. It would have to be someone who really minds about him. Someone who's prepared to risk everything to protect him.'

'And you think—' Sabina spluttered and slopped her tea just like Viv had. 'You think Robin Yardley might have... formed an attachment with a sixth former and they worked together?'

'I'm not saying anything of the kind. The person who

followed me might have been a member of staff. It was too dark
to tell, and they wore a hat. I only wish I'd challenged them.'

'Why on earth didn't you?' Sabina was all sympathy as
usual.

Anastasia hesitated, a frown furrowing her brow. 'Truth to
tell, I was a little bit scared. It was a couple of days after Natalie
was killed. I went inside the chapel and said a prayer or two to a
god I don't believe in.'

She shrugged helplessly and Bridget tutted.

'When I peered outside, the person had gone.'

'We need to find out if the gardener's been seeing someone,'
Bridget said. 'Ask the staff and students. The person concerned
won't come forward, of course, but someone might have noticed
something. We should check the grounds too. If someone's been
snooping, they might have dropped something.'

Eve's breathing grew shallower. She wondered if she'd left
any evidence behind on her secret visits to the school. And if
anyone had seen her with Robin or Simon. At least they'd know
she wasn't one of the silhouettes. Thank goodness she, Anastasia and Viv had witnessed them together. But her stomach
knotted tighter still.

45

Eve dropped Viv back outside Monty's and paused by the village green to text Robin. By the time she drew up at South-wood, ready for her interview with Martin, he'd texted back, saying it was safe to call. She rang him from her car. It took her a few minutes to relay the latest news.

'*Eve, you have to be careful,*' he said when she'd finished. '*What you did this morning was incredibly risky. Brave, and fruitful, but dangerous. It's true, Palmer can't pin being one of the silhouettes on you, but if he gets evidence we're together and you've been snooping, he might decide you've been protecting me. It would make you an accessory. He'd love to send us down.*'

Eve's chest felt heavy.

'*I understand you'll carry on interviewing people, but your questions must be about Natalie, not the investigation. From now on, if you suspect someone, call Greg. He'll manage to investigate somehow, whatever Palmer says. Promise me you'll play by the rules.*'

Eve hesitated. 'I promise.' She didn't want to take risks any more than he did, but she didn't know what was around the corner. 'Robin, Viv thinks someone was unduly interested in me in the Cross Keys. A bulky man with grizzled grey hair.'

'*Oh no...*'

'I was worried you'd say that. She noted his description and I got the plate of the van he was driving. I'm going to take it to Greg in the library the minute I've interviewed Martin Leverett. Don't worry. I won't say anything in front of Palmer or the wider team.'

'*Thanks.*' She heard him take a deep breath. '*Eve, I don't think we can meet until this is sorted out.*'

Her heart plummeted. The mystery at Southwood might be resolved in the next few weeks, but the man with the grizzled grey hair had been elusive so far, and he wasn't giving up. How could they manage a relationship if they weren't allowed to see each other? Fear for Robin's safety made her legs feel like jelly. If they stayed apart, it wouldn't be Eve the man targeted. He'd give up, and go for Robin himself.

'*He might have spotted you near my place,*' Robin was saying, all his focus on her, '*but I doubt he's got proof that we're seeing each other.*'

'I'd rather take the risk. I hate the idea of being apart.'

She could hear the catch in his voice as he answered, mirroring hers. '*I'm so sorry. I just can't let you do it. If you keep your distance, you should be safe. I'm going to call Greg too. Ask him to keep an eye on you. At least the police are still on site at Southwood. Please be careful. I love you.*'

Eve had to fight the tears pricking her eyes. 'I love you too.'

Five minutes later, Eve was inside Martin Leverett's office.

'Thanks so much for seeing me again. I hope it's not a bad time. You sounded hesitant when I called.'

'I'm sorry. We had a disrupted morning. Someone set the fire alarm off; their idea of a practical joke, presumably, but we don't need it at the moment. Everyone's nerves are torn to shreds.'

He picked at the leather inlay in his desk, his jaw tense.

'Of course. I'm sorry.' She hoped the entire school wouldn't get detention for what she'd done.

'You had some extra questions?'

She wanted to face him with what she'd surmised about his relationship with Natalie. See his reaction. If he'd killed over it, it ought to show in his eyes.

'Mr Leverett. Martin. You must believe me, I won't put this in my obituary. But I want to ask you about it because it will shed light on Natalie's character. I've heard a rumour that you and she... well, that you were close.'

The head teacher shook his head, like a shudder almost, but his cheeks flushed, and he looked down. 'What? Who on earth told you that?'

'I'm afraid I can't say.' She sure as heck wasn't going to admit she'd gone through his desk drawer that morning. 'But they were completely certain.'

He was gaping at her now.

'And it would fit with her regular visits to you and all the quiet chats you had. She might have talked about policy, but it meant the two of you were repeatedly alone together.' She paused, feeling her way. 'You said Lucia told Natalie you were having an affair with Sally Rowe, but it was all a misunderstanding. But I don't believe Lucia's the sort to spread rumours without checking they're true. Especially not about something so personal. I think she was desperate to drive a wedge between you and Natalie. She must have been convinced Natalie was intent on breaking up your marriage. And it looks that way to me too.' In reality, it took two to tango. Martin was just as responsible as Natalie was. But his motivation might be less cruel. 'It reflects on her character,' Eve added. 'I ought to convey that in the obituary, though I'd never mention specifics.'

She doubted he'd buy her reasons for asking.

'Natalie could certainly be flirtatious,' Martin said at last. 'But you won't need my testimony to tell you that. Her behaviour was all over the papers.' He was driving his nail into the beautiful, polished wood of his desk now. 'If only that had come out before we voted her in as Founders' Day Champion. There was no bond between us. Your informant must be motivated by malice.'

She'd have known he was lying even if she hadn't seen the contents of his desk drawer. He could have killed her out of frustration. She was sure he'd been obsessed. Temporarily at least. And even now Natalie was dead, the obsession wasn't quite over.

Eve looked pointedly at Martin's hand. He was still damaging his desk.

He stopped immediately. 'Natalie and I never slept together, if that's what you're implying.' His eyes were steady on hers. 'It's a very stressful time at the moment. And being head is always challenging. I've felt it, being the first male to hold the role. But I haven't looked for solace from anyone but Lucia. My mother suffered similarly as the first non-founding family principal. I think she'd have been happier elsewhere, in a less senior role, not that she'd ever admit it. The offer of a headship was simply too tempting. If we'd moved, we wouldn't be in the centre of this mess.'

46

After Eve left Martin's office, she stood looking out onto Great Quad from an empty corridor, thinking. She felt as though she was knocking her head against a brick wall. She wasn't sure what she'd been hoping for – perhaps that Martin would be shocked into confessing. She could see how close to the edge he was. If he was innocent, would he really be that tense?

Her hunch was that Martin had told the truth about not sleeping with Natalie. And now she thought about it, it made sense. The bottle of perfume he'd kept in his drawer made him seem like a desperate would-be lover. Someone making do with keepsakes. But Natalie had visited often. Spent time with him. And Lucia had been convinced she was a danger. Eve had thought and thought about her actions, but an attempt to drive a wedge between Martin and Natalie was the only thing that fitted. And Natalie's note showed she wanted to keep him onside. She'd told him reports of her affair were rubbish. It was Martin that she wanted.

He was hooked – horribly tempted, but holding back. And she was pushing, wheedling, sure she'd win him over. She knew he wanted her.

Might he have slept with Natalie by now if she hadn't been killed? He'd been stiff and formal when she turned up. Still smarting from the reports of her affair, Eve guessed. And she'd been furious at the thought of him sleeping with Sally Rowe. The slap proved that. But she could imagine them making it up. Arranging to meet in the hidden room. She could have been working away at him, and if so, he must have been tempted. He wouldn't have voted for her as champion otherwise.

Eve went outside and made her way around the quad towards the library. She shivered as the cold air hit her; the temperature had dropped since she'd entered the school. She was partway to her destination when she saw Sabina, Bridget and Anastasia appear from the tunnel that led to Old Quad.

'I can't believe no one told me,' Bridget was saying as their paths crossed. 'We need to get the carpet replaced immediately. It's disgusting.' She had a hand to her forehead.

'No one ever goes up there,' Anastasia said. 'Or they shouldn't. I fully agree it needs doing, but it's been thoroughly cleaned, and other things have taken precedence.'

Sabina shook her head as Bridget replied. 'It's the principle of the thing. When I heard it was the blow which killed her, I assumed she'd had some sort of internal haemorrhage, not that... not that...'

Eve could fill in the blanks. Not that Natalie's head had been turned to pulp. Someone must have cleaned up but the carpet would be stained forever.

One step forward. Unless Bridget was a very good actor, she hadn't killed Natalie. Eve was convinced she hadn't seen her body.

The three women swept past, Sabina looking irritably at Eve, though she'd told them she needed to be there that afternoon before she'd left.

She put her hand on the notepad inside her bag as she neared the library door. She peered through the windows of the grand room. Greg was there, as well as Olivia Dawkins and a couple of other constables. Palmer was absent, which was all to the good. She pushed the swing door open and went inside.

'Ms Mallow.' Greg was all formality. 'How can we help?'

She glanced quickly at the others present. Olivia Dawkins was nearest but she moved away at Eve's look. She was a hundred times more tactful than Palmer. Not that he set the bar high.

'Please, take a seat.' Greg motioned her to a chair opposite him at the desk he'd commandeered.

Eve handed over her notes and explained their significance in an undertone.

Greg nodded. 'It's useless to say don't worry, but I'm in direct contact with London.' His voice was low too. 'We're doing everything we can.'

'You think it's significant?'

'This description matches the one we've been working with.'

'He's a big fish?'

Greg's eyes were sympathetic. 'Try not to worry.'

The lack of a proper response sent her adrenaline levels into orbit. She put her head back and closed her eyes for a moment. When she opened them, she saw the huge silver cup she'd noticed on Founders' Day, when she'd looked above Natalie's head. Some kind of sports trophy, she guessed.

At that moment, she heard a familiar pompous voice behind her.

'Boles. I need you.'

Palmer.

'Ms Mallow, I don't know what you're doing here but I'm quite sure you've taken enough of DS Boles's time.' He was standing next to her. Greg was on his feet. Palmer added in an undertone: 'We need to make an arrest. And be quick about it.'

Greg raised an eyebrow.

'The gardener. New information. Come along.'

Greg's eyes flitted to Eve's for a moment, but Palmer was already leaving and he had to follow.

Eve felt sick. She wanted to chase after them – call Robin. Warn him what was coming. But Olivia Dawkins bustled up to her.

'I'm sorry. Had you finished? Is there anything I can do?'

'I don't think so, thanks.' She left the library and dialled Robin's number, but the call went to voicemail. 'Please ring me, Robin,' she said. 'I was just in the library when Palmer came in. He's on his way to pick you up.'

If the police checked Robin's phone records, they'd know she'd warned him, but she was past caring. Nothing mattered if she couldn't get at the truth. As she rang off, it started to rain.

She stood there in the damp feeling utterly helpless, with no idea which way to turn. Should she admit to Olivia Dawkins what she'd found in Martin Leverett's drawer that morning? But it didn't prove he'd killed Natalie and it might just make her look desperate – as though she was trying to protect Robin. It could play to the narrative he'd warned her about. Perhaps it was better to keep her powder dry until it was essential to use her secret knowledge. At least she'd taken photos.

She looked back through the library window again, unde-cided, thinking of the silhouettes she'd seen there, the night of Natalie's murder.

Her eyes rose again to the sports trophy. She remembered thinking how close to the edge it looked on Founders' Day. Imagining it dropping on Natalie's head as she gave her speech. Bringing a dramatic end to the interminable proceedings.

Then suddenly her mind focused. It didn't look that close to the edge today. Was it to do with the angle from which she was viewing it? She thought about where she'd been sitting. But no, that made no sense.

The cup was simply further back on the shelf than it had

been.

She paused, caught in thought. Surely no one made a habit of dusting up there. You'd have to use a ladder, and no one would notice your efforts. She could imagine someone polishing the trophy before Founders' Day, but not afterwards. There'd been a lot going on.

She took a deep breath and went back into the library again.

Olivia Dawkins smiled at her, as if she had all the time in the world, and only Eve to focus on. 'You've thought of something else?'

Eve explained what she'd noticed, knowing it sounded weird. This was confirmed when she caught one of the other constables who'd been left behind pointing his finger at his temple and winding it round to imply she had a screw loose. She fixed him with a stare and he turned hastily away.

Eve focused on DC Dawkins again. 'We know someone was in here pretending to be Natalie to put everyone off the scent. And I'm certain the trophy on that shelf has moved since Founders' Day. I wonder if the two facts might be related.'

'It's a reasonable question,' Dawkins said, with a look at the constable, who'd just tutted. 'And it's easy enough to check.'

Eve could have hugged her. There was a library ladder in the room. She watched as Dawkins climbed up. She had to stand right at the top to reach the alcove. Eve hoped to goodness she didn't fall. It looked precarious.

'Do you want me to do it?' the sceptical constable asked.

Dawkins didn't bother replying. She focused on the trophy as she pulled a pair of gloves from her pocket. A moment later, she was stretching for it. She could only just reach and it looked heavy. Eve resisted the urge to offer help too. For a moment, she watched as Dawkins stood on tiptoe, her fingertips inside the trophy's rim. She edged it forward, and managed to grasp the handles at last.

Pulling it towards her, she lifted it down. 'Well, well, well.'

47

Olivia Dawkins carried the heavy trophy down the library steps with a lot more poise than Eve would have managed. At the bottom, she placed it on the table and took out two large evidence bags, ready to receive the contents.

She pulled them out one by one. One long wig, and one faux leather jacket, with square shoulders. It looked a lot less expensive than the genuine article Natalie had worn, but its style was a good match. The wig had been carefully chosen too. Whoever had worn it had had time to plan.

Dawkins got the evidence safely stowed then turned to the other officer. 'Call the chief and let him know.'

After that, she took a statement from Eve, explaining the background to the discovery.

It was all Eve could do to answer coherently. Private thoughts spun in her head, and the process with Dawkins seemed to take forever. Her heart rate ramped up as the urgency she felt bubbled inside her chest. The fact was, this discovery didn't help. They already knew someone had dressed up as Natalie. They might get a DNA match if they found the wearer's hair inside the wig, but only if their DNA was on file.

And Robin still hadn't called back. Palmer was bound to have reached his cottage by now.

She needed more evidence, right that minute. The day was wearing on, the light fading. But mixed with her drive to do something was a feeling of helplessness. She had no idea where to aim her efforts.

Dawkins was smiling. 'All done. And thank you – this could be very useful.'

Eve tried to look pleased as she said goodbye and left the library, walking into Great Quad where the rain still fell. Students were dashing for cover – presumably lessons and clubs had finished for the day. Before long they'd be going in to supper. To her right through a window she saw the coven, plus Bridget Leverett. They were probably making their way to the staff common room for pre-dinner drinks. She had no excuse to join them, but she didn't want to leave. She couldn't solve a mystery that was centred around Southwood from her cottage miles away. Her hair was getting wet and a trickle of water snaked its way between her neck and collar, making her shiver again. She hadn't brought an umbrella.

She paused, uncertain what she should do.

At last, she decided to bide her time, but she mustn't be spotted. She could take a leaf out of Anastasia's book and sit in the chapel. She ought to have it to herself, while everyone followed their evening ritual.

She put her head down against the wind and rain and walked through the tunnel that led to Old Quad, then beyond to the chapel itself.

Despite having seen the coven heading in the opposite direction, she opened the old oak door slowly. The wind made it too noisy to hear if there was anyone inside. But the place was shadowy, in near darkness, and silent once she entered. She texted Robin to let him know where she was, told him she loved him and that she'd gone there to think things over.

It took a moment to find the light switches. The first one she tried illuminated the side chapel, creating a welcoming glow in the darkness. She decided to leave it at that. She didn't want the place lit up like a beacon. She just needed time to work out who to talk to next – or who to follow. She was already going against Robin's instructions, but she couldn't call Greg for help. He was busy arresting him while she stood by, uselessly doing nothing. And if she gave up, Robin might be tried and convicted. The person who'd planted his ring in Natalie's room was out to frame him. They might have other tricks up their sleeve.

She walked slowly over to the side chapel, in a daze, but a moment later she'd sat down on one of the hard polished benches, taken out her notebook and shaken herself. She had to focus. She needed to go back to the details she'd discovered – every little thing. The answer might be staring her in the face if she ordered her facts the right way.

She started off by adding the discovery of the wig and faux leather jacket to her notes, then tried to stay calm as she reread everything, starting with the silhouettes she, Viv and Anastasia had seen. She needed to piece together what must have happened after the unknown pair embraced.

The fake Natalie had taken off her wig and jacket, climbed the ladder at the back of the library and stuffed them into the trophy.

Even though it was hard to reach.

Goosebumps rose on Eve's arms. She'd been wrong. The discovery wasn't irrelevant. If you were going into the library dressed as a recently deceased woman to give yourself a false alibi, why ditch the costume before you left again? It had been fully dark, and that area of the quad deserted. You'd be seen, but only from a distance. And you'd want people to notice you. Surely when you left the library, you'd need people to carry on seeing you as Natalie. Seeing a different person leave would ruin the whole thing. It was a needless risk.

So why go to such lengths to hide the disguise?

She wrote the question down and frowned, sifting through other related notes. The person who'd gone to meet fake Natalie had looked over their shoulder before entering the building. To check no one was following them, seemingly. And yet, if they'd also been trying to create a false alibi, they'd want to be seen.

And the question remained, why hide the costume? It was almost as though the person acting as Natalie had had a change of heart. And a sudden one. But what might have caused that? The only dramatic event Eve knew of that evening was Natalie's death.

At the very edge of her mind, tiny strands of ideas were flying in the wind. Little hints of another way of reading what she'd seen, if she could just weave them together...

What if...? But no, it didn't make sense.

She shook her head. Nothing made sense. She forced herself to run with the new idea. What if it *was* Natalie's murder that caused fake Natalie to ditch her costume? There was only one way she could have heard about it after she'd dressed up: if the person who joined her knew Natalie was dead and told her so.

Icy shivers ran over Eve's body. It would explain the way the second person had stopped so suddenly when they saw what appeared to be Natalie's outline at the window. If they knew Natalie was dead, it would have been like seeing a ghost. And they'd stopped on the doorstep of the library too – hesitated for what felt like ages. Not the actions of a nervous lover perhaps, but of someone presented with a frightening and perplexing mystery. Of seeing someone you thought was gone, standing in a room in front of you.

But if fake Natalie hadn't known real Natalie was dead until the person entering the library told her, why had she imitated her? It couldn't have been for an alibi...

And then it all came to Eve, with horrible clarity. How could she have overlooked such an obvious alternative explanation?

Lucia was jealous of Natalie. She'd told her Martin was having a fling with the gym mistress but he'd denied it furiously. He'd probably convinced her, once they'd had the chance to calm down. The accusation was untrue, and he was hooked on Natalie mentally, even if he hadn't crossed the final physical line. And she wanted him to want her. If – as he said – he hadn't slept with her yet, she'd want the conquest. Eve thought of her motivation. She'd hated Southwood – sleeping with the headmaster then publicising it nationally could have brought the school crashing down. Martin and his family would be caught in the crossfire. Everything destroyed. Eve knew how driven Natalie had been. She wouldn't have given up. And she was running out of time. If she wanted to make an impact, it was now or never. So it was likely she and Martin had made up, after she'd slapped him on Founders' Day.

Lucia might have challenged her husband about his feelings, but if he denied it, it would have been stalemate. She couldn't make threats or issue ultimatums if he hadn't owned up. She'd want proof he'd fallen for Natalie – something to put her in control.

So what might she do? Dress up as Natalie, and hang around in the window of the library, knowing Martin would pass by and be drawn in? It was the sort of time he'd likely appear to join the coven for drinks in the common room. So she'd made her plan to catch him red-handed. He might bluster when he went in, make excuses, but Eve imagined shock would rob him of a suitable explanation, especially if he spoke before he realised he'd been tricked. His tone would have said it all.

But if Eve's theory was right, Martin had known Natalie was dead. That was why he'd acted as he did before entering the library. He must have thrown himself on Lucia's mercy, admitted what he'd done. Told her to get rid of the costume which would make them look guilty as heck if anyone caught her wearing it. They hadn't planned to fake an alibi – were too scared to see how helpful it might be. They must have left the building as quietly as they could and come to join the gathering in the common room for drinks. And ever since, they'd been supporting each other.

Eve made herself pause. Did the theory really hold water? Why would Martin kill Natalie? Perhaps, despite what he said, they'd finally made love in the hidden room, and he'd realised the mistake he'd made. It would have given her total control over his marriage, his future, and the future of the school. If he'd told her he'd made a mistake maybe she'd taunted him with that. Rubbed his nose in his children finding out – along with every prospective and current Southwood parent. She liked power and she hated the school. But something still niggled in the back of Eve's mind.

Coming to, Eve noticed her surroundings again. All was still and quiet in the chapel. She got up for a moment to peer out of a window towards the school, but nothing moved.

Back in her seat, she realised she was next to a plaque dedicated to the memory of Anthony Leverett, Bridget's husband and Martin's father. Bursar of Southwood School for ten years. Until his death five years earlier, when Anastasia took over. She must have moved straight into his office when he died. She remembered Lucia saying it felt like a familiar place to Martin. So many of his father's things were there still. Anastasia had put her mark on the room too, though. There was her collection of knick-knacks in the green bowl. The decorated pebble and the token, given to her by the true love that hadn't worked out. And there'd been the pipe-cleaner doll, a present from Ada.

Thoughts of the current bursar brought her back to her notes about the silhouettes in the library. Anastasia had been pretty sure the man who'd entered wasn't Martin and she knew him well. Maybe Eve was wrong. But she couldn't think of another pairing who'd fit so neatly. So maybe Anastasia was in error. Could she be that sure, really? The figures had been at a distance.

And then she identified the niggle about Martin. Natalie's killer had taken the murder weapon with them. There'd been no blunt instrument kept in the hidden room. It hadn't been a spur of the moment killing. Martin couldn't have attacked her after making love up there, then regretting it. And leaving that aside, his actions didn't make sense if he was guilty. If he'd realised she was intent on destroying him, he'd hardly still cling to the cravat he'd anointed with her perfume.

In a panic, she went back to her notebook. The answer had to be there somewhere.

48

There were so many details, but which were relevant? She focused on Martin. What if he'd found Natalie's body – because he was due to meet her perhaps – but hadn't killed her himself? Just like Scarlett, he could have been caught up in her death by accident. It was a coincidence, but it sounded possible.

Martin could still have been the second silhouette in the library. Anastasia might have claimed the figure had the wrong gait to protect him. Lucia had said he and the bursar were close. He found it easy to talk to her. Eve had wondered if that made Bridget jealous.

Once again, she thought of the poor relationship between Martin's mother and Anastasia. Anastasia said her reforming zeal had made her champion Bridget for head. It didn't matter that it was Bridget's husband who was descended from a founder, not her. They ought to employ the best woman for the job.

Yet Bridget hadn't been well suited to the position, according to Sabina. She couldn't think why she'd been chosen. Even Martin had said something similar.

Eve flipped through the pages of her notebook. Bridget

would have left to take an alternative role if Anastasia hadn't intervened.

Yet she had – despite the coolness between them, and Bridget's shortcomings.

And then suddenly, Eve felt a wave of chilly goosebumps travel over her. Disparate bits of information flew together like filings drawn by a magnet. Her cheeks felt hot. Underlying what had happened was a secret. A secret that made everything clear.

The entire family would have moved away if Bridget hadn't become head. That was important.

And Anastasia's words about Anthony. She flipped through her notebook again and found her record of the meeting. *Everyone fell for him,* she'd said. *He was tremendously good-looking and the nicest man you could hope to meet.*

Then Anastasia's recollections of his reaction to Eliza's poem. *He didn't take it badly. He felt very sorry for Eliza and worried about it for a long time afterwards.*

Yet Bridget had said – she checked her notes – *I have no idea whether it bothered him or not.*

Anthony had confided in Anastasia, not his wife.

Of course, she was well known as a calm, practical presence, but there was one more thing that came back to Eve now. An image of the love token she'd seen in Anastasia's office. Decorated with a baby rabbit and a stubby-looking bird.

Why hadn't she seen it? Not a baby rabbit, but a baby *hare* – a leveret. A play on Anthony's surname. And the bird... How could Eve not have noticed, with her love of nature? She was sure now that it was meant to be a twite – a type of finch. A dumpy little thing, with its stubby bill and long tail.

She'd noted what Anastasia said about it. She noted everything. *The token was a present from an old boyfriend. A bit twee, I know. We adored each other but our timing was terrible. It still makes me happy to have it there.*

It represented her and Anthony, together forever. He'd been married when he came to Southwood, with a young son, but she'd never stopped loving him. And he'd loved her, judging by the token. Anastasia surrounded herself with his old belongings, cared for his son, his wife and their children.

Eve looked again at the man's memorial tablet on the side chapel wall. Was he the reason Anastasia came there? Had it been him she was talking to and not the god she didn't believe in?

As she sat there, she imagined Anastasia, the calm presence who even Lucia and Natalie talked to, getting wind of Natalie's designs on Martin. She'd have seen the urgency. Natalie was dying. If she was going to create mayhem, she'd have wanted to act now. So Anastasia had too. Natalie's speech at Founders' Day came back to her. She'd said it for all to hear. *Who can resist those wonderful Leverett looks?* She'd been full of gleeful anticipation at the destruction she could cause. How frightened Anastasia would have been for Martin and his young family. All that was left of her beloved Anthony. She minded about Southwood too, but Eve was pretty sure that was secondary.

Eve got up. She needed to get out of there. Call Greg. Make him listen. She dialled as she went.

Anastasia might have known Martin planned to meet Natalie in the hidden room. If she'd tried to warn him, he'd probably reassured her – told her she was wrong, he had no feelings for Natalie. But she knew them both. His weakness, Natalie's ruthless drive and her desire to bring down the school. It made sense that Natalie had renounced her share, even though she was dying. She'd have wanted to distance herself before she torpedoed Southwood. She could present it as proof she'd always known the place was rotten. Maybe she'd have claimed Martin pursued her, not the other way about. She could make it look as if she'd been pulling back from the school, ready to put some space between them.

Eve dashed up the nave as she waited for the call to connect, hastening towards the door.

Anastasia could have arranged to get to Natalie before Martin did. Killed her, then run for it. Natalie had picked the lock to get into the hidden room. She must have arrived early to do it. She'd get a kick out of it.

Greg's number went to voicemail.

She left a message and was just switching to text mode, when the church door opened.

It was Anastasia. Standing between Eve and the exit.

Eve's hands started to shake. In the instant before the bursar turned and saw her, Eve clicked on the draft SOS message she'd had ready to send to Viv on Monday night. But then their eyes met. The bursar looked just as surprised to see Eve as she was to see her. She hadn't come looking for her.

Eve needed to stay calm. But her breath caught in her throat. She hadn't had the chance to click send. But if she did so now, Anastasia would see her desperation and trembling hands. She'd give herself away, and help might not arrive in time.

'Oh, hello.' Anastasia's smile made her eyes crinkle, just as usual.

Eve wanted to respond in kind, but her body defied her. Her heart was going like the clappers. She had to clear her throat before she could reply. 'Hello.' In the background her mind ran on, whether she wanted it to or not. She was thinking of Eliza's murder. Maybe the head of sixth form had been the other person following Anastasia, the night Eve had sneaked into Southwood. Perhaps she'd been suspicious of the bursar, looking for evidence. And at some point, she'd found it.

The bursar glanced at the lights behind Eve. 'You've been taking a leaf out of my book. Sitting in the side chapel.' Then suddenly the look in her eye changed. It was subtle, but Eve's breathlessness got worse. 'I came over for a think myself. I gather they've found the wig and the jacket someone used to impersonate Natalie. Thanks to you, in fact.'

Eve swallowed. Her throat felt like sandpaper. 'It's good news, I guess.' But Anastasia didn't think so, clearly. She'd come to the place where she found comfort to think things over. She'd be worried Martin and Lucia would be implicated in a murder they hadn't committed.

'I know you've been doing a lot of investigating,' Anastasia said. 'And you've probably got further than you've admitted.' She was standing by a table at the back of the chapel now. Between Eve and the door. 'You followed me on Monday night.'

It was a statement, not a question. As she spoke, she reached behind her and opened a cupboard, pulling something from it.

A churchwarden's mace.

49

Eve heard herself gasp in the quiet of the chapel. She woke up her phone, her hands still shaking.

'I wouldn't if I were you.' Anastasia approached her quickly now, her expression not altering much. Just as purposeful, practical and energetic as she always was. But she swung the mace in front of her, knocking the phone from Eve's hand.

In the split second before she struck, Eve pressed send on the text to Viv. The mace caught her knuckle and she howled in spite of herself. Was her finger broken?

Through the shock of the pain, panic flared. Would the text have gone before the phone smashed on the tiles? And even if it sent, would Viv take it seriously? She'd probably be in her kitchen, the radio blaring, drinking a Friday night gin and tonic.

She might not see it at all.

If only Greg Boles picked up the voicemail she'd left. But she'd only asked him to call. Not explained her thinking. And he'd be busy picking up Robin.

As Eve tried to control her reaction, Anastasia pursued her, swinging the mace so she had to move further back down the nave.

'It was Eliza who described you to me, of course. She was watching me on Monday night too.'

So Anastasia had lied about seeing Eve herself. A fresh flood of realisation washed over her. Of course, that made sense. If the bursar knew she'd had company, she'd hardly leave the chapel door ajar. She probably wouldn't have gone in there in the first place; it had left her with no escape route. Why hadn't Eve spotted that?

'If you knew it was me all along, why mention it in front of Sabina and Bridget?'

'I wanted to know if Eliza was right. And I could see she had been, just by watching your eyes.' She sighed, shaking her head. 'So I knew you were suspicious of me. Eliza was wondering if I'd killed Natalie too. It was the most ridiculous thing that aroused her suspicions. The way I cast about for somewhere to search when we were looking for Natalie on Sunday morning. I waited for her to suggest the hidden room, even though I knew how much time Natalie had spent there as a student. Eliza suddenly wondered if I'd avoided mentioning it in case it looked suspicious. And I'm afraid she was right.'

Eve remembered the scene. Anastasia closing her eyes. Apparently racking her brains. Had Eliza really died for that? 'It wasn't much in the way of evidence.'

The bursar shook her head, a wry look in her eye. 'She didn't stop there. Late afternoon on Tuesday, she came to my rooms. I could tell something had made her question my innocence, though we talked amicably enough. But she went to use my bathroom, and she was a long time. I should have guessed why. It's hard to clean up neatly after such bloody work. She found a tiny stain on my towel. No one would have spotted it if they weren't looking. But Eliza was. I could have told her I'd cut myself, but I knew it would be no good. She saw the truth and she knew she'd got me. If it was tested, I was well aware of what the police would find.'

'But she didn't call them, even though you let her go at that point.' Why had the bursar taken that risk?

Anastasia sighed. 'She preferred to use her knowledge for her own ends – as leverage. Someone was blackmailing her to stay on at the school. She wanted me to help her leave while still appearing to be here.' She shook her head. 'Martin would never have worn that. Too dishonest. And Eliza was dangerous to me. To all of us. To continued harmony at Southwood. I knew then that I'd have to kill her.'

Eve's legs felt like jelly. Anastasia was telling her everything. She knew she'd got Eve trapped. Was confident she'd never get out alive.

'You pretended to go along with her request to make her feel safe. Advised her to write the letter to the headmaster.'

'I told her I couldn't help unless she told Martin the truth. I said I was sure he'd be discreet, and we needed to gain his sympathy. After that I'd be able to persuade him to quietly let her go. And as she wrote, she drank the drugged drink. It was easy to persuade her to go for a walk to clear her head after that. Her defences were down.'

It was so cool and calculated. 'You and Martin's father had an affair.'

Eve felt sure of her ground, but Anastasia shook her head. 'I've always cared for his family. His position.

'We held back. It was a meeting of minds. We adored each other, but I knew his family and Southwood's future were paramount. We'd talk for hours, share everything. It was so hard, not giving in. For him too.'

A memory slipped into Eve's head. *He always was a perfect gentleman*, Lucia had said. *Oh yes*, Bridget had replied, taking a juddery breath. *Always stuck to protocol. Just like Southwood, he placed a strong emphasis on etiquette.*

He might not have crossed that physical line, but Bridget had lost him just as surely as if he had. His mind and his heart were no longer hers. It made her think of Martin, Natalie and Lucia.

'After all our restraint, along came Natalie,' Anastasia said, 'playing with Martin, ready to sacrifice his entire future to get back at the school. One night I came in here and talked to Anthony. Said I could kill her. I didn't think I meant it. But then I realised I could. It was a solution that made sense. Her relationship with Martin was a pale, sick imitation of mine and Anthony's. There was no love there. It was all driven by her hatred.'

She was backing Eve into the side chapel now. She knew there was no other exit but the main door. Eve glanced this way and that for something to use as a weapon, but there was nothing. And the mace's reach was long.

'People will know you're guilty. They'll miss you at dinner.'

'Already over, my dear. Time must have run away with you. We normally go to our rooms or studies around now, before meeting again for a nightcap. And people won't think I'm guilty. It will be the gardener everyone blames. They'll think he committed murder with a female accomplice, and you were the third wheel who became a liability. A girlfriend he wanted to ditch, who knew too much. After all, you're close.'

The breath went out of her. Anastasia had connected her with Robin.

'I saw you together before Natalie was killed. And I noticed your reaction when everyone was attacking him at Sabina's. Viv Montague kept glancing in your direction. She's a good friend, but not a helpful one. You're fond of Robin Yardley.' She was looking intently at Eve now. 'More than fond. I know the signs.' She took another step forward. 'People will assume you were protecting him. You loved him too much. But you were hurt by his actions – and with another woman as an accomplice too. You'd be jealous, naturally. Asking questions. Demanding reassurances. Increasingly dangerous to him.'

'The police went to arrest him. He'll have an alibi.'

'I'm afraid not. Your time of death will be approximate. It's unlikely your body will be found before Sunday. I'm the only one who makes a habit of coming here. The vicar only visits once a week.' Anastasia gave the faintest smile. 'And there's plenty to incriminate Mr Yardley. His ring, found in Natalie's bedroom, for instance. And I believe it was the fragments of mud I planted in Eliza's study that got the police excited today. I'm told the analysis has come through and it includes traces of the mulch he uses. His own recipe, I understand. It was easy enough to collect from the grounds here.' She sighed. 'When Eliza became a threat, it seemed possible I might pass her off as Natalie's killer, and her death as suicide, but I'd already planted Mr Yardley's ring. I didn't know I'd have another option. It seemed best to pursue both avenues in tandem. My caution paid off when the police decided Eliza's death was murder. As for Mr Yardley, they were keen on him from the start. The DNA identification will complete the picture.'

'DNA?' Eve couldn't stop her voice from shaking.

'I took hairs from his hat while he was gardening at Sabina's. They were found in Eliza's office this afternoon. Inspector Palmer's assured Martin the forensic analysis will be fast-tracked. The authorities believe in Southwood's importance. I understand they already have Mr Yardley's DNA on file. He clearly has a past.'

Eve longed to tell her it wasn't what she thought. That he was on the register because of his old job.

'And of course, it's common knowledge that Natalie had some kind of hold over Mr Yardley.'

It was horrible, seeing how far she'd thought this through, the details she'd put in place.

'But there is no other woman – no accomplice.'

'The police won't care. They'll search, of course, but if they draw a blank it's still a win for them. They have their killer.'

'They might get DNA from hair inside the wig DC Dawkins found.'

'But unless the DNA's on file that won't lead them anywhere. And it won't be.'

Eve was sure that was true. If Lucia said nothing, the truth would never come out. She felt like a fly trapped in a spider's web. Desperately pulling at the strands, with no chance of escape.

She had to get clear of Anastasia. Failing would be worse than just dying. Robin could be convicted of her murder, as well as Natalie and Eliza's. And she'd go down in history as shielding him from justice. Robin's old police contacts in London might not be totally sure of his innocence. They knew how much he had riding on keeping his identity secret. They might figure he'd lost control and lashed out in response to Natalie's selfish desire to unmask him.

As for Eve, even her children might never be sure she was innocent of protecting a killer.

She was horribly aware of the mace with its hard silver head. One accurate swing and she'd be dead.

She swallowed. Tried to think. She had a few advantages. She was wearing trousers and flats to Anastasia's pencil skirt and high heels.

And that was it.

The plan that came to her was basic in the extreme, but she had to take it. She was out of time.

She ducked left suddenly, but as Anastasia reacted, darting to her right to mirror Eve's move, Eve lurched in the opposite direction, leaping onto the nearest bench in the side chapel. Thank heaven they were backless, unlike the traditional pews in the main church. She leaped onto the bench behind and the one after that, then between the open pillars marking the side-chapel boundary and into the main body of the building. She felt the impact reverberate through her as she landed on the hard floor.

It was only the element of surprise that allowed her to beat Anastasia to the open space. Diagonally ahead and to the left, the chapel door was still open.

So near and yet so far. The pews were in her way, so she hurtled down the nave ready to turn at the end. Anastasia was right behind her. Too close.

The mace hit her in the back as she reached a heating grate in the floor, and she stumbled. She was falling towards the tiles. She was just conscious of the force to her chest as she hit them and then her head felt the impact.

50

It took Eve a moment to remember where she was as she came round. How long had she been out? She tried to gather her thoughts, listening for sounds and piecing together their meaning.

A door creaking. Slamming shut. Then a thunk.

Someone locking the chapel door.

Anastasia, trapping her inside. Shutting out help and witnesses. That must be the only reason Eve was still alive. The bursar realised she had time to make herself safer with Eve unconscious. Next minute the side chapel went dark. The clouds must have cleared. Moonlight lit the building's interior. Eve tried to move her head so she could see up the nave. Watch for Anastasia's approach. The pain made her feel sick.

She could hear the bursar's high heels on the tiles. Getting louder.

Just ahead of where Eve had fallen was a rug. Eve lay rigid. If only she could convince Anastasia that she was still unconscious. She needed her to get close. Through three-quarter closed eyes, Eve watched the bursar's approach, her heart thudding.

She waited until Anastasia had the weight of one foot on the rug, then grabbed its other end and tugged it with all her might, twisting out of the way as she did so. Watching as the bursar fell, crying out as her leg twisted under her.

Eve was up again, but she hadn't realised how groggy she'd feel. The dizziness almost overwhelmed her as she dragged herself forward and lurched towards the door. She fell against it, reaching desperately for the key in the lock.

But there was no key there, and behind her Anastasia had struggled to her feet, breathing heavily.

Eve fumbled about in the dark. Desperate to find a key. Trying to reach a light switch. Her fingers met dusty surfaces, smooth stone. She must be disorientated. If she could just have some light.

But looking behind her she saw Anastasia, the key in one hand, glinting in the moonlight, the mace in the other. She was limping towards her slowly, inexorably.

Eve was like a mouse caught in a trap with an owl on the approach. There was nothing she could do but watch.

At last, Anastasia was upon her and brought the mace up, swinging her arm down, aiming for Eve's head.

Eve acted on instinct, hurling herself to her left, away from the door and the mace.

The mace hit the place where her head had been and swung down, hard against the lock on the chapel door.

It gave way, coming off the door altogether. Crashing down.

The weapon was heavy and as it finally hit the tiles, Eve grabbed for it, pulling it to her with more strength than she'd thought she had left. Then, just as suddenly, she thrust it back towards Anastasia. The stick hit her stomach with force.

It was enough. Enough to get Eve out of there at least. The bursar was down. Eve dived round the door, now ajar and loose on its hinges, dropped the mace, and pulled it shut.

She was struggling for breath, feeling as though she was about to be sick. But she was in control.

From inside the chapel, she could hear the bursar hammering on the door, but she was stuck. With the lock and handle gone, she had nothing to pull. Whereas Eve had hold of the decorative door knocker. The one thing keeping her safe.

And at that moment she heard running.

Looking behind her she saw Olivia Dawkins, along with the patronising constable from earlier, and several other officers.

The chapel door was surrounded as they opened up. Anastasia's eyes were wide, the fight not gone from her. But she could see it was over. Officers were holding both her arms now.

Someone dialled an ambulance as Eve sank down on a bench, tears pricking her eyes. Everyone was asking questions, but the cacophony washed over her. All she could think of was that Robin was safe, and she was safe. She took a huge, juddering breath as relief overwhelmed her. She'd get to see him again. And hug her children and Gus. Hold each of them tight.

Things didn't move quickly in Detective Inspector Palmer's circles. When Eve reached the hospital she heard that Robin was at the police station. They'd taken a while to find him, and they couldn't release him yet. News that the bursar had attacked her wasn't enough. There was a lot of explaining to do, and interviews to conduct. They must have talked to Lucia and Martin too.

It helped that Greg Boles finally got a lead on the sleeping pills. One of the teachers admitted their jar had gone missing. They hadn't reported it in case the police thought they'd killed Eliza – the woman in question was one of many who'd argued with her. But at the news of Anastasia's arrest, they'd come forward. Then a cleaner who'd serviced the woman's room remembered nipping to fetch more linen, without bothering to lock up. She'd spotted Anastasia in the corridor on her return. She hadn't thought anything of it. The teacher kept quiet about the missing pills, so why would she? Besides, Anastasia was above suspicion.

Greg Boles talked to Eve before interviewing the bursar. He said he'd use her information to turn up the pressure.

Apparently, it worked. He told Anastasia the quicker this was resolved, the better it would be for Martin, Lucia and their children. If she'd loved Anthony, she knew what she had to do.

The bursar had deflated. Confessed. Gone from saying Eve had attacked her in the chapel to admitting it had been the other way about. Greg had already destroyed that story anyway. If Eve was the aggressor, why would she have texted Viv to ask her to call the police? And why shut Anastasia in the chapel rather than finish her off?

But it all took time, and Eve's conversations with Robin were stilted and minimal.

It was Viv that Eve spoke to properly first. She came to fetch her from the cottage hospital after she'd been checked over.

'Thanks for calling the cops.' She knew now that their appearance was down to her text, not the message she'd left for Greg Boles.

Viv hugged her gently as she helped her into the passenger seat of Monty's van. A boneshaker if ever there was one. 'I thought it was possible you'd sent the message by accident, but you do make a habit of almost getting killed, so it seemed best to err on the side of caution.' Viv got into the driver's seat and fastened Eve's safety belt for her. Eve's right hand was bandaged to bring down the swelling after the blow from the mace. At least it wasn't broken. It could have been worse. 'I guessed if you were in danger you'd be at Southwood somewhere. You worked it out, then.'

'It would all have gone smoothly if Anastasia hadn't heard about the discovery of the wig and the jacket. She must have guessed from the start that the silhouette was Lucia – and why. She was close to her and Martin. They confided in her. She was desperate to protect them. Knowing there was physical evidence that might lead back to them had her upset. And when she was upset, she always went to the chapel, to feel close to Anthony, I'm sure.'

Viv shook her head as she drove along the dark lane, braking suddenly to avoid a fox.

Eve let out an involuntary groan as her head jerked forward. 'Sorry.'

'You're very much forgiven. If it weren't for you I'd probably still be clutching the knocker of Southwood's chapel door, wondering when the heck someone would come to my aid.'

'To complete my good work, I'm going to come and stay the night at Elizabeth's Cottage.' Eve made a noise but Viv continued. 'No arguments. The doctor said you shouldn't be on your own. I promise I'll be lovely and quiet in the morning and walk Gus too.'

'All right then. You're one in a million.'

51

It was several days before she got all the news, though Robin had told her over the phone that everything had played out as she'd guessed. The coincidence of Martin and Scarlett both stumbling across Natalie's body made sense. Natalie had been in demand; they'd each been obsessed with her in their own way.

Other details were coming to light now. The hammer Anastasia had taken from a tool shed to use as the murder weapon. One of many. It hadn't been missed, even when the police asked. No one kept an inventory, and the school was full of all sorts of equipment – much of it dating back decades. On returning to her rooms, Anastasia had bagged the weapon, then taken it to the chapel that night and hidden it in a disused heating grate. Eve had watched her go, with no idea what was concealed under her gown.

The bursar wasn't holding back, now the die was cast. She'd told Greg she wanted everything cleared up so Martin and Lucia could get on with their lives. It left Eve's skin crawling – that desire to protect which had led to such horrific violence.

Now, she was round at Robin's. It was the first time she'd

been there since the night before Eliza's murder. Gus was settled contentedly at their feet.

'You've got something fresh?' She glanced at him as he poured her a glass of wine. He'd dished her a plate of sausage casserole too, with buttery baked potatoes and broccoli.

He gave her a smile she found hard to interpret. Anxious maybe? What if he had bad news? She was conscious that he'd let her come to his house. As she'd walked over, fear that it might be a farewell meal had gripped her. One last meeting before he went off to start again. She'd had to work to stop the tears pricking her eyes.

'I have. But you go first.'

Eve tried to relax and put her worries on hold as she ran through her news.

'I've spoken to Lucia Leverett. Parents are withdrawing their daughters from Southwood left, right and centre now. I think Anastasia was right: it would have blown over eventually if the killing was put down to an outsider. But now they know the murderer's descended from a founder, there's no chance of that.'

'What are Lucia and Martin's plans?'

'They're in conversation with a lawyer about arrangements going forward. Anastasia's decided to relinquish her share in the school with immediate effect, so it will all be held in trust for Ada. Normally her trustees wouldn't be allowed to make big changes before she comes of age, but there's a clause about exceptional circumstances. If one of the family lines comes to an end, they've got the flexibility to change course, apparently. Lucia doesn't think the school will continue in its current form. She's got an idea for turning it into a residential centre for children who've been bullied. And with her helping to run the place, I can imagine it being a success. She and Martin are both in trouble with the authorities of course, especially Martin, as he found Natalie's body. Scarlett's in the same boat.'

Robin nodded. 'They've got a police investigation hanging over them.'

'What do you think will happen?'

'Greg says Palmer's recommended that it's not in the public interest for the Crown Prosecution Service to take it further. You know what he's like. He'll be desperate to avoid upsetting two well-to-do families in case it affects his career. And think of the paperwork he'll avoid.'

Eve groaned. 'Why am I not surprised? All the same, I'm glad for Martin and Lucia. They fell into the situation innocently, and I think they were like rabbits in headlights. Not thinking clearly. As for Scarlett, she's paid in other ways.'

She knew Robin had tuned in to watch the head girl on the *Natalie Somerson Show* two nights earlier. They'd already spoken about it on the phone, though it was almost too agonising to discuss. Eve had tried again to dissuade Scarlett from appearing, but it hadn't worked. They hadn't been able to make her look guilty of murder, of course, but everything else had come out. Her cheating. The school's leniency. Lots of background on her rich father and his generous donations to Southwood. It seemed to be Bridget Leverett who'd lured him in as a donor. And she who'd nominated Scarlett as head girl. But Natalie's blackmail and Eliza's wrongdoing hadn't been included. Eve assumed Dirk Acton had realised she was right: he'd be in the frame for blackmail himself if he publicised what had happened.

For a second, the prospect of a future show, where Acton featured Robin's past, reared up in front of her. Once again, she tried to shut it out.

'No wonder Martin and Lucia want to start again. Lucia tells me she's insisted Bridget move out now. Martin's planning to buy her a cottage close by. I don't imagine Bridget will like it, but all the bad publicity means Lucia's got plenty of leverage.'

It was disconcerting. What had happened was so appalling,

but it had ended up freeing Martin and Lucia. Southwood had seemed like an unchangeable institution, too set in its ways to reform. But now, even the coven was no more. The school statutes provided for alternative arrangements if Southwood's main function changed.

She'd passed on all of her news. In a moment, she'd have to ask Robin for his. She swallowed, a sinking feeling in her chest.

Their eyes met. There was no putting it off.

'What about you?' She reached for his hand. 'Can they shut down the stories about your past life? And what about the man you saw in the woods?' She had to ask, even though she was afraid of the answer. 'You didn't tell me to stay away tonight. I felt like I was being eaten up from the inside when you said we shouldn't see each other.' She leaned forward. On the edge of her seat. Would he be gone tomorrow? Off to a new place with a new identity?

He looked nervous again.

'What is it?'

'News. Big news. Eve, they've caught him. The man who was following me and checking you out in the pub.'

'Robin!' She felt a lifting in her chest.

Gus rushed out from under the table at her tone, looking up at them each in turn.

'So we can carry on meeting then?' Eve was out of her seat. 'And what about the wider gang? Will it get into the media? Will others like him turn up? How much danger are you in?' She didn't care about risking it herself. It was worth it. You only got one life. But the thought of Robin vulnerable – of him suddenly being attacked in a back lane or run off the road – left her ragged.

Robin stood too, and put his arms around her. 'Back in London, I always knew there was a kingpin we were missing. Someone who had all the connections in the police, and all the links to organised crime. Someone who badly wanted revenge. It's him we've been trying to identify all these years.'

Robin still occasionally slipped back to the capital to help the ongoing investigation, but it had been so long she'd given up hope it would ever be resolved.

'Turns out, news of my whereabouts drew him out of the woodwork. The results of my intervention have been causing him problems ever since. The desire for personal revenge was his undoing.'

'You're saying the man who came to Saxford *is* the lynchpin?'

'The head of the whole operation.' He nodded. 'And on his phone and in his papers are details we barely dreamed of. Everything we need to take down the whole gang.'

Eve felt her skin tingle. Then tears prick her eyes. 'You mean...?'

He nodded. His eyes were glistening too and he pulled her closer to him. 'Yes, it's for real. The next time we eat together it can be a fish and chip supper at the Cross Keys.'

Eve did cry then.

Robin laughed through his tears. 'Don't get upset. We can go somewhere posher if you'd prefer.'

She gave him a mock swipe. 'I was worried it was bad news. You looked anxious.'

'I felt I was springing it on you. I mean, I know it's a different proposition, being a normal couple. Going out. Going for long weekends. All that stuff. I know you like your independence.'

Gus gave him a hard stare, looking up from under his bushy eyebrows.

Eve was probably looking at him with much the same expression. 'I think I'll cope.' Then suddenly she was anxious too. 'If you will, I mean.'

'Nothing would make me happier.'

52

Eve felt nervous the following afternoon. She'd invited Viv, the vicar, and Sylvia and Daphne, her neighbours on Haunted Lane, over for tea. It wouldn't normally be a cause for anxiety, but these were the people who knew she'd been secretly seeing Robin. Yet only Jim Thackeray, the vicar, knew his full backstory.

Eve had been too scared to reveal his secret past, but now she was questioning that judgement. It implied she lacked faith in her dearest friends, when in fact she'd trust them with her life. Just not with Robin's. It wasn't hers to risk.

'Does that make any sense?' she asked Gus. He looked at her uncomprehendingly. 'I really hope Viv doesn't look at me like that.'

She'd made sticky flapjacks stuffed with dried fruit and got her friends sitting down with mugs of tea before she started her explanation.

Jim seemed to appreciate how worried she was. His kind eyes were on her, and he nodded his encouragement.

When she'd finished, Sylvia laughed. 'I can see why you

didn't tell us – Daphne and Viv in particular are such blab-bermouths.'

'It wasn't that, truly. I—'

Daphne leaned forward and patted Eve's arm as she turned to her partner. 'Stop tormenting the poor woman.' She faced Eve again. 'If I held a secret that might lead to Sylvia's death I'd take it to my grave, even though I love and trust you all.'

Eve swallowed. 'Thank you.' She could hardly bring herself to turn to Viv. She wasn't like Daphne or Sylvia. She honestly wasn't sure what she'd think.

Viv looked up from fussing Gus. 'Blimey, this is classic. Can you imagine Moira's face when she sees you together? Please say we can be in the pub when you go in tonight. I know I can get her there!'

'I'm so sorry I didn't tell you.'

Viv looked surprised. 'Well, we always knew Robin had a secret past and that he had a good reason to keep it that way. I have to say I'm *slightly* disappointed. I'd got him down as an ex-spy, or a prince from overseas at least.' She put her head on one side and nodded. 'But all in all, I'm satisfied.'

By the time Eve and Robin entered the Cross Keys that evening, Eve had gone further and explained the background to Jo, Matt and Toby behind the bar, and to Viv's brother. They were all friends. She didn't want to spring it on them. But Viv had made her swear not to tell Moira.

Eve felt a mix of excitement, happiness and awkwardness as she walked in with Robin, arm in arm.

Viv was sitting at a table to one side of the bar with Sylvia, Daphne, Jim Thackeray, Simon, Polly and Moira. As they came in, Viv started clapping and suddenly everyone was joining in. Including Moira, who was taking part much more hesitantly than the rest, her eyes on Viv, her brow extravagantly furrowed.

A moment later, Robin bought Eve a glass of white wine, then put in an order for drinks all round. Moira was plucking urgently at Viv's sleeve.

Eve shifted nearer to their table.

'Dear me, Viv,' Eve heard her say. 'I realise Robin's innocent of murder and I'm sure we're all very pleased, but there are still question marks over his character and past, surely? Do you think it's wise—'

She moved closer to Robin again, amusement bubbling in her chest, mixed with defensive tension. She wasn't sure if Robin had heard the storekeeper.

She got her answer a moment later. He pulled Eve in close and glanced at Moira, smiling. 'It's a long story. Mind if we join you? I'll fill you in.'

Eve's favourite bit was the grand reveal: that he'd once been Detective Inspector Robert Kelly. She'd never seen Moira blush so deeply.

As he told his tale, other pub goers listened in. In the background, Eve could see Jo, Toby and Matt relaying the story to those out of earshot. One after another, people came and patted Robin on the back and shook his hand. The tears were back again and Robin hugged Eve all the tighter.

NATALIE ZOE SOMERSON – TV PERSONALITY AND TALK-SHOW HOST

Natalie Somerson has died in Suffolk at the age of fifty-five. A woman has been arrested for her murder.

Natalie's childhood was unsettled. She was sent to a boarding school far from home aged just seven, by a father who couldn't tolerate her presence. From there, she moved on to board at Southwood School in Suffolk, a well-renowned institution where her aunt, Anastasia Twite, was a teacher. It seemed fitting: they were both descendants of one of the school's founders, Emily Fox, and Natalie was destined to inherit a half share in the institution when Anastasia died.

But Natalie was deeply unhappy at Southwood. It seems she had few genuine friends, something that won't surprise her critics, but perhaps she'd been hurt too much to allow people to get close. It was also a troubled period in her life. She lost her mother aged fourteen, yet her father still kept her at a distance. Her upset was compounded by one of her teachers, who seemed to delight in humiliating her in front of her classmates. She also robbed Natalie of the chance to perform at a local theatre, despite her talent for acting. Although there's no doubt Natalie was a rebellious and disruptive child, it seems clear the punishments hardened her resolve and made a bad situation worse. No one who knew the details was surprised when Natalie fought back, hurting the teacher in turn. A battle ensued, which finally put Natalie in control, something she craved.

It's possible she hoped that someone would let her loose from the school she hated or at least set some boundaries. But descendants of Emily Fox were never going to be expelled from Southwood. Natalie would remain there until she graduated. She had nowhere else to go.

Perhaps her controversial approach to the guests on her show was moulded all those years ago, or earlier still, when her father sent her away. She'd lacked control over her life and manipulating her guests gave her back some power. It's no excuse – she caused much misery – but she was made miserable first.

It was a hard opening to write. Eve felt sad for the young Natalie. Her drama teacher had finally got in touch to confirm she'd clashed with Eliza over sacking her from the production of *Grease*. She said Natalie had shown promise and it was clear the decision was personal. That said, there were few redeeming features about the woman she'd become.

There was a knock at the door and Gus leaped up, barking for all he was worth. She opened up to find Robin, who was instantly mobbed by the dachshund. Both gardener and dog looked up at her after a moment. Robin was grinning.

'Walk on the beach? And then we can pick up something from Moira's for supper.'

'You know what I love – as well as you and Gus, obviously?'

He raised an eyebrow as she got her coat.

'Normality. Let's go.'

A LETTER FROM CLARE

Thank you so much for reading *Mystery at Southwood School*. I do hope you had fun working on the clues! If you'd like to keep up to date with all my latest releases, you can sign up at the following link. Your email address will never be shared, and you can unsubscribe at any time.

www.bookouture.com/clare-chase

The idea for this book began with the motive, and how self-less love might lead to desperation and evil deeds. It was also interesting to explore the pressures that might come from living in an enclosed environment, steeped in tradition.

If you have time, I'd love it if you were able to write a review of *Mystery at Southwood School*. Feedback is really valuable, and it also makes a huge difference in helping new readers discover my books for the first time. Alternatively, if you'd like to contact me personally, you can reach me via my website, Facebook page, Twitter or Instagram. It's always great to hear from readers.

Again, thank you so much for deciding to spend some time reading *Mystery at Southwood School*. I'm looking forward to sharing my next book with you very soon.

With all best wishes,

Clare x

KEEP IN TOUCH WITH CLARE

www.clarechase.com

 facebook.com/ClareChaseAuthor

 twitter.com/ClareChase_

 instagram.com/clarechaseauthor

ACKNOWLEDGEMENTS

Much love and thanks as ever to Charlie, George and Ros for the feedback and the cheerleading!

And as always, crucially, I'm hugely grateful to my brilliant editor Ruth Tross for her inspiring ideas and clear-sighted feedback. I'm also indebted to Noelle Holten for her fantastic promo work and to Alex Holmes, Fraser Crichton and Liz Hatherell for their expert input. Sending thanks too to Tash Webber for her wonderful cover designs, as well as to Peta Nightingale, Kim Nash and everyone involved in editing, book production and sales at Bookouture. It's a privilege to be published and promoted by such a skilled and friendly team.

Love and thanks also to Mum and Dad, Phil and Jenny, David and Pat, Warty, Andrea, Jen, the Westfield gang, Margaret, Shelly, Mark, my Andrewes relations and a whole bunch of family and friends.

Thanks also to the wonderful Bookouture authors and other writers for their friendship and support. And a big thank you to the dedicated and generous book bloggers and reviewers who take the time to pass on their thoughts about my work. I really do appreciate it.

And finally, but importantly, thanks to you, the reader, for buying or borrowing this book!

Printed in Great Britain
by Amazon